"*Whiskey Sour* is very good indeed."

—January Magazine

"Everything about *Whiskey Sour* is smart—smart characters, smart writing, and a smart pace that keeps you reading long after you'd meant to turn out the lights. This superb debut goes down smooth and will leave readers demanding a refill!"

—Michael Prescott, bestselling author of Dangerous Games

"An original, humorous character study of a woman on the edge of her career and personal life. *Whiskey Sour* moves at a brisk pace to a surprising and tense finale that has quite a kick."

—South Florida Sun-Sentinel

"An easy, breezy read, well written and very funny."

—Kingston Observer

"Even us non-drinkers will enjoy J.A. Konrath's detective story, with its witty dialogue and enjoyable characters. With an intriguing female as his protagonist, Konrath gives us our first glimpse of a promising series."

—Steve Alten, bestselling author of The Loch

"I found myself laughing out loud many times. The second book in the series can't come soon enough!"

—Murder Express

"A rapid-fire debut thriller . . . (with) a savvy heroine."

—Kirkus Reviews

"J.A. Konrath's *Whiskey Sour* is the best mystery series debut I've read in years. From electric excitement to laugh-out-loud humor, this book has it all."

—Warren B. Murphy, bestselling author of *Pigs Get Fat*

"Being a police officer and an occasional drinker of whiskey myself, *Whiskey Sour* immediately caught my eye—especially with a main character with the name 'Lt. Jack Daniels.' I am a big fan of Ed McBain (87th Precinct) and Robert B. Parker (Spenser novels)—so finding a book that combines both their styles was a real treat. *Whiskey Sour* is fast, fun, and witty, with humor and just the right amount of gore to keep me turning the page."

—Colin Sullivan, Texas-based police officer

PRAISE FOR
BLOODY MARY

"As sharp and tangy as its title cocktail. Snappy dialogue. Powerful action. A fabulous character to spend time with. What a recipe for a page-turner."

—David Morrell, bestselling author of *The Brotherhood of the Rose*

"If the Grim Reaper has a sense of humor, he reads J.A. Konrath . . . If you prefer your mysteries served up like a good steak—sizzling, juicy, and tasting of blood—there's not a better item on the menu."

—William Kent Krueger, author of *Blood Hollow*

WHISKEY SOUR

A Jacqueline "Jack" Daniels Mystery

WHISKEY SOUR

J. A. KONRATH

HYPERION NEW YORK

Mass market ISBN: 0-7868-9072-X

Hyperion books are available for special promotions and premiums. For details contact Michael Rentas, Assistant Director, Inventory Operations, Hyperion, 77 West 66th Street, 11th floor, New York, New York 10023-6298, or call 212-456-0133.

FIRST MASS MARKET EDITION

10 9 8 7 6 5 4 3 2 1

This book is for M.
I love you today, and everyday.

ACKNOWLEDGMENTS

The author wishes to thank (in alphabetical order): Bruce Arnoux, Mark Arnoux, Latham Conger III, George Dailey, Jeff Evens, Mariel Evens, Elaine Farrugia, Stacey Glick, Miriam Goderich, Carl Graves, Todd Keithley, Chris Konrath, Joe Konrath Sr., John Konrath, Mike Konrath, Talon Konrath, Elisa Lee, Jim McCarthy, Ursel Schmidt, Ace Streng, and Marge Streng.

Special giant-sized thanks go to Jim Coursey—my friend and sounding board; Jane Dystel—agent extraordinaire; Laura Konrath—my mother and biggest critic; Leslie Wells—world's greatest editor; and most of all to my spouse, for the ceaseless efforts and relentless encouragement.

WHISKEY SOUR

1½ oz. whiskey
1½ oz. sour mix

Shake well with ice and
pour into an old-fashioned glass.

Garnish with cherry and orange slice.

WHISKEY SOUR

CHAPTER 1

THERE WERE FOUR BLACK AND WHITES already at the
7-Eleven when I arrived. Several people had gathered in
the parking lot behind the yellow police tape, huddling close
for protection against the freezing Chicago rain.

They weren't there for Slurpees.

I parked my 1986 Nova on the street and hung my star
around my neck on a cord. The radio was full of chatter
about "the lasagna on Monroe and Dearborn," so I knew
this was going to be an ugly one. I got out of the car.

It was cold, too cold for October. I wore a three-quarter-
length London Fog trench coat over my blue Armani blazer
and a gray skirt. The coat was the only one I had that fit over
the blazer's oversized shoulders, which left my legs exposed
to the elements.

Freezing was the curse of the fashion savvy.

Detective First Class Herb Benedict hunched over a plastic tarpaulin, lifting up the side against the wind. His coat

was unbuttoned, and his expansive stomach poured over the sides of his belt as he bent down. Herb's hound dog jowls were pink with cold rain, and he scratched at his salt-and-pepper mustache as I approached.

"Kind of cold for a jacket like that, Jack."

"But don't I look good?"

"Sure. Shivering suits you."

I walked to his side and squatted, peering down at the form under the tarp.

Female. Caucasian. Blonde. Twenties. Naked. Multiple stab wounds, running from her thighs to her shoulders, many of them yawning open like hungry, bloody mouths. The several around her abdomen were deep enough to see inside.

I felt my stomach becoming unhappy and turned my attention to her head. A red lesion ran around her neck, roughly the width of a pencil. Her lips were frozen in a snarl, the bloody rictus stretched wide like one of her stab wounds.

"This was stapled to her chest." Benedict handed me a plastic evidence bag. In it was a three-by-five-inch piece of paper, crinkled edges on one end indicating it had been ripped from a spiral pad. It was spotty with blood and rain, but the writing on it was clear:

you canX caƙh ME
IM THE GINGERBREADMAN

I let the tarp fall and righted myself. Benedict, the mind reader, handed me a cup of coffee that had been sitting on the curb.

"Who found the body?" I asked.

"Customer. Kid named Mike Donovan."

I took a sip of coffee. It was so hot, it hurt. I took another.

"Who took the statement?"

"Robertson."

Benedict pointed at the storefront window to the thin, uniformed figure of Robertson, talking with a teenager.

"Witnesses?"

"Not yet."

"Who was behind the counter?"

"Owner. Being depoed as we speak. Didn't see anything."

I wiped some rain off my face and unbunched my shoulders as I entered the store, trying to look like the authority figure my title suggested.

The heat inside was both welcome and revolting. It warmed me considerably, but went hand in hand with the nauseating smell of hot dogs cooked way too long.

"Robertson." I nodded at the uniform. "Sorry to hear about your dad."

He shrugged. "He was seventy, and we always told him fast food would kill him."

"Heart attack?"

"He was hit by a Pizza Express truck."

I searched Robertson's face for the faintest trace of a smirk, and didn't find one. Then I turned my attention to Mike Donovan. He was no more than seventeen, brown hair long on top and shaved around the sides, wearing some baggy jeans that would have been big on Herb. Men got all the comfortable clothing trends.

"Mr. Donovan? I'm Lieutenant Daniels. Call me Jack."

Donovan cocked his head to the side, the way dogs do when they don't understand a command. Under his left armpit was a magazine with cars on the cover.

"Is your name really Jack Daniels? You're a woman."

"Thank you for noticing. I can show you my ID, if you want."

He wanted, and I slipped the badge case off my neck and opened it up, letting him see my name in official police lettering. Lieutenant Jack Daniels, CPD. It was short for Jacqueline, but only my mother called me that.

He grinned. "Name like that, I bet you really score."

I gave him a conspiratorial smirk, even though I hadn't "scored" in ages.

"Run through it," I said to Robertson.

"Mr. Donovan entered this establishment at approximately eight-fifty P.M., where he proceeded to buy the latest copy of *Racing Power Magazine* . . . "

Mr. Donovan held out the magazine in question. "It's their annual leotard issue." He opened it to a page where two surgically enhanced women in spandex straddled a Corvette.

I gave it a token look-over to keep the kid cooperative. I cared for hot rods about as much as I cared for spandex.

"Where he proceeded to buy the latest copy of *Racing Power Magazine*." Robertson eyed Donovan, annoyed at the interruption. "He also bought a Mounds candy bar. At approximately eight fifty-five, Mr. Donovan left the establishment, and proceeded to throw out the candy wrapper in the garbage can in front of the store. In the can was the victim, facedown, half covered in garbage."

I glanced out the storefront window and looked for the garbage can. The crowd was getting larger and the rain was falling faster, but the can was nowhere to be found.

"It went to the lab before you got here, Jack."

I glanced at Benedict, who'd sneaked up behind me.

"We didn't want things to get any wetter than they already were. But we've got the pictures and the vids."

My focus swiveled back to the scene outside. The cop with the video camera was now taping the faces in the crowd. Sometimes a nut will return to the scene and watch the action. Or so I've read in countless Ed McBain books. I gave the kid my attention again.

"Mr. Donovan, how did you notice the body if it was buried in garbage?"

"I . . . er, Mounds was having a contest. I forgot to check my wrapper to see if I'd won. So I reached back into the garbage to find it . . ."

"Did the can have a lid?"

"Yeah. One of those push lids that says 'Thank you' on it."

"So you reached into the push slot . . ."

"Uh-huh, but I couldn't find it. So I lifted the whole lid up, and there part of her was."

"What part?"

"Her, uh, ass was sticking up."

He gave me a nervous giggle.

"Then what did you do?"

"I couldn't believe it. It was like, it wasn't real. So I went back into the 7-Eleven and told the guy. He called the police."

"Mr. Donovan, Officer Robertson is going to have to take you into the station to fill out a deposition. Do you need to call your parents?"

"My dad works nights."

"Mom?"

He shook his head.

"Do you live in the neighborhood?"

"Yeah. A few blocks down on Monroe."

"Officer Robertson will give you a ride home when you're done."

"Do you think I'll be on the news?"

On cue, a network remote truck pulled into the lot, faster than the crappy weather warranted. The rear doors opened and the obligatory female reporter, perfectly made up and steely with resolve, led her crew toward the store. Benedict walked out to meet them, halting their advancement at the police barricade, giving them the closed crime scene speech.

The medical examiner pulled up behind the truck in his familiar Plymouth minivan. Two uniforms waved him through the barricade and I nodded a good-bye to Robertson and went to meet the ME.

The cold was a shock, my calves instant gooseflesh. Maxwell Hughes knelt down next to the tarp as I approached. His expression was all business when I caught his eye, drizzle dotting his glasses and dripping down his gray goatee.

"Daniels."

"Hughes. What do you have?"

"I'd put her death at roughly three to five hours ago. Suffocation. Her windpipe is broken."

"The stab wounds?"

"Postmortem. No defense cuts on her hands or arms, and not enough blood lost to have been inflicted while she was alive. See how one edge is rough, the other smooth?" He used a latex-gloved hand to stretch one of the wounds open. "The blade had a serrated edge. Maybe a hunting knife."

"Raped?"

"Not from what I can tell. No signs of semen. No visible trauma to the vagina or anus. But this isn't an autopsy." Max was fond of adding that final caveat, though I'd yet to see an instance when the autopsy didn't corroborate every one of his observations.

"The mouth?"

"No apparent damage. Tongue intact, protruding slightly. Consistent with strangulation. No bite marks. The blood in the mouth seeped up through her throat after she died. That coincides with the pooling of blood in her face. She was stored upside down."

"She was found face-first in a garbage can."

Hughes made his mouth into a tight thin line, and then reached into his pocket for a clean handkerchief to wipe the rain from his glasses. By the time he tucked it away, the glasses were wet again.

"Looks like you've got a real psycho here."

"We'll need the report on this one right away, Max."

He opened up the yellow plastic tackle box that housed the tools of his trade and began bagging the corpse's hands. I left him to his work.

More cops and newsies and gawkers arrived, and the carnival atmosphere of an important murder got into full swing. It would offend me, if I hadn't seen it so many times.

Benedict finished his impromptu statement for the media and began selecting uniforms for the door-to-door witness search. I went to pitch in. It boosted morale for the men to see their lieut pounding pavement with them, especially since it was probably futile in this instance.

The killer had dumped a body in a public place, where it was sure to be found. But he'd done it without attracting any attention.

I had a feeling this was only the beginning.

CHAPTER 2

MORNING. THE STALE SWEAT THAT CLUNG to me and the sour taste of old coffee grounds were constant reminders that I hadn't slept yet.

As if I needed reminders. I have chronic insomnia. My last sound sleep was sometime during the Reagan administration, and it shows. At forty-six my auburn hair is streaked with gray that grows faster than I can dye it, the lines on my face shout age rather than character, and even two bottles of Visine a month couldn't get all the red out.

But the lack of sleep has made me pretty damn productive.

Spread out before me on my cluttered desk, a dead woman's life had been reduced to a collection of files and reports. I was combining all the information into a report of my own. It read like a test, with none of the blanks filled in.

Twelve hours had passed and we still didn't know the victim's name.

No prints or hairs or fibers on the body. No skin under the fingernails. Nothing solid in the door-to-door reports. But this lack of evidence was evidence in itself. The perp had been extremely careful.

The victim wasn't sexually assaulted, and death had resulted from suffocation induced by a broken windpipe, as Max had guessed. The lesion around her neck was six millimeters thick. It didn't leave fibers, which would indicate rope, and didn't bite into the skin, which would imply a thin wire. The assistant ME suggested an electrical cord as a possible weapon.

Ligature marks around her wrists and ankles bore traces of twine. Staking out every store in Illinois that sold twine wasn't too clever an idea, though it was mentioned.

The stab wounds were postmortem and made by a thick-bladed knife with a serrated back. There were twenty-seven wounds in all, of varying depth and size.

We were unable to pull any fingerprints from the garbage can Jane Doe was found in. Even Mike Donovan's prints had been washed away by the rain. The contents of the can were an average assortment of convenience store garbage, except for one major item.

Mixed in with the wrappers and cups was a five-inch gingerbread man cookie. It was heavily varnished, like an old loaf of lacquered French bread that gourmet restaurants use for decoration. An elite task force of two people was assigned to Chicago's hundred-plus bakeries to try and get a match. If they failed, there was an equal number of supermarkets that sold baked goods. Double that figure to include the neighboring suburbs. A huge job, all for nothing if it was homemade.

If this weren't such a somber situation, the image of two detectives flashing around the picture of the gingerbread man and asking "Have you seen him?" would be pretty funny.

I took another sip of some coffee that the Gestapo could

have used for difficult interrogations, and felt it bleed into my stomach, which didn't approve. The caffeine surging through my veins left me nauseous and jittery. I gave my temples ten seconds of intense finger massage, and then went back to my report.

She was killed roughly three hours before Donovan discovered her body at 8:55. Depending on how much time the perp spent with her corpse, he could have killed her anywhere within a hundred-mile radius. That narrowed it down to about four million people. Take out women, children, the elderly, everyone with a solid alibi, and the 20 percent of the population who were left-handed, and I figured we had maybe seven hundred thousand suspects left.

So we were making progress.

Pressure from the mayor's office forced us to involve the Feebies. They were sending up two agents from Quantico, special operatives in the Behavioral Science Unit. Captain Bains played up the technical end, extolling the virtues of their nationwide crime web, which would be able to match this murder up with similar ones from around the country. But in reality he disliked the Feds as much as I did.

Cops were fiercely territorial about their jurisdictions, and hated to have them trampled on. Especially by bureaucratic robots who were more concerned with procedure than results.

I went for another sip of coffee, but the cup was mercifully empty.

Maybe one of the leads would pan out. Maybe someone would identify the Jane Doe. Maybe the Feds and their super crime-busting computer would solve the case moments after they arrived.

But a feeling in my gut that wasn't entirely coffee-related told me that before we made any real progress, the Gingerbread Man would kill again.

He'd done too much planning to make this a one-time-only event.

Herb walked into my office, carrying an aromatic cup of hot Dunkin' Donuts coffee, a dark roast by the smell of it. But the way he poured it greedily down his throat made it apparent he hadn't brought it for me.

"Got the serum tests." He dropped a report on my desk. "Traces of sodium secobarbital found in her urine."

"Seconal?"

"You've heard of it?"

I nodded. I'd researched every insomnia remedy going back to Moses. "I've read about it. Went out of vogue when Valium came around, which went out of vogue with Halcion and Ambien."

I hadn't ever tried Seconal, but had given the others a shot. The depression they caused was worse than the sleepless nights. My doctor had offered to prescribe Prozac to combat the depression, but I didn't want to go down that slippery slope.

"Needle puncture on the upper arm was the entry point. ME said two ccs would put a hundred-and-fifty-pound person under in just a few seconds."

"Is Seconal prescribed anymore?"

"Not much. But we caught a break. Only hospital pharmacies carry injectionals. Because it's a Control two class drug, every order has to be sent to the Illinois Department of Professional Regulations. I got a list of all recent orders. Only a dozen or so."

"Also check for thefts from hospitals and manufacturers."

Benedict nodded, finishing his coffee. "You look like a bowl of crap, Jack."

"That's the poet in you, fighting to get out."

"You keep pulling all-nighters and Don is going to hit the bricks."

Don. I'd forgotten to call him and tell him I was staying late. Hopefully he'd forgive me. Again.

"Why don't you go home, get some rest."

"Not a bad plan, if I could."

My partner frowned. "Then go spend some time with your gentleman friend. Bernice is constantly on me about working too much, and you're here twenty hours a week more than I am. I don't see how Don puts up with it."

I met Don in a YMCA kickboxing class about a year ago. The instructor paired us up for sparring. I knocked him down with a snap-punch, and he asked me out. After six months of dating, Don's apartment lease ran out, and I invited him to move in—a bold move for a commitaphobe like me.

Don was the polar opposite of me in the looks department; blond, tan, with deep blue eyes and thick lips that I would kill for. I took after my mother. Not only were we both five feet six inches tall, with dark brown eyes, dark hair, and high cheekbones, but she was a retired Chicago cop.

When I was twelve, my mother taught me the two skills essential to my adult life: how to use a liner pencil to make my thin lips look fuller, and how to group my shots from forty feet away with a .38.

Unfortunately, Mom relayed very little information when it came to the care and feeding of a boyfriend.

"Don goes out a lot," I admitted. "I haven't seen him in a couple of days."

I closed my eyes, fatigue working slender fingers through my hair and down my back. Maybe going home would be a good idea. I could pick up some wine, take Don out to a nice lunch. We could try to openly communicate and work out the problems we'd been avoiding. Maybe I'd even score, as Mike Donovan had put it.

"Fine." My eyes snapped open, and I felt a surge of enthusiasm. "I'm going. You'll call if anything shakes loose?"

"Of course. When do the Feebies show?"

"Tomorrow, noonish. I'll be here."

We nodded our good-byes, and I stretched my cramped body out of my chair and went to go make a sincere effort with the man I was living with.

After all, the day could only get better.

Or so I thought.

CHAPTER 3

H<small>E HAS THE WHOLE THING ON</small> video.

It's playing right now on his forty-inch screen. The shades are drawn and the volume is maxed. He is alone in the house, sitting on the couch. Naked. The remote is clenched in a sweaty fist.

He leans forward and watches with wide eyes.

"I'm going to kill you," he says on tape.

The girl screams. She's on her back, tied to the floor, jiggling with fear. Completely his.

The light in the basement is clinically harsh; his very own operating theater. Not one freckle or mole on her nude body escapes his attention.

"Keep screaming. It turns me on."

She chews her lips, her body shaking in an effort to keep quiet. Mascara leaks down her face, leaving trails of black tears. The camera zooms in until her eyes are the size of bloodshot volleyballs.

Yummy.

The camera zooms back out, and he locks it into position on the tripod and walks over to her. He's naked and visibly aroused.

"You're all the same. You think you're hot shit. But where's all that confidence now?"

"I have money." Her voice cracks like puppy bones.

"I don't want your money. I want to see what you look like. On the inside."

She screams when he picks up the hunting knife, fighting against her bonds, her eyes bugging out like a cartoon. Nothing but an animal now, a frightened animal fearing for its life.

It's a look he's seen many times.

"Please-oh-God-no-oh-God-please . . ."

He kneels down next to her and wraps his free hand in her hair so she can't turn away. Then he tickles her throat with the edge of the blade.

"So pretty. I'm only giving you what you deserve. Don't you realize that? You're an example to the others. You thought you were famous before? Now you'll be even more famous. The first one."

She trembles before his power, fear radiating from her body like heat. He sets down the knife and fetches the extension cord.

This is the good part.

"Beg for your life."

More screaming and crying. Nothing coherent.

"You'll have to do better than that. Do you even remember me?"

She catches her breath and stares at him. The moment of recognition is like candy.

Sitting on his couch, he pauses the tape on the scene, eating up her terror. Fear is the ultimate turn-on, and this is the real thing. Not an actress in some fake S/M porno flick. This is the genuine article. A snuff film. *His* snuff film. He lets the tape play.

"You can't treat men like that. All of you think you can do that to me and get away with it."

He twists the cord around her neck, pulling it tight, getting his shoulders and back into it.

It isn't like in the movies. Strangulation isn't over in fifteen seconds.

She takes six minutes.

Her eyes bug out. Her face turns colors. She bucks and twists and makes sounds like a mewling kitten.

But slowly, sweetly, the fight goes out of her. Oxygen deprivation takes its toll, knocking her out, turning her into an unconscious blob.

He releases the cord and splashes some water on her face to wake her up.

She's even more terrified when she comes to. She fights so hard, he thinks she might break the twine. Her voice is raw and painful-sounding, but the screaming goes on and on.

Until he strangles her again.

And again.

He does it four times before something in her neck finally gives and she can't breathe even when he takes the cord off.

She writhes around on the floor, a private death dance just for him. Wiggle and twitch, gasp and moan. Her eyes roll up and her tongue sticks out and she turns colors.

He climbs on top and kisses her as she dies.

Though excited and aroused, there is still more work to do before he can fully enjoy her. He goes off screen and comes back with the plastic tarp.

This next part is messy.

He uses the hunting knife like an artist uses a paintbrush. Slowly. With care.

Then he adds his signature.

He's out of breath, slick with sweat and blood.

Satisfied.

For the moment.

"One down, three to go," he says to the television.

All in all, a successful production. Perhaps a little quick, considering the weeks of careful planning it has taken to get to this point. But that can be blamed on excitement.

With the next one he will pace himself better. Make it last. Do the cutting while she's still alive.

He'll grab the next girl tomorrow and try out some new things.

In the meantime he rewinds the videotape to watch it again.

CHAPTER 4

"D ON, I'M HOME."

I hid the wine bottle behind my back in case he was sitting in the kitchenette next to the front door.

He wasn't.

"Don?"

I did a quick tour of the place. It didn't take long, because my apartment was about the size of a Cracker Jack box. Except there was no prize inside.

But I wasn't discouraged. If he wasn't home, I could catch him at the health club. Don had vanity issues. True, he had a good body, but the amount of time he invested in it seemed disproportionate to the benefits.

I went to chill the wine, when I noticed the note on the fridge.

> *Jack,*
> *I've left you for my personal trainer, Roxy. We just*

*weren't right for each other, you were too into your
stupid job, and the sex wasn't very good.*

   *Plus your tossing and turning all night drove me
crazy. Please pack up all my stuff. I'll pick it up Friday.*

   *Thanks for fixing those parking tickets for me, and
don't worry. Roxy's place is about ten times bigger
than yours, so I'll have somewhere to stay.*

   Don

I read the note again, but it wasn't any nicer the second
time. We'd dated for almost an entire year. He'd been living
with me for six months. And now it was over, ended with a
brief, indifferent letter. I didn't even warrant the standard "I
hope we can still be friends" line.

I hit the freezer and took out an ice tray. Three cubes
went into a rocks glass, along with a shot of whiskey and a
splash of sour mix. I sat down and thought, and drank, and
thought some more.

When the cocktail was finished I made another. I was wad-
ing deep in the self-pity pool, but there was little sense of loss.
I hadn't loved Don. He was a warm body to hold at night and
a partner for restaurants and movies and occasional sex.

The only man I'd ever loved was my ex-husband, Alan.
When he left me, the pain was physical. Fifteen years later,
I'm still wary about giving another person that much control
over my heart again.

I eyed the half-finished drink in my hand. When Jacqueline Streng married Alan Daniels, she became Jack Daniels.
Ever since, people have given me bottles of the stuff as gifts,
each probably thinking they were being clever. I was forced
to develop a taste for it, or else open up my own liquor store.

I gulped down the rest of the cocktail and was about to
pour another, when I noticed my reflection in the door of the
microwave. Seeing myself, sitting at my cheap dinette set

with my sleepy red eyes and my limp hair, I looked like a finalist in the Miss Pathetic America Pageant.

Lots of cops I knew drank. They drank alone, drank on the job, drank when they woke up, and drank themselves to sleep. Law enforcement officers had a higher rate of alcoholism than any other profession. They also had the most divorces and the most suicides.

Divorce was the only statistic I cared to add to.

So I took off my blazer and my shoulder holster, replaced my skirt and blouse with a pair of jeans and a sweater, and went out to explore Chicago.

I lived on Addison and Racine, in a part of town called Wrigleyville. Rent was reasonable because it was impossible to park anywhere, especially since the Cubs started hosting night games. But I had a badge, so any fireplug or no-parking zone was fair game.

The neighborhood was loud and active, as expected. At any given time there were at least ten drinking-age college students per square foot, barhopping among the area's forty-plus watering holes. Great if you were in your twenties. But a mature woman like me was out of place in these trendy clubs, where techno music shook the foundations and drinks like "Screaming Orgasms" and "Blow Jobs" were the house specials.

Don had once dragged me into a bar called Egypto, where the only lighting in the place came from several hundred Lava lamps lining the walls. He bought me a drink called a "Slippery Dick." I told him the drink wasn't stiff enough. He didn't laugh. I should have known then.

So for a woman of my advanced years, Wrigleyville gave me only two real choices: the bar at the Westminster Hotel, or Joe's Pool Hall.

I'd only been at the Westminster once, out of curiosity. It turned out to be the kind of place where old people gather to die. The entertainment that night had been Dario, a small hairy man in suspenders with an electric accordion. He did a disco version of "When the Saints Go Marching In" while geriatrics polkaed furiously. I felt old, but not that old.

So I wound up at Joe's. They had good beer priced cheap and a dinginess that yuppies avoided. When I pushed open the door, I wasn't assaulted by industrial dance music. Just the clackety-clack of pool balls and an occasional laugh or swearword.

My kind of place.

I went up to the bar, resting my forearms on the cigarette-scarred counter and propping a foot on the brass railing. A fat bartender took my beer order, which set me back a whopping two bucks, with tip.

I pulled off the bottle and took in the surroundings, searching for an open table through the dim lighting and the cigar smoke.

All twelve were occupied, all but two with doubles action.

Of the singles, one was being worked by an elderly black man who was having a heated discussion with himself. At the other table was a bald guy in jeans and a white T-shirt. He was a few years my junior and looked vaguely familiar.

I picked up a cue from a nearby rack and walked over.

He was hunched over the table, his stick gliding on the solid bridge of his thumb and forefinger, eyeing the cue ball with intense concentration.

"This may sound like a come-on, but haven't I seen you somewhere before?"

He took the shot without looking up, banking the three ball into a side pocket. Then he righted himself and squinted at me, and I suddenly knew who he was.

"You arrested me six years ago."

That's one of the dangers of being a cop. People you think you remember from high school turn out to be felons.

"Phineas Troutt, right? Tough to forget a name like that."

He nodded.

"And your name had something to do with booze. Detective José Cuervo?"

His face was blank, and I couldn't tell if he was joking or not.

"Jack Daniels. I'm a lieutenant now."

I noted his body language. His blue eyes were steady, and he held himself in a relaxed stance. I didn't feel threatened by him, but at the same time I was aware I'd left my gun at home.

"You had brown hair before," I said. "Long, in a ponytail."

"Chemo. Pancreatic cancer." He pointed his chin at my cue. "Can you use that thing, or do you hold it for some Freudian reason?"

That seemed like a challenge to me, and I was feeling a bit reckless. I recalled the bust vividly, because it had been the easiest arrest of my career. It had been an 818—gang fight in progress. When we arrived on the scene, Phineas dropped to his knees and laced his hands behind his head without even being asked. Strewn around him were four unconscious gang-bangers in need of medical attention. Phin claimed they jumped him, but since he was the only one without anything broken, we had to bring him in.

"Loser racks and buys the beers."

"Fair enough."

We played eight ball, calling shots, putting the eight in the last pocket called. He beat me an average of two games to one, so I wound up paying for most of the games and buying most of the drinks. We hardly talked, but the silence was companionable, and the competition was good-natured.

By the eighth game, the alcohol was starting to affect me, so I switched to diet cola. Phin, as he preferred to be called, stuck with beer, and it didn't seem to affect him at all. Even after I'd sobered up, he continued to whup my butt.

I liked it that way; it made me play better.

Day became night, and Joe's began to fill up. Lines formed at all the tables, forcing us to relinquish ours.

I thought about asking Phin if he wanted to get a cup of coffee, but it sounded too much like a date, and I didn't want to give the wrong impression. Instead, I offered my hand.

"Thanks for the games."

His grip was warm, dry.

"Thank you, Lieutenant. It's nice to have some quality competition. Maybe we'll have a chance to do this again?"

I smiled. "Damn right. Bring your wallet, because next time you'll be buying most of the beers."

He smiled, briefly, and we went our separate ways. I made a mental note to check outstanding warrants on him. If he was wanted for something, I wasn't quite sure what I would do. I liked the guy, even if he did have a rap sheet. These days it was rare for me to like anything. Could I arrest a pool buddy, especially one dying of cancer?

Unfortunately, yes.

Once home, my bed was uncomfortable, my mind refused to relax, and the clock mocked me with each passing minute.

I was tired, exhausted actually, but thoughts kept flashing through my skull and wouldn't let me be. They weren't even profound thoughts; just random flotsam.

I tried counting backward from ten thousand. I tried deep breathing and relaxation exercises. I tried to imagine myself asleep. Nothing worked.

Time marched forward, taking me with it.

By the time I was feeling the slightest bit drowsy, the sun peeked in through the blinds and I had to get up to go to work.

I sat up and stretched my tired bones, and then went into

my morning exercise routine. A hundred sit-ups, with a promise to do two hundred tomorrow. Twenty push-ups, with a similar promise. Thinking about doing some barbell curls and rejecting the idea because the barbell was hidden in the closet. And then off to the shower.

I'd survived my first night without Don, and it wasn't nearly as bad as it might have been. It could only get easier with time.

Then I saw his toothbrush on the bathroom sink and was depressed the rest of the day.

CHAPTER 5

CUTTING OR SLICING DOESN'T WORK, because it's impossible to close it up afterward.

The way to do it is to pinch each side of the wrapper by the seam and pull gently. This is tricky—opening the candy without ripping the package. Even the smallest tear is no good. People aren't stupid. No one will eat candy with a torn wrapper.

Working on the candy itself is the exciting part. "Fun Size!" the bag proclaims. "Dinky" was a more appropriate description. The mini candy bars are scarcely a bite each.

But one bite is all it takes.

His average is good; he only ruins four wrappers out of twenty-four. He sets the chocolate on a tray and opens up the package of sewing needles. Needles and pins work best. They don't mar the surface going in; just leave a tiny hole that is easily covered up with a dot of melted chocolate. He uses four needles per candy bar, on cross angles, so no matter where it's bitten, at least one will draw blood.

After doing ten candy bars with needles, he cracks his knuckles and feels warmed up enough for some harder work.

Fishhooks take finesse. He holds the candy lightly in a latex-gloved hand and picks up a hook with needle-nose pliers. Pushing the barb into the bottom of the candy, he inserts the hook bit by bit, angling the pliers in a curving motion so the entire fishhook disappears through the entry hole.

It is difficult work, but he's had years of practice. His personal record is eleven hooks in one small candy bar. He liked to prepare for Halloween weeks in advance, and when the big day arrived, he'd find a neighborhood house that was empty and set up his bowl full of lethal treats next to their door. Sometimes he also put a sign that said Only Take One! next to the bowl. A nice ghoulish touch.

After rigging five pieces with fishhooks, he opens a box of X-Acto knife blades and pushes several of those into the remaining bars. X-Acto blades leave a bigger entry hole, but with a cigarette lighter and an extra chocolate bar, he can hide the hole from even the most intense inspection.

After finishing all twenty candies, he places them carefully back into their wrappers. A few drops of Super Glue seal them back up. Then he puts the bars into the plastic bag they came in, one by one, through a small one-inch slit in the side. When he's done, he puts four untainted candies from a second bag into this one, so it holds the correct total of twenty-four.

Holding it in his hand, it looks like an ordinary bag of candy bars, ready to be consumed.

He plugs in a hair crimper, lets it get hot, and then carefully crimps closed the slit he's made in the bag. The crimper melts the plastic edges together somewhat unevenly, so he trims away the excess plastic with a razor blade.

Perfect.

Now it's time to see whom the treat will go to. He turns his attention to the photos on the table, flipping through them to find the two he wants.

They are both close-ups of faces. He'd taken them at the 7-Eleven the other day, while standing in the crowd and watching the stupid pigs trample around his crime scene. One is of a fat man with a mustache. The other is of a thin woman with nice legs.

One of these is the officer in charge of his case. They were the only two cops there who weren't wearing uniforms, so they had to be the top guys. But which one is the head honcho? The one who, by the luck of the draw, has become his nemesis?

A simple phone call to the police will reveal who heads the case, but he doesn't want to call from his home phone. The pigs can trace phone calls instantly, and he doesn't want it to lead back to him somewhere down the line.

Nothing will lead back to him.

His plan is flawless. Perfect. Every last detail has been worked out. Stalk. Abduct. Destroy. Dispose. Repeat. He has the perfect cover, has their schedules down pat, even has a contingency plan if the police ever find him. Not that they will, but it pays to plan ahead.

So he takes a walk to the nearest pay phone, on the outside of a Mini-Mart, and calls Information to find out what police station is nearest to Monroe and Dearborn—the corner where he dumped the first whore.

Armed with the district number, he calls the officer on duty and identifies himself as a reporter from the *Herald*.

"Can you spell out the name of the detective in charge?"

"Daniels, first name Jack."

"Jack Daniels? For real?"

"Yes, sir."

"Is he on the heavy side, has a mustache?"

"No, that's Detective Benedict. He's Daniels's partner. Jack is a woman. Short for Jacqueline, I think. She's a lieutenant."

"Thanks."

Hanging up, he feels excitement crackle through his body like electricity. He rushes back home to his pictures, leafing through them until he finds one of Daniels leaving the scene in her crappy Chevy Nova.

"I know who you are." The Gingerbread Man rubs his finger over her face. "And I know what you drive. But I'll know more. Much more."

He smiles. Chicago thinks a simple bitch like that can catch him?

Think again.

He checks his watch. Nine in the morning. He isn't going to grab the second girl for another two hours. What time does the good lieutenant go to work? Is she there right now?

He decides to check. Picking up the bag of candy with pliers to avoid leaving fingerprints, he carries the gift to his truck and takes a meandering path to the 26th District.

It looks like any other building in Chicago, except this one houses cops rather than offices or apartments. There is a parking lot next to it with a big sign that reads "Police Vehicles Only." On his third trip around the lot, he spies Jack's Nova, near the back, between two patrol cars.

"Hey, buddy!"

A cop flags him down. He almost hits the gas in panic, but when the pig approaches, it's obvious what he wants.

"It's on me, Officer." The Gingerbread Man smiles,

handing the cop his selection. "I appreciate you keeping the city safe."

The pig doesn't even thank him, waddling off down the street, letting the biggest arrest of his life drive away.

The Gingerbread Man parks in front of a meter and puts on some leather gloves. Cradling the bag of goodies in his jacket, he walks briskly back to the police station and enters the parking lot as if he belongs there. Two uniformed patrolmen give him a glance, and he nods a hello, confident and at ease. They return the nod and walk on.

Adrenaline threatening to make his heart explode, he approaches Jack's car and pulls the slim-jim out of his pants leg. It's a long strip of thin metal with a forked end. He forces it between the driver's-side window and the weather stripping, and jams it down into the inner workings of the car door. By feel, he finds the lock mechanism and pushes down.

Up pops the button, in about the same amount of time it would have taken to open it with a key.

The interior smells faintly of perfume. Even though he's in a hurry, he climbs behind the wheel and savors the moment.

Violation is such a rush.

"I'm in your car, Jack."

He sniffs the steering wheel. Hand cream and hair spray.

It tastes salty.

On the floor is an empty cardboard coffee cup. He picks it up and licks the smudge of lipstick on the rim.

His eyes close, and he can see Jack, tied up in his basement, naked and bloody and screaming.

Such an excellent idea.

Another look around proves the parking lot is still empty. He places the package on the passenger seat and searches through the glove compartment for the lieutenant's vehicle registration. He memorizes the address, grinning at how easy this is.

"I'll be seeing you, Jack."

His lingering has put him a few minutes behind schedule. He doesn't want to be late grabbing the second whore. He has a bunch of new things he's just aching to try out with her.

He makes sure no one is watching, then he gets out of the car and strolls back to his truck, a spring in his step.

What a day this is turning out to be.

CHAPTER 6

I WAS FINISHING MY THIRD CUP of coffee when the FBI walked in.

They didn't immediately announce themselves as Feebies when they entered my office, without knocking. But both wore tailored gray suits, Harvard ties, spit-shined shoes, and crew cuts. Who else could they be—yearbook committee?

"Lieutenant Daniels?" The one on the right continued before I acknowledged him. "I'm Special Agent George Dailey. This is Special Agent Jim Coursey."

Special Agent Coursey nodded at me.

"We're from the Bureau," Special Agent Coursey said.

Special Agent Dailey nodded at me.

Dailey was slightly taller, and his hair a shade lighter, but that minimal difference was negligible. They could have been clones. And knowing our government, they might have been.

"We're both ViCAT operatives of the BSU."

"The Violent Criminal Apprehension Team of the Behavioral Science Unit."

"We've done a profile of the perpetrator, and we have a printout of possible related cases with percentile rankings of same suspect likelihood."

"Are we going too fast for you?"

I said, "You're early."

They looked at each other, then back at me.

"The sooner we give your people an idea of what we're looking for, the sooner we catch him," Dailey said.

Coursey dropped his briefcase onto my desk and snapped it open, pulling out a packet of neatly stacked paper. He handed me the top sheet.

"Are you familiar with profiling?"

I nodded.

"Profiling of repeat and recreational killers is done with the ViCAT computer at Quantico." Dailey had apparently missed my nod. "We enter specific details about the murder, including but not limited to the condition of the corpse, location it was found, method of demise, signs of ritualism, physical evidence, witness testimony, and any beforehand information about the deceased. The computer analyzes the data and gives us a rough description of the suspect."

"For example," Coursey took over, "our suspect is a male Caucasian, between the ages of twenty-five and thirty-nine. He's right-handed, and owns a station wagon or truck. He's blue collar, probably a factory worker, possibly in the textiles industry. He is an alcoholic, and prone to violent rages. He frequents western bars and enjoys line dancing."

"Line dancing," I said.

"He also wears women's underwear," Dailey added. "Possibly his mother's."

I felt a headache coming on.

"As a juvenile he set fires and committed relations with animals."

"With animals," I said.

"There's a high probability he's been arrested before. Possibly for assault or rape, probably on elderly women."

"But he's impotent now."

"He may also be gay."

I lifted my coffee cup to my lips and found it was empty. I lowered it again.

"He hears voices."

"Or maybe just one voice."

"It could be the voice of his mother, telling him to kill."

"Maybe she just wants her underwear back," I offered.

"He may be disfigured or disabled. He might have severe acne scars, orscoliosis."

"That's a curvature of the spine," Dailey added.

"Is that a hunch?" I asked.

"Just an educated guess."

I thought about explaining the joke to them, but it would be wasted.

"He may have been dropped on his head as a child," Coursey said.

He probably wasn't the only one.

"Gentlemen." I wasn't sure where to begin, but I gave it a try. "Call me a skeptic, but I don't see how any of this is going to help us catch him."

"First of all, you should start staking out western bars."

"And local textile factories that have hired someone with a criminal record within the last six months."

"I could stake out the zoo too," I said. "He may be sneaking in at night and committing relations with animals."

"I doubt it." Coursey furrowed his brow. "The profile says he's impotent now."

I rubbed my eyes. When I finished, the two of them were still there.

"Of course, the profile may change slightly as more data becomes available," Dailey said.

"If he kills again."

"When he kills again."

They looked at each other and nodded smartly.

I wondered, in all seriousness, what would happen if I pulled my revolver and shot one of them. Would the other one arrest me, or would he wait to see if my profile showed the proper aptitude for the crime?

"Here's the statement we're releasing to the press." Coursey handed me another piece of paper. "Now that we're assigned to the case."

"We still have jurisdiction." I let some irritation show. "No state borders have been crossed."

"Not yet. Until then, we're just consultants."

"Simply a tool for you to use."

"To help make things run smoother."

There's a laugh for you.

"This"—Dailey handed me more papers—"is a list of reasons why we've pegged the murderer as organized rather than disorganized. You're familiar with the concept of grouping serial criminals as either O or DO?"

I nodded. He went on, paying me no heed. I had a feeling this entire meeting could have been conducted without my presence.

"DO, or disorganized criminals, usually have little or no planning stage. Their crimes are spur of the moment, either lust- or rage-induced. Signs of guilt or remorse can usually be found at the scene, such as something covering the victim's face; an indication the killer doesn't like the accusation of a staring pair of eyes. Clues in the form of physical and circumstantial evidence abound, because the DO type doesn't stop to cover them up, or only does as an afterthought."

"I'm familiar with the labels." I stated it, distinctly, precisely.

"The organized type," he went on. Perhaps I hadn't been clear enough. "Usually spends a lot of time on the planning stage. The perp may spend days beforehand fantasizing about the murder, plotting out every detail. He won't leave evidence intentionally, and usually the victim bears no sign of savage, uncontrollable violence. The injuries, while they can be sadistic, are more focused and controlled."

"We've come up with one hundred and fifteen reasons why we believe this killer is the organized type," Coursey said. "And we'd like to take an hour or so to go over them with you."

I was ready to fake a heart attack to get them to leave, when Benedict walked into my office, saving me the trouble.

"Jack, we got a lead on that Seconal. Sixty milliliters were purchased by a Charles Smith on August tenth of this year at the Mercy Hospital pharmacy."

"Have we found him?"

"He gave a fake address. There are seventeen Charles Smiths in Chicago and twelve more in the rest of Illinois, but it looks like the name is fake too."

"What about the doctor?"

"That's how we nailed it down. The doctor's name was Reginald Booster."

The name was familiar.

"The unsolved murder from Palatine a couple months back?"

"That's him. He was killed at his home on August ninth. I had the file faxed to us and I've called his daughter. We're meeting her at the house at one."

"Let's go." I stood up and grabbed my jacket, thrilled to be actually doing something on this case.

"We'll go over this when you get back," Dailey said.

It sounded more like a threat than a promise. I left without acknowledging them, but felt no moral victory in being rude.

They hadn't noticed.

H E KNOWS WHERE SHE LIVES.
He knows where all of them live, but this one was easier to find than the others. It was just a matter of looking her up in the phone book. T. Metcalf. Did women really think they were fooling anyone by only allowing the first initial of their name to be published? Who else but women did that?

He watches her apartment from his truck. Theresa Metcalf. The second whore to die. He's parked across the street, binoculars aimed at her window, peering through her open blinds. There's movement in the apartment. He knows it's her, getting ready for work.

He has her schedule down better than she does. As usual, she's running late. When she finally hits the street, it will be in a rush. But she never runs, and she never calls a cab. Work is five blocks away. She always walks the same route. Human beings are creatures of habit. He's counting on that.

He looks at his watch again. She's later than normal today. His palms are sweating. It's been a thrilling morning so far; preparing the candy, leaving it for Jack, getting her address. Now comes uncertainty.

The Gingerbread Man leaves very little up to chance, but grabbing a person has too many variables to account for them all. He'd originally intended for Theresa to be the first, but when the day came to snatch her, she'd uncharacteristically walked to work with her roommate.

Potential witnesses, the weather, traffic, and unpredictable human nature all conspire to make an abduction very delicate and tricky. He doesn't know if she carries Mace. He doesn't know if she has a black belt in karate. He doesn't know if she will scream and attract attention. All he can do is plan as best he can, and hope for luck.

He watches the blinds close in the window. Good. She'll be coming down the stairs in a few minutes.

"You open?"

He quickly drops the binoculars and looks to his right. A boy, no more than ten, is staring in at him. Black kid, big head, wide eyes.

It had been a long time since he'd killed a child. Almost another life. Before prison. The last one was a little girl. She'd been playing in front of her house. He grabbed her on impulse. She was so fragile and small. Screamed like an angel.

"What do you want?"

"Bomb Pop."

He reaches into the cooler behind him and pulls out a Bomb Pop. First sale of the day, not including the freebie he'd given that cop earlier. It sells for two dollars. He pays a dime wholesale. Since he works independently and the truck is his, the only overhead is gasoline. Not only does he have the perfect urban camouflage, but he's even making a profit.

The kid pays him in change, counting it carefully. Little

shit has no clue how close to death he is. Just a quick tug on the shirt, and the boy could be his. He scans down the street for witnesses and sees nary a soul.

But not today. Today he has other plans.

The kid lopes off, licking his ice cream.

The front door to the apartment opens, and the whore strides out. He runs through the grab one more time in his head. Pull out in front of her. Jump out. Stick her with the needle and haul her in back. Shouldn't take more than ten seconds. Then he'll have her for his use, for as long as he can keep her alive.

Tapping his foot, impatient, he lets her get a block ahead of him before he starts the truck. His hands are sweating and he has a sudden attack of the giggles. The syringe is in his pocket, filled with fifty milligrams of Seconal. Not much, but a little goes a long way. He'll pump it straight into her arm, and it'll begin to take effect within five seconds.

First she'll become drowsy and disoriented. Then she'll begin losing muscle control. It takes about five full minutes before she will be under completely, but until then he should be able to handle her without difficulty. Seconal has a soothing effect, and so far everyone he's used it on has remained compliant, if not downright helpful.

He practiced on winos when he'd first gotten the Seconal. There are plenty littering the streets of Chicago, begging for handouts. The first one he gave six ccs, killing him almost instantly. He halved the dosage, and the next one never woke up. One to 1.5 milliliters turned out to be the right dose for women, depending on how chunky they were. These whores aren't chunky. They're racehorses. Whorses. He giggles.

The alley is coming up. He pulls into it ahead of her, taking in everything. There's no one nearby. Perfect. She approaches the truck without even noticing it.

Wait! She's crossing the street! He's watched her walk to

work almost a dozen times, and she's never crossed until she reaches the intersection. His mind races. Call it off, or improvise?

"Theresa?"

He's out of the truck, coming at her on an angle, syringe palmed in his right hand.

"Theresa?"

She stops and looks at him. He smiles brightly. Smiles disarm people. His pace is fast, but he puts some bounce in his step and tries to look in a hurry rather than threatening.

"I thought it was you. Charles, remember?"

He says it at normal speaking level, which is too low for the twenty-foot distance between them.

"Pardon me?"

She cranes her neck forward a bit. Her posture isn't defensive, but her expression is confused. She isn't sure if she recognizes him or not.

He takes two more steps. "I'm sorry, you don't remember me, do you? I'm Charles."

Her eyes narrow slightly, trying to place him. "Sorry, I . . ." She shrugs.

"You mean you don't even remember the truck?" He takes three more steps and makes a grand sweeping gesture toward his ice cream truck. "I thought you'd remember the truck."

"Look—I'm late for work . . ."

"At Montezuma's. That's where you work, right?"

"Have I served you before?"

"No." The Gingerbread Man grins. The smile is genuine now. "But you will."

The girl doesn't like his leer and subconsciously shifts her weight away from his approaching form. He detects the subtle change, and knows that if she bolts or screams, he won't get a second chance.

"Here, let me . . ." Reaching into his pockets, he pulls out a handful of quarters. Trying to look clumsy, he lets the change spill from his hand and all over the curb.

"Aw . . . my boss is gonna kill me!"

He kneels down and begins picking up coins, hoping he looks really pathetic.

He must, because she only watches for a few seconds before coming over to help.

"Thanks. This is a whole morning's work here."

She crouches down, picking up a quarter. "What did you say your name was?"

He checks for witnesses. A guy on the end of the street, walking past, not paying attention.

"Charles."

"And where do I know you from?"

She reaches out to hand him some coins. He snatches her wrist and yanks her to him, jabbing the needle home, hugging her close so to any casual observer it looks like an embrace.

She tries to twist, but he has sixty pounds on her and his hold has taken away her leverage. Leaving the syringe still sticking in her arm, he brings his hand up to the back of her head and crushes her face to his, drowning out the cry welling up inside her with a kiss.

He tastes fear. She has the nerve to try to bite him, and that gets him excited. He likes to bite too. He sinks his teeth into her lower lip, and then her body begins to relax.

Half pulling, half carrying, he gets her over to the truck. A cab rolls past, but doesn't slow down. Once she's in back, he handcuffs her to the metal bar he's bolted to his freezer. Then he removes the needle from her arm and puts it back in his pocket.

Theresa Metcalf shakes her head, as if she is trying to clear it. When she notices the handcuffs, she screams.

In the driver's seat, Charles flips on the music. A recorded pipe organ version of "The Candyman" trumpets through the speakers at full volume. He checks his mirrors and carefully backs out of the alley. She screams again, but he's confident that he's her only audience.

"I scream, you scream, we all scream for ice cream." He giggles.

Quite a day. Quite a day indeed. And quite a night it will be as well.

He's bought three new videotapes. He's planning on filling them all.

"Wait till we get back to my place," he tells T. Metcalf. "Then you'll have something to scream about."

She is too drowsy to hear him.

CHAPTER 8

H OW DID YOU KNOW," HERB SAID, smacking his lips, "that I was in the mood for candy?"

I glanced over at Benedict. He was clutching a bag of chocolate, eyes twinkling.

"Do you keep an emergency supply in your jacket?" I asked.

"Me? These are yours. They were on the seat."

"Where?"

"In your car here, on the passenger seat."

I started the Nova and frowned, puzzled.

"They're not mine. Was there a note?"

"Nope. Just candy. Maybe it was Don."

I shook my head and pulled out of the parking lot.

"Don left."

Benedict mulled it over, cradling the candy in his hand. "How do you feel about it?"

"I don't know."

"Did you love him?"

"I don't know."

"Do you miss him?"

"I don't know. Yes. Maybe. I'm not sure. No."

"Remind me never to get romantically involved with you."

I turned left on Jackson and headed toward Mercy Hospital, where Herb had traced the Seconal prescription and where the late Dr. Booster had kept an office until the ninth of August. The Booster case was still listed as open, even though the investigation had gone cold. The detective in charge was a Palatine cop named Evens. Herb had left him a message, telling him to get in touch.

"So who gave you the candy?"

I shrugged. "Haven't the slightest. Maybe someone put it in my car by accident."

"Accidents like that never happen to me."

"Have you checked your car? Maybe you have a bag too. Maybe your entire backseat is crammed full of chocolate products."

"Stop it. You're getting me excited."

I tried to think it through. My car was unlocked when we got in. Had I left it unlocked? I must have. How likely was it that someone broke into my car just to leave me candy? Especially in a police parking lot.

"Mind if I . . . ?"

"Go right ahead."

Benedict ripped open the plastic bag and withdrew a mini bar, holding it up to his nose.

"Smells okay. I don't think they're laced with arsenic."

"Would that even matter to you?"

"Probably not."

My partner opened up the candy and popped the entire

bar into his mouth. He chewed for almost a full minute, making cooing noises.

"Maybe it was Bill, in Evidence." Benedict's mouth was still half full. "He's always been sweet on you. This could be his way of expressing his love."

"Bill is almost seventy."

"Beggars can't be choosers, Jack. Want one?"

"I'll pass. But feel free."

He grunted a thanks and opened another.

"There's no one you know who would give you candy?"

"Nobody. I'm all alone in this big cruel world."

"Geez, Jack. That's really sad."

"If there were an award for the world's biggest loser, I wouldn't even win that."

"At least you don't dwell on it."

I hit the gas and cruised through an intersection just as a yellow light was turning red. It was an unnecessary risk, but I didn't get to be a lieutenant in the male-dominated world of Chicago law enforcement without taking chances.

"You could try Lunch Mates," Herb said.

"What?"

"It's a dating service."

"Jesus."

"I'm serious." He took a bite of the candy, smacking appreciatively. "You make an appointment to meet with an agent and answer questions about yourself. Then they arrange for you to meet for lunch with a compatible man. It's all prearranged so there's no pressure."

"I could also meet men by putting on some hot pants and walking along Twenty-third and Stony. At least I'd be the payee instead of the payer."

Benedict popped the rest of the chocolate into his mouth.

"I just read an article about it in the *Chicago Reader*. It seems like a good idea."

"Only weirdos meet people like that."

"Not at all. Just people with full-time careers who are sick of the bar scene."

"They'd match me with some weirdo."

"I think that both parties have to agree to meet before the lunch takes place. What have you got to lose?"

"My dignity, my self-respect . . ."

"Bullshit. You don't have any dignity or self-respect."

"Jesus."

I hung a left and swung into the parking lot of Mercy, where I parked in a loading zone. As Benedict and I extracted ourselves from the less-than-spacious confines of my beater, a parking lot attendant sauntered over, oozing attitude. I flashed my badge. Instant respect.

We strolled up to the doctors' building, a large oppressive brick edifice that competed for the ugly award with the equally oppressive hospital. They stood side by side, large and brown, with crumbling brickwork and rusty fire escapes. Chicago was a city filled with great architecture, but every garden had a few weeds.

"I see you couldn't leave your compulsion behind," I said to Herb, indicating the candy in his hands.

"I was thinking about passing it around the children's ward. That is, if you don't mind."

"Not at all. I must say I'm touched by your unselfish nature."

"Bernice says if I gain any more weight, she's cutting off the nookie."

"The No Nookie Diet."

It was a welcome shock to find the interior of the doctors' building both brightly lit and pleasant. After consulting the front desk, we were directed to the fifth floor.

Dr. Booster had been a general practitioner. He shared an

office with Dr. Emilia Kuzdorff and Dr. Ralph Potts, an OB-GYN and a pediatrician, respectively. We got into the elevator with an attractive blond woman and her sniffling daughter. Watching the child sniffle made me aware that I had a slight runny nose as well. Serves me right for not dressing properly.

I searched my pocket for a Kleenex—while on the job, I didn't carry a purse. Too cumbersome. That's why I favored blazers with big pockets. Today I was wearing a gray Donna Karan and a matching skirt, with a blue blouse and black flats. Heels were another hindrance to the job.

Sadly, my pockets were without any tissue. I briefly considered using Benedict's tie, which was a green-and-orange–striped monstrosity that was too wide by at least thirty years. It was also covered with chocolate stains. Herb may be out of style, but he's messy to make up for it.

Benedict must have guessed my intent, because he produced a pack of tissue from his pocket for me.

We located office 514 with no major difficulties. Dr. Booster's name was still on the plaque next to the door. The waiting room was full of screaming children and frustrated mothers. I approached the front desk and got the attention of a nurse.

"I'm Lieutenant Daniels. This is Detective Benedict. We have a few questions concerning Dr. Booster."

She looked up at me with the greenest eyes I'd ever seen. It took me a moment to realize they must be contacts.

"Have you caught him?"

"No, ma'am. Not yet. You knew Dr. Booster?"

"I worked for him for seven years. He was a good doctor. He didn't deserve that."

"Can I get your name, ma'am?" Benedict had his notepad already in hand.

"Rastitch. Maria Rastitch."

The phone rang. She picked it up, said a few words, and transferred the call.

"We're hoping to look at a patient list."

"We already supplied that other officer with a list."

Which we'd seen. There was no Charles Smith. No one even had Charles as a first name.

"We wanted to see a list that cross-referenced names with prescriptions. Dr. Booster wrote out a prescription for a large amount of Seconal before he died. Were any of his patients taking Seconal?"

She frowned and swiveled her chair over to the computer. After a few seconds of punching keys she shook her head.

"Nope. No Seconal."

Benedict said, "How about patients of Dr. Kuzdorff and Dr. Potts?"

"This includes them. There's no one. Years ago we used Seconal for sleep disorders, but flurazepam is the preferred method of treatment now."

"Do you have copies of all Dr. Booster's prescriptions?"

"The ones he fills out here, yes. It would be on the computer. Our database lets us pull information by patient name, social security number, illness, visitation date, appointment date, and prescription."

"Is it possible that the doctor wrote a prescription after office hours?"

"For Seconal? It would be odd. It's a Control two drug. I don't see why he would prescribe it at all, in the office or out of it."

"But it's possible?"

"Sure. All he'd need is the prescription paper."

"Doesn't the pharmacy call here to confirm prescriptions?"

"Sometimes. But if it's after office hours, they may fill it without calling. The hospital pharmacy never calls. The pharmacists there know all of the doctors."

I handed her my card.

"Thank you, Ms. Rastitch. Please call if you think of anything that may help. If it isn't too inconvenient, we'd like to speak to a few other employees."

"Not at all. I'll announce you."

Herb and I spent another hour talking to Booster's staff and fellow doctors. They all echoed what the green-eyed nurse had said. No one knew why Booster would write a prescription for Seconal, and no one knew any patient who took it.

But Booster had written the prescription, as confirmed by the Illinois Department of Regulations, and someone calling himself Charles Smith had filled it and presumably used it in the abduction of our Jane Doe. If no one in Booster's office remembered him, maybe the pharmacist who filled the prescription would.

Benedict and I left the doctors' building, walking over to its ugly twin, where the hospital pharmacy lay in wait. There was a line. But one of the many perks of having a badge was the ability to bypass lines. This seemed to irritate the dozen people we cut in front of, but you can't please all the people all the time.

The pharmacist looked like I'd picture a pharmacist to look: balding, fortyish, WASP, with glasses and a white coat. His name was Steve, and he informed us he'd been working there for three years.

"Were you working here last August tenth?"

He double-checked his schedule and informed us that yes, he was indeed working that day.

"Do you remember filling out a prescription for sixty milliliters of liquid Seconal on that date?"

His brown eyes lit up. "Yes. Yes, I do. It practically depleted our stock."

"Could you describe what the individual looked like?"

He furrowed his brow. "It was a man, I remember that much. But what he looked like? I'm drawing a blank. I fill hundreds of prescriptions a day, and that was two months ago."

"Was there anything unusual about his appearance? Very tall or short, old or young, skin color, eyes?" Herb asked.

"I think he was white. Not old or young. But I'm not sure."

"Was he a hunchback?" I asked, bringing up the FBI's profile.

Benedict shot me a glance, but honored my rank by not questioning me in front of a civilian.

"You mean like Quasimodo?" Steve asked.

I felt silly, but nodded.

"No, I would have remembered it if he was."

"Did he also get syringes with the Seconal?"

"I'm not sure. Let me check."

He went to his computer and hit a few keys.

"Here's the prescription." Steve pointed at his screen. "Under the name Charles Smith. He isn't listed anywhere else in our computer. No needles, either. All he got from us was the Seconal."

"Do you have the original handwritten prescription?"

"Nope. We throw them away at the end of the week."

"How do you know if a prescription is real or faked?"

"I suppose it's possible to counterfeit prescriptions, but who else but a doctor would know how many mgs of tetracycline are used to fight a respiratory infection? As for the Class B and C drugs, the ones that could be sold on the street, we call on them."

"Did you call for this one?"

"No. I remembered considering it, but it was eight in the evening and Dr. Booster's office was closed. I also recognized Dr. Booster's signature. Even though the amount was strange, it seemed authentic."

I sniffled, puzzling it over.

"Catching a cold?" Steve asked.

"Not on purpose."

"I'd suggest an over-the-counter antihistamine. Stay away from nasal sprays. They're addictive."

"I'll keep that in mind." I handed him my card. "If it's convenient I'd like you to come in after work today and sit down with a police artist. See if we can get a picture of this guy."

"I really don't remember him."

"Our artist is good at helping people remember. This is extremely important, Steve. This Charles Smith has been linked to the brutal murders of two people. Anything at all you can give us is more than we had before."

He nodded, promising to stop by. Herb and I left to the sour looks of the people we'd cut in front of. One old woman in particular gave me a sneer that could curdle milk. I considered sneering back, but that would be petty. We left the hospital without incident.

"What about the candy?" I asked Benedict when we got into my car. "What happened to giving it to sick kids?"

"I decided that candy is bad for the teeth and generally all-around unhealthy. Not something sick kids should be exposed to."

"How gallant of you, bearing that unhealthy burden all yourself."

"Want one?"

"Yeah. If you can part with it."

"Just one. I'm looking out for your health, Jack."

He handed me a candy bar and I pulled out of the parking

lot. Keeping one hand on the wheel, I tore the wrapper off with my teeth and was about to pop it into my mouth when Herb yelped.

At first I thought he was vomiting.

But it wasn't vomit.

It was a lot of blood.

CHAPTER 9

HERB GOT ELEVEN STITCHES IN THE mouth. A shot of Novocain made it painless, but watching the curved needle stitch in and out of his squirming tongue was torture to see. I could have waited by the emergency room entrance, but I wanted to witness what some sick bastard had done to my friend.

"Thanth." Benedict nodded at the doctor when the last knot was tied.

I eyed the bloody candy bar in the metal tray next to Herb's bed. The edge of an X-Acto knife peeked out through the caramel, shining in the fluorescent light.

"One more favor, Doc. I know this is unorthodox, but I don't have access to an X-ray machine at the station."

I explained my request and he agreed, sending me and Herb out into the waiting room. While Benedict filled out forms, I went through my mental files of all the enemies I'd made throughout my life.

There were more than I'd care to mention. Anyone I'd ever busted from my patrol days up until now could have nursed a grudge. I've also pissed off a few people in my personal life. But I couldn't think of anyone, even murderers I'd put away who swore they'd break out and kill me, who would leave me such a horrible gift.

It could have been just bad luck. Some random freak I never met decides to express his hatred for cops by dropping off treats in the police parking lot. But an earlier call to the district killed that theory. No one else seemed to have gotten candy. I faced the disturbing truth that it was meant for me specifically.

"How about rethent catheth?" Herb asked.

"Recent cases?"

He nodded. Herb's lower lip had swelled up from the stitches, causing him to pout. His tongue was also swollen, making him look like his mouth was full. But a full mouth was the normal look for Herb, so it didn't detract too much.

"The only cases we've had in the last few weeks are gang deaths and suicides. Except the Gingerbread Man case. But how would he even know who I am?"

"Newth?"

"I don't think I've been mentioned in the news."

He shrugged. A line of drool was running down his chin; Herb was still too numb to feel it. I made the universal wiping motion on my own face, and he got the hint and cleaned himself off.

"Do you want to keep our appointment with Dr. Booster's daughter, or call it a day?"

"Bootherth daubder."

I nodded, glancing to the right as Benedict's doctor approached. In one gloved hand was the bag of candy bars. In the other was a manila folder.

"This may sound callous," he said, handing us the folder, "but you got very lucky. Not only could it have been much worse, but it might have been fatal. I've never seen anything like this."

I opened the folder, taking a look at an X ray of the twenty-one remaining candy bars, including the one I'd almost bitten into.

"Jethuth," Herb said.

"We counted over forty needles, thirty fishhooks, and ten X-Acto blades." The doctor shook his head. "Only one candy out of the bunch was untampered with. If a hook or a blade got lodged in the throat, it might have easily severed an artery."

I stared mutely at the X ray, feeling myself grow very cold. Someone had spent a long time doctoring up this candy. Hours. I tried to imagine that person, hunched over a table, inserting fishhooks into chocolate bars. All this trouble, hoping I'd eat just one. Or maybe hoping I'd pass them out to people. I thought about Herb, almost dropping off the candy at the children's ward. Both my hands clenched.

"So, Doctor"—I tried to keep a lid on my rage—"if we find the person who did this, in your professional opinion, could we charge him or her with attempted murder?"

"Lieutenant, there's no question in my mind. I would say that you'd have a better chance of surviving a gunshot than one of these candy bars."

I thanked him, making sure I got his card in case we needed to talk again. Herb and I walked out to the parking lot in silence, leaving Mercy Hospital for the second time that day.

"Lunch?" I asked.

Benedict nodded. Eleven stitches in the mouth weren't nearly enough to stop him from eating.

Before we ate, we stopped at Herb's house so he could get cleaned up. I waited in the car. I liked Bernice, his wife, but her idea of small talk was asking dozens of personal questions, none of which I felt like answering at the moment.

When Herb came out, his bloody shirt had been replaced and he wore a new tie, this one too thin by at least twenty years.

We went to a sub place, where I got a meatball sandwich and Herb got a hoagie with double meat and cheese.

"How is it?" I asked.

Benedict shrugged. "I can't tathte anything. But it smellth great."

After feeding ourselves, we headed for Reginald Booster's house in Northwest suburban Palatine. To do that we had to get on Interstate 90 going west. It was also called the Kennedy. The other big expressways in Chicago were the Edens, the Eisenhower, and the Dan Ryan. Naming them after politicians didn't make them any more endearing.

The Kennedy had been under construction for the last two years, so the normally awful traffic was twice as bad. But then there has never been a time when at least one expressway wasn't being repaired. "Expressway" was a misnomer.

Even with my cherry on the roof and the siren wailing, I couldn't get past the single-lane traffic. Driving up on the median was another perk of being a cop, but the medians were swarming with construction workers and yellow machines. I beared it, but I didn't grin.

Benedict went over the file with me as we drove, his lisp improving as he practiced his enunciation. On August 9, a person or persons unknown broke into Dr. Reginald Booster's house at 175 Elm Avenue in Palatine. Booster lived there alone, his wife having passed away three years earlier in a car accident. The perp tied up Dr. Booster and slit his throat. Before death, he was stabbed in the chest and abdomen area twelve times, not deeply enough to kill.

The reason I'd recalled Booster's name was that he was all over the news as the "Palatine Torture-Murder." The media loves a torture-murder.

Booster's body was discovered the next day by a weekly maid. There was no sign of anything stolen. No suspects, no witnesses, no apparent motive.

"What was he tied up with?" I asked Benedict.

He flipped through the report. "Twine."

Twine fibers were found embedded in Jane Doe's wrists and ankles. A possible link.

"Was the weapon serrated?"

"No. The wounds were smooth. But they weren't as deep as the girl's."

I thought about this. "The jagged edge on a hunting knife, it doesn't start until a few inches up on the blade. At the tip, it's like a double-edged knife."

"So it could be the same knife."

"How did he get in?"

"Means of entry unknown. Place was locked when the maid arrived. She had a key."

"Did they run that angle?"

"To death. The maid, no pun intended, was clean. In her deposition, she mentioned Booster sometimes kept his patio door open at night to let the breeze in."

That struck me as odd, but I was a city girl. Suburbanites didn't have a lock-and-key mentality. Pay half a million for a house in a nice neighborhood and you figure crime will never happen to you.

"No prints at the scene, right?"

"No. But a few smudges on his body that could indicate latex gloves."

"Does the daughter live there now?"

"Nope. She lives in Hoffman Estates. She's a kindergarten teacher."

"Brave woman," I said, recalling all of the screaming children back at the doctor's office.

"So what was that bit with Quasimodo at the pharmacy?"

"Oh. That was Tweedle Dum and Tweedle Dumber."

"The Feebies?"

"They're profiling again."

Herb shook his head. He'd had some run-ins with the Féderalés last year on a murder case. Sixteen-year-old girl shot in the head, the same MO as another murder in Michigan. The FBI BSU ViCAT profile predicted the killer was a sixty-year-old white male truck driver, former enlisted man, bearded, and a bed-wetter.

The perp turned out to be two clean-shaven black gang members under eighteen, with no military experience between them, both untroubled by enuresis. Neither Herb nor I had much faith in profiling. In fact, neither of us had much faith in the FBI.

"So they profiled the Gingerbread Man with a curved spine."

"It's just a hunch," I said.

Herb didn't laugh at the joke either, but at least he got it.

"Well, maybe we'll get an ID now," Herb said. "People are bound to recognize the name Quasimodo."

"Why is that?"

"Because he rings a bell."

I winced.

"That one actually hurt."

"Well, Hugo your way, and I'll go mine."

"Let's not talk for a while."

We came to a toll booth and I found forty cents in change in my ashtray. State troopers didn't have to pay tolls, but us lowly city cops weren't immune. Yet another reason to avoid the suburbs.

The Kennedy intersected Route 53 with the usual cloverleaf, and I took the leaf going north toward Rolling Meadows. Finally out of construction traffic, I released some pent-up tension and gunned the engine. It didn't startle Herb too much. Probably because the acceleration on my Nova was comparable to pushing a boulder up a hill.

Palatine Road going west took us off the expressway and into the heart of middle-American suburbia. I drove past housing developments, and strip malls, and shopping centers, and more housing developments, and a strip mall development, and finally found Elm Street without difficulty.

It was a little before two o'clock when we pulled into Dr. Booster's driveway, sandwiched between two mature spruces. The house was two stories and brown, partially obscured by an overgrowth of trees and bushes that needed trimming. The unkempt lawn was covered with brown leaves, and they crunched underfoot as we walked up to the front door.

Melissa Booster answered after the first knock, apparently having seen our approach. She was robust—add a hundred pounds to Rubenesque and you'd have her figure. I suppose the PC term would be glandularly imbalanced or calorically challenged. She wore a red housedress that hung on her like a set of drapes. Her makeup was simple and expertly applied, and her brown eyes crinkled at us through the layers of doughy skin that made up her face. Her three chins waggled in a cheerful smile and she invited us in.

"Sorry we're late." I offered my hand. "I'm Lieutenant Daniels, this is Detective Benedict."

"No apologies needed, Lieutenant. It's been a while since the police have contacted me. I'm happy to know the search is still on."

She spoke in the singsong voice that people used when reading to children. I suppose that being around five-year-olds all the time made it hard to switch off. We followed her to the living room, where she sat us on a sofa in front of a dusty table and waddled off to the kitchen, insisting on getting us coffee.

Herb nudged me quietly. "That's a whole lot of woman."

"Spoken by a man with a forty-six-inch waist."

"Are you referring to my washboard stomach?"

"Don't you mean washtub stomach? Shh, she's bringing doughnuts."

Melissa Booster returned, carrying two mugs of coffee on top of a Dunkin' Donuts box.

"I hope I'm not offending you." She handed me a cup.

"Miss?"

"With the cop/doughnut thing. I don't want to play on a stereotype."

"No offense at all." I smiled.

"Got any jellies?" Benedict reached for the box. He fished out something sticky and emitted a satisfied grunt. Other people would be wary of food after taking a bite out of an X-Acto knife blade, but not Herb.

"I'm sorry about the house." Melissa plopped her bulk down on the love seat opposite us. The framework screamed in protest. "The maid never came back after finding Dad dead, and things have gotten dusty. This is the first time I've been back myself. I guess enough time has passed, but I've kept putting it off. Any new news?"

"Possibly. We're following a lead on another case that may be related. Did your father ever fill out prescriptions off duty?"

"Sure. Whenever there was a family get-together he brought his prescription pad with him. Half the hypochondriacs in Illinois are related to me. That's probably why Dad became a doctor."

"What did he prescribe for family members?"

"The usual. Painkillers, sleeping pills, laxatives, cold medication, acne cream, birth control, all the standards. The current hot ones were Propecia and Viagra. He didn't seem to mind the family doing it to him. Both my grandmothers thought he was a saint."

Benedict finished enough of his doughnut to aid in the inquiries.

"Did he ever prescribe injectionals?"

"You mean like for diabetics?"

"Any at all."

"Not to my family. Most of my relatives would faint at the thought of getting a shot."

I sneezed thoughtfully, if such a thing is possible.

"How about Seconal?" I asked. "It's a powerful sedative, like Valium."

"Not to our family. Not that I know of."

"We believe your father may have written a very large prescription for Seconal the night he died, possibly for someone who knew him. Do you know anyone named Charles or Chuck?"

"Sorry, no."

"Any relative with that name, or friend of your father's?"

"No. Not that I know of."

"Ms. Booster . . ."

"Melissa."

"Melissa, this is a hard question, but do you think there was any chance that your dad may have been selling prescriptions?"

She shook her head, as if saying no to a child. "Dad? No way. Look around you. It's a nice house, but not extravagant. My father made good money, but it's all accounted for. He lived within his means. Besides, Dad just wasn't like that. I had it drilled into my head from a baby on that medication and drugs were very serious and dangerous."

She reached into the doughnut box and removed a powdered, biting into it gently.

"Would he have had a prescription pad in the house?"

"Probably. His desk is in the den. Would you like to see it?"

"Please."

Melissa placed the doughnut on the table and rocked twice on the sofa, pulling up her considerable body on the third try. We followed as she waddled to the den, down a hallway, and into a room the size of a large closet.

"Actually, this is just a large closet," Melissa said. "Dad put a desk in here and it became the den."

She didn't enter, probably because if she did, she wouldn't have room to turn around. I thanked her and went in alone, leaving Herb behind to small talk.

The desk was old and bore the traits of many years of faithful use. It was a rolltop, with five drawers and half a dozen cubbyholes to squirrel away bills or mail. I gave it a quick toss, finding a lot of junk for my efforts, but no prescription pad.

"A prescription pad wasn't listed as items in evidence taken during the original investigation, was it?"

Benedict glanced at me and shook his head, then resumed his conversation with Melissa. They were talking, go figure, about food.

I went to the file cabinet next to the desk and commenced a once-over, finding tax forms, a few medical charts, and a smattering of appliance instruction manuals. No prescription pad.

"Pardon me." I interrupted an argument about stuffed pizza. "But which room was your father's body found in?"

"In the master bedroom. It's down the hall and up the stairs to the right. If you don't mind, I really don't want to go in there."

"I understand."

Herb gave me a look, but I shook my head, indicating he didn't have to tag along. I found the bedroom without difficulty. It was large, with two picture windows, a king-size four-poster bed, and a matching armoire and dresser. The curtains, bedding, and carpeting were all color coordinated, tan and dark brown.

The bed was unmade. Next to it was a chair, part of the bedroom set where Mrs. Booster would sit and do her makeup, and where Dr. Booster was bound and murdered. The Palatine PD had taken the twine used to tie him, but the chair remained, still stained with blood. The carpet under it was equally stained, brown and splotchy.

If Booster was found here, chances were good this was where he wrote the prescription. I checked the top dresser drawer.

Sitting on top of some underwear, waiting for me, was a prescription pad and a pen. Using a pair of tweezers I keep in my jacket for this purpose, I picked up the pen and placed it in a plastic bag, which I also keep in my jacket. Then I tweezed the prescription pad, holding it up to the light. The top sheet had indentations on it, left over from the pressure of the pen used to write the previous prescription.

If I wanted to play Sherlock Holmes, I could lightly rub a pencil over the paper. The lead would fall into the depressions, giving me a readable impression of the missing sheet above it.

But the lab boys would have fits if I did that. These days,

infrared do-hickies and other complex stuff could read it without getting graphite all over everything. I bagged the pad and went through the rest of the drawers, searching for other clues. I came up empty, but the little optimistic knot in my belly refused to go away.

Downstairs, Herb and Melissa were in a heated discussion about where to get the best chili dogs. I butted in, sharing my discovery and promptly giving Melissa a receipt for the items I took.

"So he was killed for a lousy prescription?" Her eyes glassed over and she began to sob. Two months wasn't enough time to get over the death of a parent. Some people never get over it.

Benedict, having shared his thoughts on food, now shared a hug with the young woman. She calmed some, and even managed a watery smile in the middle of her tears.

"Please find the man who killed my daddy."

I could have said "We'll do our best" or "We'll stay in touch." But instead, I nodded and replied, "We will."

Then Benedict and I got back into my car and began the long and tedious trip back to Chicago.

CHAPTER 10

AT 2:35 THAT AFTERNOON THERESA METCALF regains consciousness.

Then he begins.

He tries many new things.

By 5:15 she can't scream anymore.

By 6:45 she's finally dead.

THE FBI WAS WAITING TO SHOW me more paperwork when we got back to the station. Benedict had deserted me, electing to bring both the lethal candy and the pad and pen to the lab. Occupying my office without permission was annoying enough, but Special Agents Heckle and Jeckle had also appropriated my desk.

"Good news, Lieutenant," Dailey said. "The ViCAT computer has given us a list of possible suspects."

I frowned. "That's my desk."

They looked at each other, then back at me. I wondered if they practiced that move at home.

"There isn't any other place to put all of this data."

I knew a place they could put it, but I played nice and resisted the urge to tell them.

"I need some coffee." I turned around, intending to leave. There was an excellent coffee place on the other side of town.

"Got some." Dailey opened his briefcase, on my desk, and took out two polished aluminum canisters. "Regular or unleaded?"

Both Coursey and Dailey chuckled. Exactly three chuckles each, and then they stopped simultaneously. Eerie.

"Regular." I sighed, sitting in the chair opposite of mine.

Dailey took a Styrofoam cup from his briefcase and filled it with the steaming contents of container number one.

"Cream or sugar?"

I shook my head and forced a polite smile.

"Let's begin." Coursey cleared his throat, preparing for lecture mode. "There have been several terminal occurrences over the past ten—"

I had to interrupt. "Terminal occurrences?"

"Murders."

Jesus.

"As I was saying, there have been several terminal occurrences over the past ten years in the United States that may have possible connections to the Jane Doe found here two days ago."

Dailey jumped in. "Serial or recreational killers usually have distinct patterns and modus operandi that make it possible, with the help of Vicky—"

"Vicky?" I asked.

"The ViCAT computer."

"Ah."

"That make it possible, with Vicky's help, to find links between victims."

"You mean terminal occurrences," I corrected.

"Exactly."

I sipped my coffee, and noted with annoyance that it was very good.

"You read through our report on why we believe the perp is organized rather than unorganized, correct?"

"Absolutely." I recalled dropping it in the garbage on the way to my car.

"Here's another report, a list of related crimes that Vicky has linked with the pattern established by our RK here."

"RK?"

"Recreational Killer."

"Ah."

I wondered if there was a special branch of the FBI whose sole function was to make up acronyms.

"Vicky has also listed probability percentile rankings."

Dailey nodded smartly, as if waiting for a cookie or a pat on the head. They must have taken my silence for deep thought, because they waited patiently for me to say something before they went on.

"Mmm," I said.

They went on.

"There are seven possible connections on this list."

"We'll give them to you in ascending order of probability."

"First, on May first in 1976 in Hackensack, New Jersey, there was a double shotgun homicide where the suspect was unknown."

I wouldn't be baited.

"What's the connection, you're thinking?" Dailey asked.

Actually, I was thinking that once, when I was younger, I had actually considered joining the FBI. We're all entitled to moments of stupidity, I suppose.

"The connection is that after the murders, the bodies were mutilated," Coursey said.

"With a fork," Dailey added.

"Six point three percent probability it's the same guy." Coursey nodded smartly. I think they practiced nodding smartly in the mirror.

I rubbed my eyes, getting some eyeliner on my fingers. For what I paid for eyeliner, it shouldn't come off that easily.

"Gentlemen, I have a lot of work to do. If you'll just leave the paperwork, I'll go over it as soon as I can."

"Your captain assured us that you'd give us your full cooperation, Lieutenant."

"And I intend to, Agent Dailey."

"I'm Coursey."

"I intend to, Agent Coursey. But my captain also expects me to have all of my reports done on time. I have a backlog of six cases I still haven't transferred, and there were two more shooting deaths in my district last night that need to be attended to."

"Were those shotgun deaths?" Coursey raised his eyebrows.

"No. Now thanks for your help, but right now I've got other things to do."

I stood up. Dailey and Coursey did their looking at each other thing, and then got to their feet as well.

"I just hope we treat you with greater courtesy when the jurisdiction for this case is turned over to us." Dailey nodded curtly.

Coursey added a curt nod of his own.

"I'm sure you will." I walked around my desk and sat down in my chair, which was unpleasantly warm. They gathered up their respective papers and headed for the door, but a lingering thought made me stop them.

"Guys—your computer, Vicky, does it handle more than just terminal occurrences?"

"Yes. It is also a nationwide database for felonies such as rape, arson, and bank robberies."

"How about poisoning? Product tampering?"

They nodded as one. I told them about the package I'd

gotten earlier, ending the story by showing them the lethal X ray.

"Would your computer be able to locate other tamperings like this one?"

"I believe so. Can we keep this?"

I nodded, giving them directions to the lab so they could check out the goods themselves. Maybe, for the first time, the FBI would help out rather than get in the way. Hope springs eternal.

I wasn't lying about the backlog of cases, and after making a few calls and filling out a few reports, I transferred them all so I could devote my full attention to the Jane Doe murder. Going over the case again from the beginning didn't yield any new information, but it helped me organize the info I did have.

Lab report pending, I was 99 percent sure that Dr. Booster and our Jane Doe had been killed by the same perp. He was calling himself the Gingerbread Man, and after forcing Booster to write him a prescription for Seconal, he used it to abduct Jane Doe.

The note and the cookie were messages to the police, and there was a good indication that there would be more deaths. Sixty mls of Seconal was enough to knock out twenty to thirty people. Why ask for that much if he didn't intend to use it?

I scribbled a note to myself to call the DEA and check to see if they had any stats on Seconal ODs. I also wanted to call up Vice and see if Seconal had been used in any recent rapes. Jane Doe may be the first murder, but she may not be the first person our perp used Seconal on.

I picked up the packet of pictures from the crime scene and looked through them for the hundredth time. Something in my subconscious made me linger on a photo of the girl in the garbage can, her rear end sticking out. I studied it further. There was garbage covering almost the whole body, except for the buttocks. But why so much garbage, if it hadn't been in the can for more than an hour or two?

Maybe he arranged the garbage like that. Almost as if he were saying that he threw away a piece of ass. The FBI called it posing, and I was surprised I hadn't received a lecture on that as well. Positioning the body like this was the perp's way of showing how clever he was, and how much contempt he had for the victim. So did he take the time to do this in plain sight, or . . .

I picked up the report with the itemized list of all the garbage found in the can with the body. Mixed in with the cans and bags and wrappers and bottles were twelve receipts. The prices on the receipts were noted on the list, but not what I was after.

I picked up the phone and called Evidence.

"Bill? Jack Daniels."

Bill had been caretaker of the evidence room since I was a rookie. He was older than God.

"Jack? How are you? I was thinking about you this morning, in the shower."

"You should be ashamed, a man your age."

"Chris is on his break. You could come down now. We'll go behind the storage lockers."

I laughed. "You're too much man for me, Bill, but I could use a favor. I need you to look up something from case 93-10-06782. Receipts that were found in the garbage can with a body."

"That the Jane Doe got all cut up?"

"Yeah."

"Hold on."

He put down the phone, and I heard the sliding gate unlock and imagined him walking through the aisles of shelves in the evidence room, looking for the proper case number. I finished my coffee while waiting, then regretted my haste because now I'd have to drink the awful station slop. Eventually I would break down and get a coffeemaker, because the stuff from the vending machine tasted like brewed sewage.

I put off getting more coffee and looked at the latest sheet the Feebies left. Their number one suspect match had a 48.6 percent probability rate that it was our guy. The murder and mutilation of three women with a hunting knife was unsolved, and I was ready to call the Feds and ask for more info on this case when I noticed it took place in 1953. In Nome, Alaska. I filed the paper, throwing my empty coffee cup in after it.

"Jack?"

"Yeah?"

"Ooohh, your voice makes my toes curl. I found the receipts for you, lamb chop. What do you need?"

"Look at one. Other than the date, does it have numbers in the upper corners?"

"Yeah. Two. The left-hand corner, 193, the right one 277."

"Try another receipt."

"Left 193, right 310."

"Keep going."

He read all twelve receipts, and the number in the left-hand corner was 193 in eleven out of the twelve. On the odd one, the number was 102.

"Can I do anything else for you, honey? Anything at all?"

"That should do it. Thanks, Bill."

"My pleasure."

I got on the horn with Information and was charged thirty-five cents to get the number for the 7-Eleven on Monroe and Dearborn. I already had the number somewhere, but like all public servants I'd been rigorously trained to waste taxpayers' money at every opportunity.

"Seven-Eleven," answered a voice with an Indian accent.

I found the deposition on my desk of the manager who'd been watching television while the Jane Doe was dumped in front of his store.

"Mr. Abdul Raheem?"

"No. This is Fasil Raheem. Abdul is my brother."

"This is Lieutenant Daniels, Chicago Violent Crimes. I'm sure your brother told you about the body discovered in your outside trash."

"He has not stopped talking about it. Is it true he chased the murderer away by showing him karate moves he learned from Van Damme movies?"

"I believe he was watching TV the whole time."

"I thought as much. What can I do for you?"

"Tell me what the two numbers are in the top corners of your receipts, please."

"Simple. The top right-hand number is the order number. The top left-hand number is the store number."

"Are you store number 193?"

"No, Lieutenant. We are store number 102. I believe store 193 is on Lincoln and North Avenue. Let me check the book."

He hummed to himself, tunelessly, and I felt a tingle of excitement in my gut because my hunch had paid out.

"I was correct. Store 193 is on Lincoln and North Avenue."

"Thank you, Mr. Raheem."

I hung up, satisfied. Benedict strolled in, handing me a sheet of paper. It was a photocopy of Dr. Booster's prescription pad, except now it had writing on it.

"That was quick."

"We used fingerprint powder on it, and it clung to the depressions. No prints, but the writing stood out."

The prescription was for sixty mls of sodium secobarbital, written out by Dr. Booster.

"Handwriting matches previous prescriptions he'd written." Herb held up the Booster case file.

"So he was killed for the prescription, like we'd guessed."

"It gets better. We found something else." Benedict handed me another photocopy. "This was written twenty or so pages into it. Maybe it was just a doodle, or maybe Booster had left a note for us while the killer was there."

It was a chicken scratch, only two words, practically illegible. It said "Buddy's Son."

"So the killer is Buddy's son?"

"Could be. Or maybe his buddy's son. Or maybe it has nothing to do with anything. I called Melissa Booster and she doesn't know anyone named Buddy."

I puzzled over it.

"How about the patient list? Someone with the first or last name Buddy?"

"I checked. Nothing even close."

"Let's have Booster's entire life checked out, see if he ever knew someone named Buddy."

"Tall task."

"We'll give it to the task force." I grinned, changing the subject. "I know how the killer dumped the body in the can without being seen."

Benedict raised an eyebrow. I've always wanted to be able to do that; raise one eyebrow in silent inquiry. Unfortunately, both of my brows are hooked up to the same muscle, and whenever I try to raise one I do an involuntary Groucho Marx waggle.

"He swiped a garbage can from a 7-Eleven on Lincoln, took it home, and arranged the body in it, then dropped it off at the 7-Eleven on Monroe and took the other can with him. He could have switched cans in twenty seconds, if he had a ramp and a hand truck."

"Maybe a garbageman?"

"Maybe. Check through Booster's patient list again, check out occupations; garbagemen, mailmen, delivery men, anyone who drives a truck. Check with the DMV as well, run down all truck owners on his list."

The phone rang, and I snatched it up and slapped it to my ear.

"Daniels."

"This is Detective Evens, Palatine PD. I hear you're picking through the Booster case."

I ran it down for him, ending with the discovery of the prescription pad.

"I can't believe we missed it."

"You weren't looking for it. Does the name mean anything to you?"

"Buddy? Nope. Can you fax it over, along with the prescription form? My cap's gonna rip me a new one for not finding this."

"How many interviews did you do?"

"Over thirty. Friends, neighbors, relatives. Anyone who knew the guy since high school."

"Any suspects?"

"You've got the report."

"It doesn't list hunches. Any interview strike you as an oddball?"

"Half of his family were oddballs. But not in the murdering sense. Everyone liked the guy. We couldn't find a reason someone offed him."

"I take it you'll be looking closer now."

"Now that we know he died for a prescription? Hell yeah. Now I can start pulling in dealers, junkies, a whole slew of people."

"We're looking for someone who owns or drives a truck. I could float some manpower your way, you need it."

"Nope. This murder really pissed people off here. Palatine's a nice little town. We got more than enough guys who'd like to take another crack at this case."

"Keep in touch, Evens."

"Right back at you."

I put the phone back in the cradle and sneezed. I fished out another of Herb's tissues. "So let's check out the 7-Eleven on Lincoln, see if they saw anything. Did you run into the Feebies at the lab?"

"Yeah. Thanks for sending them. I had to fake a case of diarrhea to get away from them and their nonstop monologues."

"Did it work?"

"No. They followed me into the can."

"Any prints on the candy?"

"None that we could find. But they're going to run some tests."

"How's the mouth?"

"It hurts, but I've got my taste back. You up for a bite?"

"I've got more reports to go through, then I was going to call it a day."

"Since I'm going out, I'll check the 7-Eleven on Lincoln. If memory serves, it's right next to a great Mexican place."

Herb's stomach rumbled, seconding the motion.

"See you tomorrow, Herb."

"Bye, Jack."

Benedict left. I attacked the pile of paperwork in front of me, including typing up the results of our hospital visit and our trip to Melissa Booster's. This was the computer age, but

I still used a standard electric typewriter, aware that fellow officers regarded me as a dinosaur in that aspect. Even if I did go high tech, I don't see what good a computer would do me. Ten words a minute is ten words a minute, no matter what I'm typing on.

When I was done I remained sitting there, staring at the page.

There wasn't anything else I could do at work, but I had no compelling reason to go home. I had no family there, no boyfriend waiting for me. It was just a place where I kept my meager possessions, ate, and tried in vain to rest.

"All I've got is you," I told the report.

The report didn't answer.

I sighed, then got up and left, resigning myself to yet another sleepless night.

CHAPTER 12

His cellmate had spoken of this place, during the long, boring night hours when rambling was the only way to kill time.

"Just go to the bartender, bald guy named Floyd. Tell him you need a TV repaired."

The Gingerbread Man had taken it with the same grain of salt he took all prison bullshitting. Besides, if he ever needed someone taken care of, he was more than happy to take care of them himself. If doing time taught him anything, it was self-reliance.

But this situation is different. He doesn't want to be connected with the act in the slightest way. Doing the job personally, though rewarding, is too risky. Besides, it feels godlike to be pulling the strings while staying safely behind the scenes. It adds more awe to his persona.

The idea came to him after violating the whore. He really hurt her. Brought her so close to death so many times. Payback for the humiliation, for the defiance, for picking on the wrong guy.

After he had finished, when he was lying naked with the body, he thought of his adversary, Jack Daniels.

Had Jack gotten the candy yet? Had she eaten it? Maybe she shared it with her squad, and fifteen or twenty pigs all got deadly little surprises. He had to know.

So he placed another call from the pay phone.

"This is Peters from the *Herald*. I'm following up on an anonymous tip. Were any police officers injured at work today?"

"We're not disclosing any details at this time."

"So you're confirming the rumor?"

"Sorry, this is part of an ongoing investigation."

"How about off the record?"

"Off the record, we got a detective with eleven stitches in his mouth."

"A detective? My source said it was a lieutenant."

"Your source is wrong."

So Jack hadn't eaten any. All that work for nothing.

The Gingerbread Man seethed. He'd imagined her with needles in her tongue, and this was a giant letdown.

There had to be another way to get her attention. To show he was taking their rivalry seriously. To put her in the hospital without exposing himself to unnecessary risk.

And then he remembered this place.

The tavern is dark and smells like cigarette smoke, even though it's empty this time of day. Behind the bar is a skinny guy named Floyd, the man his cellmate told him about.

The Gingerbread Man hands Floyd a photograph of Jack, the one he'd taken during the crime scene visit on Monroe. He also gives him Jack's address, license plate number, the calling card, and five hundred bucks.

The normal price to beat someone senseless was four hundred, but Jack is a cop, so it's higher.

Leaving the calling card is risky, but there's been no mention of it in the papers yet. He wants Jack to know who did this to her. Even more, when this is all over, he wants the cops and the world to know that they could have stopped him, if they'd only been smarter.

But they'll only see the connection after he's long gone.

Floyd takes everything, making an obvious effort not to look directly at his face. Smart business.

"Whaddaya want done to her?" he says, eyes on a TV at the end of the bar.

"Break her knees." The Gingerbread Man grins. The idea that Jack will be forever crippled is appealing. When he calls on her, she won't be able to run.

Floyd says he'll get someone on it right away, maybe even tonight.

In the meantime, he has to dump the whore. It's been a delightfully busy day, and he's tired, but if he keeps her around too long she'll begin to stink. More than one killer has been caught because neighbors complained of the smell coming from the death house.

So he has to do the garbage can trick again. Labor intensive, but effective. While it would be much easier just to dump her in the sewer, he wants the body to be discovered right away. The networks will eat it up.

Something for Jack to watch on TV while she's recuperating in the hospital.

CHAPTER 13

MY ANSWERING MACHINE WAS BLINKING WHEN I got back to my apartment. It was Don. He didn't want me back, but he did want the rest of his furniture, and for me to arrange having it put into storage. I was to call with the storage location.

Right. And then I might also slip him a few bucks.

I decided to be fair and meet him halfway. I called him back and got a deep female voice on the answering machine that identified itself as Roxy. I informed her and Don that I would move all of his things . . . out into the hall.

He had a lot of crap, and it took almost two hours. When I was finished the apartment looked barren. Except for my grandma's rocking chair, a beanbag, the bed, and my cheap dinette set, every other stick of furniture was his. I was shocked to find out I only had one lamp. It was a crappy lamp too, with a switch that didn't work unless you wiggled it. I must have had more lamps before he moved in, so what the hell happened to them?

The only conclusion I could draw was that once he moved his things in, he began moving my things out. I suppose I never noticed because I never paid much attention. Or maybe it was because I was rarely home.

It's a wonder he left me.

I checked the fridge for food products and managed to put together a salami and mustard on rye. The mustard was Don's, some imported brand that cost more per ounce than silver. It was too tangy. When I was done with the sandwich I tossed the mustard into the hall with the rest of his things.

Flipping through my mental appointment book, I checked out my itinerary for tonight. It would be a titillating evening of television, then tossing and turning in bed trying to fall asleep.

Be still my beating heart.

I considered making a drink and drawing a bath, but then I was seized by a fit of spontaneity and decided to actually go out and do something. Two nights in a row. I'm such a party animal.

Changing into jeans and a sweatshirt, I once again took the route to Joe's Pool Hall. The night was crisp, and it being Friday, the streets were packed with kids. I passed a group of guys who were tossing out catcalls to every girl that passed.

They didn't catcall me at all, the little snots.

Joe's was busier than usual, but Phineas Troutt had secured a corner table, methodically pocketing ball after ball. He wore khakis and an open flannel shirt over his T-shirt. I bought two beers and carried them over.

"Are you looking for a game, or do you want to play with yourself all night?" I asked.

He banked an eight into the side pocket.

"You willing to put money on it?"

"I got two bucks says I kick your butt."

"That's a boastful two bucks."

I let him see the color of my money, tossing two singles on the rail as if they were hundreds. Phin sunk his final ball and squinted at me.

"Loser racks. And if memory serves, you lost our last game. The last several, in fact."

I handed him a beer.

"All part of the hustle. I'll own your car by midnight."

He took a pull on the bottle.

"Thanks. I'm really glad you stopped by."

"Got a thing for older cops?"

"Actually, I have to piss like a racehorse. Didn't want to leave the table because I'd lose it."

He excused himself and trotted off to the bathroom.

While he was occupied, I racked the balls and executed a sledgehammer break, pocketing a stripe and a solid. I chose to keep solids, putting in three more before Phin returned.

I pointed to the far left pocket and knocked another solid down.

"I see you've taken advantage of my absence by cheating your ass off."

I politely told him to engage in a carnal impossibility, and pocketed another solid.

Running a table isn't easy. Not only do you have to sink the balls, but you have to position the cue ball to have a shot at the next ball. I had a good eye for the game, and knew how to plan ahead, but sometimes my talent wasn't up to my knowledge.

I chalked my cue and walked over to my next shot, a tricky bank into the far corner. Just as I brought the stick back, I was shoved roughly from behind.

"What the hell?" I turned around, irritated.

Staring down at me was a very big and very ugly man. He

had scar tissue for a face, and a flat, crooked nose that was no stranger to being broken. I could smell the mean on him like I could smell the booze. As he narrowed his little eyes at me, I was reminded of Bluto from Popeye fame. Except that Bluto was smaller. And a cartoon.

"You spilled my beer, you little bitch."

He said it loud enough for the whole bar to hear, spittle flecking off his fat lips.

Phin, who is no shorty himself, grabbed the guy's shoulder and looked up at him.

"Cool it, buddy. She's a cop."

The big man shrugged Phin off, focusing on me again.

"What are you gonna do about it?" Bluto snarled. Then he spit on my shoes.

We all live by rules. Cops have more rules than most, especially when dealing with irrational people. One of those rules was never to provoke them, especially when they're bigger than a small town.

But rules, as they say, are meant to be broken.

"You need a breath mint," I said evenly. "I'd suggest you go buy yourself a pack. Right now."

Bluto sneered. I was aware that people around us had stopped playing to watch. Like a fool, I hadn't worn my gun, even though regulations stated I should wear it off-duty. But I wasn't even sure that a gun would make a difference with this guy. He had to go six seven, and anything short of a bazooka probably wouldn't slow him down.

"You want me to leave, pig?" He smiled.

Then he sucker punched me in the gut.

I barely had time to clench my abs and twist my torso to deflect some of the blow. It still knocked me off my feet, and I wound up on all fours, trying to suck in a breath.

Phin was already in motion before I landed. Doing his Sammy Sosa impression, he smashed Bluto across the back of the head with the heavy end of his cue, getting for his efforts a cue in two pieces.

The big man turned on Phin, throwing a hard roundhouse that hung in the air forever. Phin ducked it and gave him a smack to the jaw that didn't even make the giant blink.

I shook away a few stars and got to my feet, knees wobbling under me. A woman didn't get to be a Violent Crimes lieutenant in America's third largest city without being able to take a punch.

Or without knowing how to punch back.

I threw a hard right into the man's kidney, trying to drive my fist through him, putting every one of my hundred and thirty-five pounds behind it.

Bluto grunted, doubling over. Phin took the opportunity to kick him in the face. Something small bounced off me that I later found out was a tooth.

The giant hit the ground, and that would have been the end of it if the bastard hadn't had friends.

They were the type of guys an asshole like this was bound to hang out with. One had black hair, slicked back, and a grubby little goatee. I counted five earrings, all of them skulls, and a matching skull pinkie ring.

The other was shorter and stocky, his fair hair in a crew cut. He wore a tank top that revealed heavily muscled arms, slathered with tattoos of guns.

I had never noticed that my favorite bar boasted a rather shitty clientele.

Tattoo Boy moved in toward Phin quick and loose, like a trained fighter. He threw a right that was so quick, I thought for sure it would take Phin out.

But Phin was fast too, and he rolled into the punch, taking it on his shoulder. I saw Phin jam an elbow into the guy's chin and then I had to deal with my own problem.

He came at me low, goatee curved in a grin. I raised my fists and clenched my teeth.

"I'm a cop, you jackass."

"I eat cops." He ran his tongue over brownish teeth and charged at me.

I brought up my knee, smacking him in the center of his ugly face, and I couldn't resist grunting, "Eat this."

I could feel his nose go mushy, but he still had enough momentum behind him to lift me up and onto the pool table. He landed on top, bleeding all over my shirt and face, throwing wild windmill punches at my sides.

As he hammered away, I tried to roll over. No good—I was pinned. I shoved, straining with all I had, but he was too heavy.

Then his hands found my throat.

I pulled at his fingers, but couldn't pry them off. To my left, on the table, several balls were jostled by our struggle. I wrapped a hand around the eight ball and smashed it into the side of his skull.

His eyes rolled up and he crumpled onto the edge of the pool table. Odd ball, corner pocket.

I sought out Phin, who was having difficulties of his own. Bluto had gotten back up, and he gripped Phin around the neck while Tattoo Boy circled, looking to land a jab through Phin's swinging fists.

"Police! Don't move!" I yelled.

They kept moving. Some guys had no respect for authority.

I weighed the eight ball in my hand, planning on pitching a slider at Bluto's back. My baseball days were long behind me, but I figured he was so big a target I couldn't miss.

I missed.

Luckily, Phin didn't need to be rescued. He pivoted on his hip and judo- threw the big man onto his back.

Tattoo Boy moved in, but Phin swiveled around and caught him on the chin with the heel of his foot.

Tattoo Boy ate the floor. But Bluto, who seemed extremely angry at having been thrown, got to his feet and picked Phin up. Not in a bear hug, but as if Phin were a sack of potatoes. He hoisted my friend up over his head, ready for a slam dunk.

I launched myself at the giant, tackling his midsection, my head and hands sinking into doughy flab. He umphed, and dropped Phin on top of me, then began a kicking frenzy on our prostrate forms.

I caught one particularly vicious boot to the head that made my vision swim. While I scrambled to get away from the flying feet, I noticed Tattoo Boy had gotten back up, and he was approaching with a look on his face that was anything but pleasant.

This is what I get for trying to have a social life.

Phin untangled himself from me and rolled gracefully to his feet, diving at Bluto, hooking a forearm into the giant's throat.

Tattoo Boy flexed his pecs, making the machine guns dance. I got up slowly and blinked away the tiny motes dancing before my eyes.

"You're under arrest," I tried.

He laughed at me, flexing again. Must have spent a lot of the time in the gym to have definition like that.

I put up my fists and feinted with a left, bringing the right cross into his jaw. It didn't seem to bother him much. I followed up with a right-left combination, working the body. He shot out with a jab of his own, catching me above the eye.

"Jack!"

I turned to see Phin soaring at me, his face total panic. He flew past and smacked hard into Tattoo Boy. They rolled to the floor.

"Now it's your turn," Bluto spat. He grinned, exposing several gaps where teeth used to live, and picked up a bar stool like it was made of balsa.

I backpedaled until I found a stool of my own. Bluto charged, raising his stool above his head and bringing it down on me like a war hammer. I managed to block it, but the force knocked me onto my ass. Pain shot up from my coccyx to the base of my skull, traveling along my spine like a lightning bolt. My vision blurred. I blinked away tears. Never, in my whole life, had my butt hurt so much.

A huge hand reached down and grabbed my sweatshirt, hauling me up to my feet. I focused on the other hand, cocked back in a fist the size of my entire face.

Not able to twist away, I turned my head down. Knuckles met the top of my skull. Everything went black for a moment. Then I was on the floor.

I heard sirens in the distance, getting closer. Bluto was howling, holding his bleeding right hand by the wrist.

I blinked. Phin walked up to the giant, taking a pool cue from a nearby table. He bounced the heavy end of the cue off of Bluto's temple. Bluto's eyes fluttered briefly and then he crumpled to the ground.

Phin tossed the cue to the floor and picked up his beer from the table rail. In all the excitement, it hadn't fallen off. I looked to the right and saw Tattoo Boy sprawled out like a throw rug, his leg at a funny angle.

And the good guys win it in overtime.

"You okay?" Phin asked.

"Assholes ruined the best pool game of my life."

He took a sip of beer and then handed me the bottle. I drained the rest.

People began to gather, coming out of their hiding places now that the trouble was over. I took a few tentative steps forward, testing my body. I hurt in a dozen places, especially my butt and my head, but nothing seemed broken.

Cop mode switched on, and I went to Tattoo Boy and patted him down for weapons. He had a switchblade, which I took. I did the same with Goatee, and got a knife and a set of brass knuckles for my efforts.

Finally, I bent over the sleeping giant and my heart skipped a beat.

In his jacket pocket, broken in three large pieces, was a gingerbread man cookie.

CHAPTER 14

THE QUESTIONING BEGAN AT THE HOSPITAL. After a doctor looked me over and declared I'd live, I joined my fellow officers in the interrogation process. Captain Bains had shown up, as had Benedict, the Feebies, several people from the mayor's office, and the assistant state's attorney.

We went by the book and wore our kid gloves to avoid messing up a possible conviction. A judge was called and warrants were issued to search the suspects' homes. Lawyers were present during questioning, and in a rare turn of events, they felt full confessions were in the best interests of their clients.

The guy with the earrings had sustained a concussion from the eight-ball sandwich I'd fed him, and he'd be out for a while. But Bluto and Tattoo Boy were conscious and able to talk. And talk they did.

But when all was said and done, with all of our caution

and persistence, we were left with little more than when we'd begun.

Bluto and his buddies had been hired to break my legs. They'd been given a photo of me, my address, and cash to share among them. I'd been tailed to Joe's from my apartment, which they'd been watching, and after finishing their intended beating they were supposed to leave the gingerbread man cookie with me.

They didn't know the man who hired them. They didn't know about the Jane Doe murder. Their residences were searched and came up clean. Their alibis for the time of Jane Doe's murder were tight. Their only crime, other than assault and battery on a police officer, was extreme stupidity at having stumbled into so much trouble for so little cash. It wouldn't even begin to cover their doctor bills, let alone legal representation.

They'd been brokered by a man named Floyd Schmidt, who operated a goon-for-hire service out of a bar on Maxwell Street. Floyd was initially uncooperative when we brought him in, but he quickly agreed to talk about anything and everything to avoid being implicated in the Jane Doe murder.

A man had come to see him at the bar, offering five hundred dollars to cripple me. Floyd could give no description other than the fact that he was white, average height, between twenty and forty years old.

"I swear, I never looked at the guy. This business, you look at people, they get uncomfortable, don't want to use your services."

No one was too surprised.

The gingerbread man cookie was the same type as the one found with Jane Doe's body. The picture of me had been processed by someone in a private darkroom rather than a commercial house. We managed to recover two of the original hundred-dollar bills used to pay for Floyd's service. We used an ALS to try and photograph fingerprints, but only lifted a set from Bluto.

In other words, we had zip.

I was exhausted, aching, and generally cranky. Herb suggested I go home. Seeing no reason to argue, I did.

And of course, I couldn't sleep.

Some Tylenol helped with my various aches, many of which had stiffened up since the fight. But even with my energy meter at 0.0, I couldn't completely relax.

He was out there. He knew where I lived. He knew I was after him.

He even took a picture of me.

While it was a close-up, I could tell it was taken at night, while raining, and I'd been wearing my trench coat. It was yet to be determined the type of camera and lens he'd used, but I knew when he'd taken it. At the Jane Doe crime scene.

The Gingerbread Man had been there. He'd picked me out as his adversary. And now he was playing some kind of warped game.

The Feebies had touched on it during a break in the interrogation process.

"There's a high certainty that this man was also the one who gave you the candy," Dailey had said.

"Vicky should have a printout this afternoon on similar product-tampering cases."

"This man has singled you out as his enemy. Be prepared for some personal contact anytime soon. A letter, or a phone call. Maybe he'll even meet you face-to-face, without you knowing it's him."

"You should be under surveillance, Lieutenant."

I politely declined, saying it hadn't escalated to that level yet.

But now, alone in bed, I couldn't help but feel a bit paranoid. In all the years I'd been hunting down killers, I'd never had one decide to hunt me.

The thought left me anything but drowsy.

I replayed the videotape of the Jane Doe crime scene in my head, an easy feat to do because I'd seen it dozens of times. I hadn't noticed any of the onlookers carrying a camera, but another viewing was certainly warranted.

I switched over from my back to my side, which was a bad thing to do because I immediately took note that Don wasn't next to me. When I'd arrived at the apartment a little earlier his furniture and things had been removed from the hallway. It had been Don, rather than a thief, because he'd left me a message written on my door in black marker.

"Your an asshole, Jack," had been the message.

Spelling was never one of Don's strong points.

But I still missed him. Or maybe not him exactly. I missed having a warm body lying next to me. I suppose we had more of an arrangement than a relationship. I got to hold him at night, and he got a free apartment.

There have been marriages built on less.

I flipped onto my back, staring at the ceiling, trying to let sleep overtake me. Gradually, slowly, eventually, drowsiness set in, pulling me into sleepyland.

Then the phone rang.

I bolted out of bed like a startled fawn and had the phone to my face before I was fully awake.

"Daniels."

"Hope I didn't wake you, Jack. We've got another one."

I closed my eyes and gave my head a shake. The clock told me it was a little past noon.

"Where?"

"A 7-Eleven on Addison," Benedict said. "About a block away from you."

I blinked and nodded, weighing the news.

"Be there in five."

"There's something else. Maybe you should prepare yourself."

"What do you mean?"

"He left another note. It's addressed to you."

"What does it say?"

Herb cleared his throat and read in a monotone.

"'Number Two. Dear Jack, I saw you at Joe's. Not bad for a bitch. I didn't get my money's worth, but it was fun anyway. Too bad that bald guy helped you out. I think you would look beautiful in a wheelchair. But there's still time for that.'"

I said, "Christ."

"There's more. 'I will keep killing these sluts. It's my mission. I've left you another present, but it's deeply hidden. Run, run, as fast as you can, Jack. You can't catch me . . . but I'll catch you. The Gingerbread Man.'"

"The crowd, Herb. Make sure we get close-ups of everyone. I bet the little weasel is there right now, watching. See you in a bit."

It only took a few minutes to throw on a suit and get over there. I didn't even need to drive. The crime scene was practically in my backyard.

Four squad cars had preceded me, parked in front of the entrance to the store, cutting off the lot. Several uniforms were securing the scene, taping it off. Another was keeping the crowd and the growing number of reporters at bay. I hung my badge around my neck and entered the circus.

Herb, who always managed to beat me to crime scenes even if they were only a block away from me, was standing next to the garbage can at the storefront. The lid was off, and something bloody was sticking out into the air. In Herb's hand was the note, bagged in a large Ziploc.

I found a tissue in my pocket and wiped my runny nose, trying to overtly scan the crowd. If I was obvious about it, I might scare our man away. And I was sure he was nearby, watching.

No one jumped out at me.

"You look like a train wreck," Herb offered.

"Thanks for caring."

I turned my attention to the garbage can. It was another woman, her ass rising up out of the refuse like a bloody mountain. Without trying to absorb too much detail, I could see that her buttocks, vagina, and rectum had been mutilated almost beyond recognition.

My stomach began to twist and I looked away, grateful that my nasal congestion masked the death smell.

This was someone's daughter. She'd suffered, died, and was now rotting away. All for the amusement of some sick son of a bitch.

"Who found her?" I asked Benedict.

"Owner. Guy named Fitzpatrick. He's the one who called it in. Patrolman recognized the MO, called up our district."

Which was an indication of how big this case was. Districts in Chicago were incredibly jurisdictional, and only an order from the police superintendent could force them to relinquish cases to one another. The order had been given after last night's fiasco.

"Witnesses?" I asked.

"Not yet."

"Owner inside?"

A nod.

I left the body and pushed open the glass door, Herb in tow. Fitzpatrick was sitting in a chair behind the counter, a sad expression painted on his face. He was portly, balding, and had several food and beverage stains on his work shirt. Two uniforms flanked him, one of them taking notes.

"Mr. Fitzpatrick," I announced, "I'm Lieutenant Daniels. This is Detective Benedict."

"Help yourself to some coffee, Lieutenant. Everyone else has. They say I'll be closed all day."

Much as I longed to pity the man and his temporary loss of income, I held firm and didn't break into tears.

"We should have things taken care of here in an hour or so," I told him. "Besides, with the news coverage, the whole neighborhood will be by later to see your shop. I'm sure more than one of them will buy something."

He brightened greatly at the entrepreneurial potentialities. Maybe he was thinking of having T-shirts made up.

"When did you notice the body, Mr. Fitzpatrick?"

"I noticed the lid was off. Sometimes kids, they steal them. God knows what they do with garbage can lids."

"What time was this?"

"At five to twelve, maybe a little after. There was no one in the store, so I went outside to look for the lid and I saw . . ." He made a gesture with his hands at the garbage can through the storefront window. "Then I came in and called 911."

The patrolman on his left, with a name tag proclaiming he was Officer Meadows, glanced at his notebook.

"Call came at eleven fifty-seven. Jefferson and I arrived on the scene at twelve oh three."

"Did you notice anything unusual beforehand?" I asked Fitzpatrick.

"No, nothing really."

"How about earlier today? Did any garbage trucks come into your lot? Vans? Anything out of the ordinary?"

"Nothing, except some guy who almost died in my store about an hour ago."

Benedict did his eyebrow thing, prompting an explanation.

"Some kid. Teenager. Had some kind of fit or seizure or something. Threw himself down on the floor by the pop machine, started shaking and foaming at the mouth. I thought he was gonna die right there."

"Did you call for an ambulance?"

"I was gonna. But the kid told me not to. Had these attacks all the time. After a minute or two he just got up and left, no problem."

I nodded at Herb, who went off to phone Mr. Raheem at the first 7-Eleven to check for a similar happenstance. Some guy foaming at the mouth would easily draw attention away from the parking lot.

"Can I have the surveillance tapes?" I pressed. "The ones for the last two hours?"

"Sure. But that kid didn't dump no body. I watched him leave."

"How much later did you notice the lid off the garbage can?"

"Few minutes, I guess."

I turned to Meadows. "Print him after he gives the deposition."

"I didn't do nothing!" Fitzpatrick thrust his jaw at me.

"We're doing that to rule out your prints if we find any on the garbage can."

He nodded, as if he knew that all along. I went back out into the fray, my headache pulsing with every heartbeat, my eyes feeling as if they'd been rubbed in sand. Maxwell Hughes was peering at the body in the can with professional detachment that can only come from constantly being around corpses. On his nod, two gloved assistants tipped the garbage can over.

The girl plopped onto the sidewalk, cocooned in a shell of bloody garbage. Two uniforms moved in, bagging and tagging, while Hughes knelt down and searched for a pulse that he knew wasn't there.

I walked over, staring down at the body, trying to imagine it walking and talking and being a person. I couldn't do it. Death robs people of their personalities. It turns them into, for lack of a more sympathetic word, an object rather than a human being.

This girl had hobbies and dreams and hopes and friends. But none of that meant a thing anymore. All that was left was the further indignity of an autopsy, in the hopes that her corpse would somehow lead to her killer.

From dreamer to evidence. And it was no easy trip.

I'd seen a thing or two. Shotgun deaths. Gangland murders. A guy who killed his kid with a hot iron. But as the garbage was peeled away, I had to turn away for fear of losing my stomach.

It was obscene, the traumas inflicted on this poor girl.

"We're missing some parts," Hughes said to his men. "I'm looking for two ears, four fingers, and all ten toes. Check inside cans and wrappers."

"Tell me this was done after death," I said to Max.

"I don't think I can appease you there, Jack." He spoke sadly. "See these cuts on her palms? From her own fingernails digging in while she clenched her fists. Consistent with most torture deaths. I don't see any ligature mark around her neck like the first one either. My guess would be she died of shock as a result of massive blood loss."

I blinked away the image of organs oozing up through the slits in her belly.

"Lieutenant," someone said.

Happy to focus on something else, I gave attention to one of the patrolmen sifting through the trash. He was holding, in his gloved hand, a gingerbread man cookie.

I wiped my nose and rubbed my temples and stared a

challenge into the crowd of onlookers, daring one of them to meet my gaze. None did.

"I talked to Mr. Raheem." Herb was putting away his cell phone. "He also had a kid in the store who had some kind of attack, about two hours before Donovan found the body."

I gave myself a mental kick in the ass for missing that.

"The surveillance tape?"

"We've got it in Evidence. We checked it up until an hour before the body was found. Maybe we should check the whole thing."

"We know this guy hires outside help. He proved that with me last night. He might have hired the same kid to do both distractions . . ."

"Then maybe he has a partner."

"And maybe we have a lead."

It was still iffy at best. The kid might not have a record, and we might never find him. Even if we did, there was a chance that he was hired the same way Floyd was, with little or no information about our perp.

But at least now we had something to do other than wait for new victims.

Herb eyed me sympathetically. "You want to meet me later, get some rest first?"

"Naw. Wouldn't be able to sleep anyway. I could use something to eat, though. Hungry?"

"When am I not hungry?"

I looked at his stitches. "Doesn't it hurt to eat?"

"Hurts like hell. But a man doesn't give up breathing just because he has a cold. I know a place that serves great falafel."

"Falafel?"

"No, I don't feel awful." Herb grinned. "I feel pretty good."

I gave him deadpan. Herb pouted.

"Come on, Jack. I've been waiting two weeks to use that joke."

"Should have kept waiting."

We took Herb's car, buying some White Castle cheeseburgers at a drive-thru and eating them back at my office. I called up Evidence, and Bill was only too happy to bring up the surveillance tape from the first 7-Eleven.

"I hear you're a free woman again, sugar buns." Bill grinned at me, showing off his unnaturally white dentures.

"I'm not free, but my rates are reasonable."

"How much for, say—three and a half minutes?"

"I don't talk money. You'll have to settle it with my business manager."

"You can have her for two bucks," Herb said. "That includes my cut."

Bill grinned wickedly, and I watched in amazement as the sixty-eight-year-old rolled his hips. They made a cracking sound.

"Unfortunately," I cut in before he pounced, "the taxpayers require my time first."

"You're a tease, Jack, getting an old man all hot and bothered and then turning him away."

He pinched my cheek and walked out.

I turned to Herb. "Thanks for informing Bill of my recent availability."

"Payback for siccing the Feds on me. You want the last burger?"

I shook my head and popped the tape in the VCR. As expected, the quality was poor. It was black and white, grainy from having been reused several hundred times, and speeded up so one six-hour tape could accommodate an entire day.

There was a time code in the lower left-hand corner, in military time, and I rewound to 1800 hours and let it play.

Lo and behold, at 18:42 a young man entered the store, made a beeline for the magazine rack, and then fell over and started shaking like a leaf. The two other patrons who were in the store, along with the clerk, went over to take a closer look.

The seizure lasted almost two minutes, or about twenty seconds on the speeded-up copy we had, and then the kid got up and left the store, keeping his head down, avoiding the overhead camera with obvious experience.

"If that was a real seizure, I'm trying out for the ballet," Benedict said.

I pushed the image of Herb in tights out of my mind and rewound the tape, letting it run in slow motion so it was closer to real time. As evidence, the tape was practically inadmissible. The picture quality was that bad. I took it out and plunked in the tape from the 7-Eleven earlier today, hoping for a better quality.

Sometimes wishes come true.

This time the tape was in color, crystal clear. Rather than the annoying pan back and forth of the previous tape, this tape used four different cameras to record four different parts of the store, which broke the screen up into quarters.

"This is more like it," Herb said.

I rewound to the part where the kid walked in, and he gave us a perfect full frontal face shot. Then he went from one screen to the next, and we watched as he popped something into his mouth and went into the familiar convulsions.

"Looks like he's spitting something up."

"Alka-Seltzer. It's an old trick, makes you look like you're foaming at the mouth."

"Let's get some uniforms up here to look at this."

Benedict got on the horn and rounded up half a dozen or so officers on duty. They piled into my office and watched the tape. No one recognized the kid.

"This has got to be an MO he's used before," I told them. "Probably shoplifting, maybe causing a distraction while his partner made off with some goods. Ask around, see if anyone's heard of a petty thief who fakes seizures."

After they'd left, the desk sergeant called and informed me that we now had a composite sketch of our suspect, drawn from descriptions given by Steve the pharmacist and Floyd the leg-breaker broker. Herb went down to get it, because the vending machines were en route. I put in the video of the first crime scene and scanned it for gawkers with cameras. Nothing.

Benedict came back a few minutes later, sans foodstuffs but with telltale chocolate smears in his mustache. He handed me the sketch, which was vague enough to look a little like every average middle-aged white man in the world. The eyes were closer together than most, and the head was more triangular, giving the perp a ratlike appearance. But under low lighting conditions, after a couple of drinks, the picture might have been of Don, or Phin, or half my squad. We could rule out Herb because the face was lean.

The phone rang, and Benedict graciously picked it up for me.

"It's Bains." He hung up the receiver only seconds after putting it to his ear. "He requests the company of your presence in his office as soon as you have a moment."

I got up and stretched, wincing as all of my aches and pains came to life. Perhaps the captain wanted to discuss the fight last night, or our progress on the case, or my brush-off of the Feds, or my unauthorized overtime, or to tell me he liked my outfit.

I was right on four of the five.

"Jack, have a seat."

I sat across his desk and faced the man. Captain Steven Bains was short, stout, about ten years my senior, and had a hair weave that looked unrealistic because it had no gray in it, whereas his mustache did. He finished peering at the paper in front of him and removed his reading glasses to look at me.

"You weren't carrying last night."

"I know. Maybe it was a good thing, because if I had my piece I might have killed one or more of them."

"Wear it from now on. It looks like this guy is gunning for you."

I nodded.

"Tell me about the second victim."

I ran it down for him, and he asked questions when appropriate.

"The pressure is mounting," he said when I finished. "The police superintendent and the mayor's office want to turn the case over to the Feds."

I made a face. "We're not lacking for manpower or resources. The only thing we're lacking is leads, because this guy doesn't give us any to follow."

"That's why I refused. But after the media kicks into gear today, it won't be long before my authority is usurped. If you want to keep this one, Jack, you'll have to dig up something more to go on."

"We're doing a restruct of the second vic. Maybe we'll get an ID."

"Hedge that bet."

I knew what he meant. In 99.9 percent of murder cases, the killer knows the victim, and links can be found. But the Gingerbread Man could be picking up random women. If that were the case, even positive IDs might not help us catch him.

"Any idea what he meant in the note, about leaving you another hidden present?"

"No. Another victim, maybe? But he doesn't hide them, he likes to put them in public places. Maybe . . ."

I rolled it around in my noggin. *I left you another present, but it's deeply hidden.* He's implying that the present was there, with the body, hidden deep. Deep in the body?

"What if he hid something inside the bodies?"

"Wouldn't the autopsy have picked it up?"

"Maybe not something deeply hidden."

Bains picked up the phone and got the assistant Medical Examiner, Phil Blasky. He asked him to recheck the first Jane Doe, looking for anything that might have been placed inside the body.

"He's on it." Bains hung up and scratched his mustache. "Special Agents Coursey and Dailey spoke with me yesterday."

I waited.

"They told me they don't believe you're giving them your full cooperation."

I chose my words carefully. "The FBI would profile Hitler as Jewish."

Bains smiled briefly, an unusual move for him.

"No one likes an asshole, Jack, until you have to move your bowels."

"I'll do my best."

"And the letters, I want them analyzed."

"They're at the lab now."

"I meant by a handwriting expert."

"We're already sure that the letters match."

"That's only part of it. The mayor's office is sending an expert to look over the letters to get a profile of our suspect."

I made a face. "Another profile? Are we going to consult a psychic next?"

"I'm sure you'll give him your full cooperation, Lieutenant." Bains said it with the full weight of his authority. Then he dismissed me, and I stood up to leave.

"Jack?"

"Cap?"

"Watch out for the overtime too. You're no help to the case when you're too exhausted to see straight."

I left, irritated. Being on the force for over twenty years, I'd had my share of big cases, and the corresponding media and political pressure. But being forced to work with the FBI, and now some snake oil handwriting expert, made my work all the more difficult.

"Look at it this way," Benedict said when I filled him in. "You get paid whether you catch the guy or not."

"Your attitude leaves something to be desired, Detective."

"It's just a job, Jack. Don't take it personally. It's what you do to make money, so you can live your life. I want to catch this guy as much as you do. You saw what he did to those women. Hell, look what he did to my mouth. But when I walk out that door, I leave work behind."

"This particular work seems to be following me wherever I go."

Herb frowned. "Get some rest. Take a day off. Call up that dating service and find a nice guy and get laid. Do something, for God's sake, other than police work. Fifty years from now, when you're dead and buried, you want the epitaph on your tombstone to read 'She was a good cop'?"

I thought about it.

"Fine," I decided. "I'll take the afternoon off. Can you manage the store while I'm gone?"

"Consider it done."

"I'll see you later."

"Live your life, Jack. You've only got one."

I nodded and left.

When I got home, I spent the next four hours thinking about the case.

CHAPTER 15

I T'S ALL IN THE PLANNING.

If you plan out every detail, you can get away with anything. The trick is to delay the gratification until the planning is complete. That's why he's been caught in the past—because the thrill of the crime overrode common sense. But that won't happen again. He now thinks of planning as an appetizer. Foreplay. It has become fun in its own right.

He's planned this spree so well that he'll be able to kill all four girls within a week, while still allowing himself time to enjoy each one. It's a tight schedule, made even tighter by the sudden interest he's taken in Jack Daniels, but the months of plotting and watching and waiting are paying off. By next week he'll be history, a Chicago legend, leaving behind a legacy of terror and unanswered questions.

He had to dispose of T. Metcalf that morning, wanting to keep her a bit longer but unable to deal with the smell. It's risky, dumping the body that way twice in a row, but it adds to his supernatural mystique. He's looking forward to the headlines.

Charles sits on his basement floor amid the barrels of gasoline, and stares at the gory red spot where he violated the corpse only hours ago. Tomorrow he'll have another one to take her place. Until then, he has more planning to do.

Jack is the cause of it.

He's expected all along to attack the cop in charge of his case. But he's dwelling on Jack more than he expected to.

Maybe the media is the cause of it, and all the attention he's getting makes him want to show off. Television mocked him, now it fears him. Justice.

Or maybe, after weeks of scheming and plotting, the idea that Jack wants to stop him before he's finished makes her just as bad as those whores who forced him to undertake this mission in the first place.

What is Jack doing now? How is the case progressing? Is she living in fear, worried she'll be attacked again? Does she feel helpless and powerless? Is she angry because she can't do anything to stop him?

Maybe he'll give her a call and find out. It's time to kick it up a notch, give her some personal treatment. She wants to go up against him? Fine. She's going to regret that decision, for the rest of her life.

Which won't be very long.

But why call, when he can drop by? After all, he knows where she lives.

The Gingerbread Man closes his eyes and begins to plan.

CHAPTER 16

I WOUND UP TAKING A NAP, which was a mixed blessing. It re-freshed me somewhat, and gave me some much-needed rest, but when my eyes opened, it was only five o'clock in the evening and I knew I'd never get to sleep come bedtime.

So I smoothed the wrinkles from my suit, took some pain medication and some cold medication, and went back to the only office in the city that never closed.

Herb was gone when I arrived, home with his wife and his life, work no longer on his mind. The ME's report was waiting for me on my desk, another rush job courtesy of the mayor's office, and I took a sip from my vending machine coffee and sat down to peruse the atrocities inflicted on another poor girl.

The first bit of news that leaped out at me was the time of death. The ME placed it at about seven P.M. the previous night. The killer had kept the body around for a lot longer than he'd kept the first one.

He'd hurt this one a lot more as well. This girl had thirty-seven wounds of various lengths and depths, but the ME indicated that several of the wounds had been reopened. Microscopic steel fragments matched those from the previous vic, indicating the same knife had been used. Histamine levels, coupled with a partially bitten-off tongue and the fingernail marks on the palms that Hughes pointed out, indicated they were premortem. She'd been tortured, the ME estimated for as long as four hours.

Death was caused by massive blood loss. Hopefully shock had spared her some pain. There were fibers found in wounds on her wrists and ankles, twine once again.

She was missing all of her toes, her labia minora and majora, four fingers, and both ears. None of them were recovered. No semen was found, but the obvious sexual nature of the crime inferred that rape might have occurred, and the perp either pulled out or used a condom.

Her urine contained traces of sodium secobarbital, the needle puncture mark on her upper left arm.

No identification was found, and the girl was officially dubbed Jane Doe #2. An expert mortician worked on her face and hair for almost two hours to make it appear as lifelike as possible. Then a digital photograph was taken, and the eyes were electronically drawn in on a computer.

This restruct picture was given to the media in time for the six o'clock news, along with a similar photo of the first Jane Doe. If anyone knew either girl, or had any information related to the case, they were asked to call the task force number. Herb had set up a unit of six desk officers to field calls, all of whom had been sufficiently briefed on the case to be able to weed out the crackpots and thrill-seekers.

The second note had been written in the same ink, on the same paper. No prints, hairs, or fibers were found on the note.

The two 7-Elevens were eight blocks apart. I thought about putting plainclothes cops on stakeouts of every convenience store in Chicago, but we would have needed five hundred people to cover the hundred-plus stores around the clock. Instead I put teams on the fifteen stores within a twenty-block radius of the first crime scene, and then drafted a flier to hand out. It told convenience store employees to keep their eyes out for anyone trying to steal garbage cans, drop off garbage cans, or fake a seizure in their shops.

After drawing up the letter, I called down to the desk sergeant and had her round up all the uniforms in the building. The night shift was treated to the same video of the Alka-Seltzer kid as the day shift, with similar results. No one recognized the suspect or the MO.

I hadn't even hit a third of the cops in the district yet, but my optimism was beginning to sag. Mug shots were now filed on computer rather than in books, and I did a quick search of young white male shoplifters and came up with more than eight thousand hits. Even with help it would take a zillion years.

I took a deep breath and let it out slow. If there was any connective tissue between what we had so far and our perp, I was too dense to see it. I was no closer to catching this guy than the day I'd taken the case.

I put in the videotape of the second crime scene and viewed it, seeing for the first time Benedict remove the note from the body, which had been stapled to Jane Doe #2's buttocks. After that it only got grimmer, made even worse because the picture quality was so good.

The first crime scene was videotaped at night while raining, by someone who had problems differentiating between focus and zoom. This video was clean, clear, and in your face. When the tape ended I had no desire to watch it again right away.

But I did watch it again. And again after that, numbing myself to the gore and trying to find something, anything, that might give me a clue.

During the fifth or sixth viewing, my mind began to wander. Was this how I was destined to spend the rest of my life? Benedict was home right now, with his wife. Maybe they were watching TV together, or making love. Or, most likely, eating. But whatever they were doing, it was together. They were sharing their lives. I was here, alone, watching the end of someone else's.

So what's the alternative? Go home, clean myself up, and hit the bars? Sure, I could let myself get picked up, kill the lonelies for a night. But I needed something more substantial than a quick, informal lay.

What I needed, what I've been missing for damn near fifteen years, was to be in love. And I didn't think I'd find it at the bars.

I thought, wistfully, about my ex-husband, Alan.

Alan was something special, that one-in-a-million guy who liked holding hands and sending flowers. He rarely lost his temper, was a whiz in the kitchen, and loved me so completely that I was never cold, even during the brutal Chicago winter.

I take full responsibility for ruining our marriage.

I met him on the job, back in the days when I walked a beat. He came up to me on the street, told me someone had lifted his wallet. I couldn't say he was especially handsome, but he had the kindest eyes I'd ever seen.

We dated for six months before he proposed.

In the beginning, our marriage was great. Alan was a freelance artist, so he was able to make his own schedule, ensuring that we always had time to be together.

Until my promotion to the Violent Crimes Unit.

Prior to this, Alan and I had planned to have children. We

were going to have a boy named Jay and a girl named Melody, and buy a house with a big backyard, in a good school district.

But much as I wanted that, I also wanted a career. Maternity leave meant time away from work, and a newly ranked detective third class needed collars to make second grade.

My work week jumped from forty hours to sixty.

Alan was patient. He understood my ambition. He tried to wait until I was ready. Then a major career setback forced me to spend even more time on the job.

Alan left me a week before I made detective second. That was also the week my insomnia started.

I buried the memories. Regret wasn't going to get me anywhere. Only one thing would.

I picked up the phone, put it back down, and picked it up again. Swallowing what little pride I had left was harder than I thought, but I managed. The taxpayers financed a call to Information, and ten seconds later I was dialing Lunch Mates, hoping they'd be closed at this hour.

"Thanks for calling Lunch Mates. This is Sheila, how may I help you?"

Her voice was so buoyantly optimistic that I felt a wee bit better about my decision to call a dating service.

"I guess I wanted to make an appointment, or schedule a visit. I didn't really expect you to still be open."

"We have late hours. After all, human relationships don't just run from nine to five. May I have your name, miss?"

"Jacqueline Daniels. Jack, for short."

She tittered politely. "Wonderful name. Your occupation, please?"

"Police officer."

"We have many clients in the law enforcement field. Were you looking for a match also within the department?"

"Christ, no . . . I mean . . ."

"No problem. It's hard to date in the same profession. That's why all those famous actors and actresses are always getting divorced. Sexual orientation?"

"Pardon me?"

"Are you looking to meet a man or a woman?"

"A man."

"Wonderful. We have many good men to choose from."

Her ability to put people at ease probably made all the losers she dealt with feel a lot better about themselves. It was sure working with me.

"Are you free at any time soon to come in for an orientation?"

"Yeah, uh, maybe tomorrow? Lunchtime, if possible?"

"How about twelve o'clock?"

"Fine."

She gave me directions, we made a little more small talk, and she'd bolstered my ego enough to make me feel good about hiring a service to find men because I was too incompetent to find one on my own.

"See you tomorrow at noon, Ms. Daniels. We'll get all of your information then, along with giving you an overview of our company. We'll also be taking a picture of you. You're free to bring in any pictures of yourself, if you'd like."

Other than my driver's license, I didn't think I had any pictures of myself.

"Will there be a videotape?"

More musical laughter. "Oh, no. We don't make videos of our clients. We simply get to know them, then come up with likely matches to meet for lunch. We have thirty-five agents here, and each handles between fifty to a hundred clients. Our agents set up lunch dates within their own client list. If they go through their whole list without a suitable match, the client is given to another agent."

That sounded like being the last kid picked for a backyard football game. I could picture some poor fat girl being traded from agent to agent every month, and the image made me wince.

"Well, I'll see you soon then."

"Good evening, Ms. Daniels."

I hung up, my confidence still high. Then I realized I'd forgotten to ask about the cost of this service. That helped kill the optimism buzz.

I knew an ex-cop who used an expression whenever something bad happened. He was a real creep, but as the years passed I've come to respect the honesty of his words. Whenever he'd failed a test, or gotten a reprimand, he always said, "It's just one more layer on the shit cake."

With all the layers I'd built up over my life, I suppose one more didn't matter too much.

The phone rang, and I slapped the receiver to my face.

"Jack? I was wondering if you'd still be there."

It was the assistant ME, Dr. Phil Blasky. He was one of the best in the business, we used him on practically every high-profile case. In person, he was a thin bald man with an egg-shaped head, but his voice was a rich opera baritone, similar to that of James Earl Jones.

"Hi, Phil. Looks like we're both burning the midnight oil."

"You've gotten the second Jane Doe reports? I messengered them over."

"Just reviewed them. I guess the mayor is pressuring you folks as much as us."

"Jack . . ." Phil's voice dropped an octave, which made it low enough to rattle teeth. "I've been working late to investigate that lead Bains told me about. Checking the bodies for anything hidden in them. I found something in the stab wound of the second Jane Doe, and then went back to the first one and found the same thing."

"What?"

Phil took a breath. "It's semen, Jack."

"Pardon me?"

"The guy's sperm. I found it in the deepest stab wound on each victim. Got a chemical hit while swabbing them out. I never would have found it if I hadn't been told to look."

I let this sink in. "You mean he raped the stab wounds?"

"The wounds have some tearing along the edges, so that's a good assumption."

"While they were still alive?"

"We're not sure. But there's a possibility of it, yes."

"Where?" I had to ask.

"Both of them in the stomach."

"Can we type him?"

"The lab is trying now. But that's a long shot. It's mixed in with a lot of blood, and has been decomposing for days."

This was the present he said he'd left me. Jesus.

"Thanks, Phil."

"Catch this psycho, Jack."

Phil ended the call.

I gripped the phone until that annoying off-the-hook signal came on and reminded me to hang up. The images swirling around in my brain were almost too horrible to imagine.

I'd been stabbed once, years ago, by a gang-banger with a switch blade. Knife went into my belly. I had minor surgery to stop the bleeding, was off my feet for a month. The pain had been one of the worst I'd ever experienced, a combination of a cramp, an ulcer, and a third-degree burn. The thought of a man violating that wound . . .

I shuddered. Then I got up and rewound the crime scene tape to watch for the umpteenth time, my determination fiercer than ever.

CHAPTER 17

HE CALLS FIRST, FROM A PAY phone a block away. A machine answers. Perfect. He drops the receiver, not bothering to hang it up, and walks over to the front door of Jack's apartment building.

With a discreet look in either direction, he begins to press buzzers. On the eighth button he gets someone on the intercom.

"I'm from Booker's Heating and Cooling. Here to look at the furnace."

He's buzzed in.

It's an old building, straight middle class. The halls are clean and recently painted, but there's no doorman, no security camera, and the lighting is low wattage to save the landlord on his electric bill.

It can't get any easier.

Jack lives on the third floor, apartment 302. He takes the

stairs, reasoning he's less likely to encounter someone in the stairwell than on the elevator. But even if he does, he's dressed for the part; a stained brown jumpsuit, a toolbox, and a name tag that reads "Marvin."

The Gingerbread Man makes it to Jack's floor without seeing a soul. The hallway extends out in either direction in an L shape, and he easily locates the right apartment.

He knocks on it softly. There's always the chance that Jack is home and just didn't pick up her phone. There's also the possibility that she has a dog. Knocking should make the dog bark, unless it's very well trained.

But no one answers, and nothing barks. He takes a thin billfold out of his back pocket and opens it up, selecting an appropriate tension wrench and lock pick.

Foreplay.

Opening deadbolts is almost as easy as opening car doors. He has the penal system to thank. He went to jail on a B&E charge. Even though he had killed before, he was naive in the ways of properly committing a crime. Prison turned out to be the perfect school for honing his skills.

It takes him forty seconds to knock back the tumblers. The deadbolt turns with a satisfying snick, and the Gingerbread Man enters the home of the cop assigned to catch him. He locks the door and looks around.

It's perfect. No dog, no witnesses, and Jack has even been good enough to leave the lights on for him. He tugs on his latex gloves and giggles. Now for phase two of the plan.

He does a quick tour of the apartment, not knowing how much time he has until she gets home. It doesn't take long to deduce the bedroom closet is the best hiding place. It's roomy, has a hamper that he can sit on, and is only a few steps away from the bed. Plus, there's no window in the bedroom, no chance of anyone looking in. He gets to work.

Opening his aluminum toolbox, he takes out the rechargeable drill and a quarter-inch bit. He makes a hole in the closet door about three feet from the floor. Then he rubs off the splinters on both sides with a small file, and uses a roll of duct tape to pick up all the sawdust on the carpet. Next he sprays some WD-40 on the closet hinges, until it opens and closes as silent as death.

Satisfied with the setup, he goes to the bathroom and empties his bladder.

He enters the closet and shuts the door behind him. The adrenaline is pumping like hot oil through his veins. Sitting on the hamper, he has a perfect view of Jack's bed from the hole in the closet door. He removes the gun from the bag, an old .22 with the serial numbers filed off, and practices opening the door and creeping up to the bed.

On the third try he's confident he can sneak up to the sleeping lieutenant without making a sound.

He sits back on his perch in the closet and waits, letting the fantasy build. Hopefully he won't have to use the gun. He needs it just until he can jab her with the Seconal needle. Once he's sure she's completely out, he can tie her up and take his time with her.

He becomes aroused thinking about it.

His video camera is in the toolbox. He didn't take the bulky tripod, but the thought of doing it handheld is exciting. He can get some intimate and gory close-ups.

His eyes gradually adjust to the dark. He removes a sandwich he's brought along and eats, planning the evening's festivities in his head.

He didn't bring his hunting knife—didn't want to risk getting stopped on the street with that incriminating piece of evidence on him. But he has the twine, some pliers, a soldering iron, and the drill. When it comes time to give Jack her present, he's pretty sure she has a knife in the kitchen large enough to make a deep hole.

It's a shame he'll have to gag her—he so wants to hear her scream.

He finishes the sandwich, wondering if Jack has a cheese grater.

The front door opens.

He grips the gun in his hand, making sure it's cocked. His palms are sweaty in the latex gloves. His heart beats so loud that he thinks he can hear it.

"Relax," he tells himself.

Eye pressed to the hole in the closet, he waits for Jack's entrance.

CHAPTER 18

I ENTERED MY HUMBLE ABODE AT close to ten o'clock, lugging take-out Chinese. A full night loomed ahead of me, and I hoped a full stomach would get me drowsy.

But when I looked at the pineapple chicken, my stomach turned. I put it in the fridge for later, making myself a stiff whiskey sour instead.

My stomach didn't like that either, but it helped take some of the edge off. In fact, when I finished it I actually yawned. Encouraged by this good omen, I headed for bed.

I stripped down to my underwear, letting my clothes fall where they may. I put my gun on the nightstand next to my bed and replaced my bra with an old T-shirt. Then I climbed under the covers and killed the lights.

My mind had to be blank. That was the key. If I had nothing to think about, I had nothing to keep me awake. I imagined a vast field of wheat, blowing in the breeze, enclosed by a tall fence. Outside the fence were a million and one thoughts—the case, the dating service, the Jane Does, and on and on. But my fence was too tall, too strong, and I wouldn't let them in.

I was on the very edge of sleep, ready to tumble fully into it, when the phone rang.

"Daniels."

"Jacqueline? I assumed you'd be up."

I blinked twice. Much as I craved sleep, some things were more important.

"Hi, Mom. How's everything?"

"Everything's wonderful, sweetheart. Except that scoundrel Mr. Griffin won't fix this hole in my porch screen, and I've got mosquitoes the size of geese flying around my room. I didn't wake you, did I? I know you're a night owl, and long distance is free after ten o'clock."

I yawned. "I'm up. You know you can call anytime, Mom. How's the weather in Orlando?"

"Beautiful. Hold on a second."

There was a smacking sound, and a cry of triumph. "I finally found something *People* magazine is good for—swatting mosquitoes. How's Don?"

"I left him."

"Good. He was an idiot. Believe me, dear, I understand the need for sex as much as anyone. That's the only reason I let that old fool Mr. Griffin keep coming by. But you can do so much better. You take after me—beautiful, intelligent, and a crack shot. You know, the first four years I was a police officer, they wouldn't even let me wear a gun?"

I smiled at the familiar story. "And when you finally did get one, you scored higher than every guy in the district at the range."

"Who would have ever guessed that one day I'd look

back on my forties as if they were my youth." Her voice dropped an octave. "Jacqueline, I fell yesterday."

I sat up in bed, alarms going off in my heart. She didn't say it casually. She said it like all seventy-year-olds say it, with weight and reverence.

"You fell? How? Are you okay?"

"In the shower. Just a bruised hip. Nothing broken. I went back and forth about telling you."

"You should have called right away."

"So you could put your life on hold to fly out here and take care of me? You think I'd allow that?"

Mary Streng was the queen of self-reliance. Dad died when I was eleven. Heart attack. The day after we put him in the ground, Mom got a job with the CPD. She started in Records, eventually moved up to Dispatch, and by the end of her twenty years she'd risen to detective third class and worked property crimes.

No, she wouldn't have allowed me to fly out there.

"You still should have called."

"I saw a show about this on *Oprah*. Adult-age children, caring for their feeble parents."

"You're far from feeble, Mom."

"Role reversal, they called it. There was a woman on who changed her mother's diapers. I'll eat my .38 before I let it come to that, Jacqueline."

"Please, Mom. You don't have to talk like this."

"Well, that's still a ways off. All I did was bruise my hip. I can still get around. It just limits some of the things I can do with that naughty Mr. Griffin."

"Mom . . ."

"Look, I just wanted to tell you. I have to go now. *Real Sex 38* is almost on HBO. I'll call you soon. Love you."

And she hung up.

Sleep was miles away.

I remember my father like I remember old movies; just a few quotable lines and a general impression. He died when I was too young to get to know him as a person.

But my mom . . . my mom was everything to me. She was my best friend, my mentor, my hero. She was the reason I became a cop.

Mothers shouldn't be allowed to get old and fragile.

I purposely pushed it out of my head to avoid getting maudlin. Instead, I focused on my Lunch Mates appointment tomorrow. They'd be taking a picture, and I still looked like I'd gone a few rounds with Mike Tyson. What guy would go out with a woman with bruises all over her face?

I got up and went to the bathroom, checking the vanity. Maybe a little foundation here, a little concealer there . . .

So the face would be okay, but what to wear?

I mentally ran through my wardrobe. My best outfit was the Armani. I normally couldn't afford designer clothing, and had picked this up at an outlet store. The price tag was hefty, even with the discount, but it gave me confidence when I put it on. I had several blouses that matched, and wondered if I should go with the loose silk one, or the tighter cotton one.

Only one way to find out.

I went to the closet.

CHAPTER 19

Excitement has given way to frustration, and finally anger. Juices flowing, locked and loaded, he's only moments away from sneaking out of the closet to pounce on her, when the phone rings.

He endures a syrupy conversation between Jack and her mom, so thick in parts that he feels like gagging. Then he waits stock-still for Jack to go back to sleep.

But she doesn't.

The little bitch stares at the ceiling, tossing and turning like her panties are a few sizes too small.

For an hour, he waits.

And for an hour, Daniels refuses to snooze.

Every few minutes she'll close her eyes, and just when he's ready to move, they'll spring open again.

The most infuriating part is that her gun is right next to her on the nightstand. He knows that Jack will shoot him before he can even get the door open.

He could try to fire through the closet, but that's too risky. It's only a .22, and if he misses, he's pretty sure that Jack won't.

He grinds his teeth in rage, then forces himself to stop because it's noisy. The muscles in his neck and back are cramping. His eyes are beginning to blur from peeking through that tiny hole. And worst of all, he has to piss again.

Then, like an answered prayer, Jack gets out of bed and goes to the bathroom. Away from her gun. The time to strike is now.

He's about to ease open the closet when the bitch is back again. But instead of going to bed, she's coming this way.

The Gingerbread Man stifles a giggle. Imagine Jack's shock when she opens up her closet and he shoves a gun in her face.

Standing erect, he grips the pistol and prepares to spring.

CHAPTER 20

I WAS HEADED FOR THE CLOSET when I remembered my new sweater. It was a brown wool pullover, L.L.Bean, and it made me look soft and feminine. That would work just fine, and then I could save the Armani for the actual date, assuming I get one.

I went over to my dresser to find the sweater, along with a pair of jeans. Satisfied I wouldn't look like another desperate nine-to-fiver for my picture tomorrow, I turned to go back to bed, when something made the hair on my neck stand up.

Someone was in the closet.

I wasn't sure how I knew. A vaguely defined sense. An alarm on an instinctive, subconscious level. But I felt paralyzed, a deer in headlights, and my stomach dropped down to my ankles.

Then, action.

Hoping I didn't give myself away during my brief catatonic pause, I took two steps toward the nightstand and my gun.

Like a whisper, the closet door rolled open behind me. My intruder yelled, "Don't move!"

I moved anyway. I dove for the pistol, my hand wrapping around the butt just as the shot rang out. I felt a sudden pressure in my thigh, like I'd gotten kicked.

I belly flopped on the bed and rolled, gun in hand, squeezing off two shots in the general direction of the closet. A shadowy figure ducked the bullets and scurried out my bedroom door.

Keeping my gun trained on the doorway, I felt behind me for the lamp on the nightstand and switched it on.

My leg was covered with blood.

The entry wound was four inches above my knee, on the inside of the thigh. The flow was steady, but not pulsing. There was no pain, only numbness. But the pain would come, I was sure of that.

I picked up the phone to dial 911, but there wasn't any dial tone.

"Hi, Jack."

It hit me almost as hard as the bullet had. This wasn't some burglar, after my cash and VCR. It was him—the Gingerbread Man. And he was on the phone in my kitchen. I hit the disconnect button twice, but couldn't get a dial tone with the extension off the hook.

"Hello, Charles."

"How do you—oh, you must have traced the prescription. Clever, Jack. But you have to know I wouldn't be dumb enough to leave my real name."

His voice was soft, gravelly.

"Yeah, you're a regular Einstein. How long were you stuck in that closet, sitting on my dirty laundry?"

"I hope I didn't hit an artery. I wouldn't want the fun to end so soon."

"Maybe you should come in here and check for yourself."

"I'm not going anywhere. I'll check on you soon enough. After you've lost some blood, and your reactions have slowed down."

The pain hit. Red and angry, making my vision swim. It felt as if I'd been impaled by a white-hot pickax. I held the phone between my ear and shoulder and clamped my hand down over the wound. Hopefully someone in the building heard the shots.

"I hope you stick around." Speaking through my teeth. "Cops should be here any second."

"Why should they come? A few loud bangs? Could have been a television turned up too loud, or a car backfiring."

"I'm calling from my cell phone right now."

"You mean this one, in your purse next to the microwave?"

Dammit. I tried to sit up, my bed soggy with blood. The killer was right. If I lost too much, I'd pass out. Then he'd come back and finish the job.

"Ooh, look—pictures. This must be Mom. Maybe when I'm done with you, I'll take a trip to Florida. She fell, I understand. So sad. But I bet I can get her on her feet again."

I bit back my response, focusing all my energy into getting off the bed. The pain made me cry out, but I managed to get on my feet and limp over to my dresser. I pulled out a braided belt and looped it around my leg, over the wound.

"What do you think, Jack? Should I pay Mom a visit?"

"You know what I think, Charles?" I jerked the tourniquet tight and winced. The room began to spin. "I think you're a sad, small little man who didn't get enough love when he was a baby. Either that, or you were dropped on your head."

He giggled.

"You don't know what you're talking about. People like me are labeled as psychotics. But it's a cruel world, Jack. Only the strong thrive. And I'm one of the strong. I'm no more psychotic than a shark, or a lion, or any other predator at the top of the food chain. And I'm head and shoulders above you and the rest of the world because I know what I want, and I know how to take it."

"Dropped down a whole flight of stairs, it sounds like."

I had to sit, or risk passing out. The pain was a writhing, living thing, full blown and making any movement agony.

"You sound sleepy, Jack. Maybe you should lie back, take a little nap."

It didn't seem like bad advice to me. My breath was coming a little quicker, and I was cold, but beyond the pain a kind of peace was settling in. A nap might do me good.

"Shock," I said aloud.

I wiped some sweat off my face and gave my cheek a slap. I was going into hypovolemic shock, a condition caused by extensive fluid loss. If I passed out, I was dead.

But in my condition, there was no way I could attack him. So what the hell could I do?

I had more bullets in my dresser. I half hopped, half dragged myself over to the drawer and replaced the two rounds I'd fired. I had a plan, kind of, but to make it work I had to keep him distracted.

"So what's the real reason you're killing these girls, Charles? Did your scoutmaster get too frisky on a camping trip?"

"Cliché, Jack. Everyone wants to look for the reason. Like there's a switch that can be turned on to make a person a killer. But maybe it has nothing to do with environment, or genetics. Maybe I simply enjoy it. I know that I'll enjoy giving you my special present. Think I can use that bullet hole in your leg?"

"Possible," I mumbled, pulling myself to the door. "It's a really small hole."

My bedroom led out into a short hall. The kitchen was to the left, out of view. But that wasn't my goal. It was a straight shot into the living room, and to my window with the view looking out over Addison.

"You little bitch." Men never took teasing about their penis size well. "I'm going to make you scream so loud, your throat bleeds."

"Promises, promises." I held my gun in both hands, took aim, and fired four shots into my window.

The glass exploded outward, hopefully peppering the sidewalk below. It was night, and my neighborhood was always crawling with barhopping kids. If that didn't warrant a call to 911, I didn't know what else would.

Apparently my assailant thought the same thing.

"We'll finish this later, Jack." His voice was curt. "See you soon."

And he finally hung up the phone. I cocked my ear and heard my front door slam shut.

I was still on the floor, gun clenched in my fist and fighting to stay awake, when the cops arrived.

CHAPTER 21

EVERYONE AGREED I'D BEEN LUCKY.

The bullet entered my thigh at the sartorius muscle and exited through a muscle called the gracilis. The wound was clean, without bullet fragmenting or ricocheting, narrowly missing the femoral artery. I needed three units of blood, but the scar would be minimal. I should be out of bed in a day or so.

Since my arrival at the hospital last night I'd been reconstructing the entire episode in my head, trying to remember every detail of our conversation. Herb helped, taking everything down, asking questions to help jar my memory.

We moved on the leads quickly.

First, my mom was effectively protected. At the onset I'd insisted upon nothing less than moving her to a safe house. Mom would have none of it, naturally. We compromised; she would stay at a friend's house for a few days. I didn't have to ask to know that she meant the ubiquitous Mr. Griffin. I met him once last year; he was stooped over, walked with a cane, and had arthritis in both hands. A far cry from the man my mother described as "Insatiable—he's like a machine."

Hopefully he'd mind her bad hip.

My door showed no signs of forced entry, nor did the door to the apartment building. He could have somehow gotten a key, or more likely, knew how to pick locks.

Every tenant in the building was questioned, and someone had buzzed in an unknown maintenance man earlier that day to work on the furnace. This was being checked out.

My apartment was gone over with a fine-toothed comb, literally. A great deal of excitement was generated over the discovery of some semen stains on the bedroom carpet, until I reminded everyone that I used to have a sex life.

All fingerprints found were either mine or Don's. There were enough hairs and fibers picked up to take weeks to sort through, and I wasn't very optimistic. Even if they did manage to find one of the killer's hairs out of the several thousand vacuumed up, it wouldn't help too much—unless he had his name and address written on it.

I installed a burglar alarm.

In a tremendous show of faith in me, or as some saw it, a tremendous lack of ambition, Captain Bains refused to bend to political pressure and kept me on as head of the case. His logic was simple. I was the strongest link to the killer. Chances were high that the Gingerbread Man would contact me again.

A round-the-clock surveillance was begun on me, and I received a cellular phone with their number on speed dial. Three teams would rotate the watch, and I was to inform them of everywhere I went. The code word we'd picked was "peachy." If I was in trouble, I'd use the code word and the cavalry would come rushing in.

I was picking at a hamburger that tasted like it had been

steamed, when Herb came into my room, his fourth visit in twenty-four hours.

"I see I've arrived coincidentally at dinnertime." He pulled up a chair.

"Some coincidence. You're the one who filled out my menu card."

"Is it good?"

"I'm not sure. Somehow they've managed to drain every nuance of flavor from it."

"Hmm. May I?"

I allowed him access to my food.

"It tastes like it's been steamed." This fact didn't stop him from polishing it off, along with my applesauce, my green vegetable, and the rest of my juice.

"I saw some gum stuck under the table there, if you want dessert."

"I love a free meal."

"Free? They're charging me forty-five dollars for that feast there. A forty-five-dollar hamburger. It gives me a headache thinking about it."

"Want me to call for some aspirin?"

"I can't afford the aspirin. I'd have to put them on lay-away. Now help me up so I can use the can."

"I thought you weren't allowed out of bed until tomorrow."

"You want to warm up my bedpan for me?"

Herb helped me up. The pain in my leg made my eyes water, but I kept my footing. The best way to describe it was like a charley horse, but sharper. Maybe I'd break down and get some aspirin after all.

When I'd finished bathroom duty I sat in a visitor's chair opposite Herb, wincing when my knee bent.

"Are you sure . . ."

"I'm fine," I told him. "I don't want my leg to get any

stiffer than it is. I want out of this hospital. I hate waiting around like this."

"This is your first time, isn't it?"

"I've been shot at before. This is the first time the bullet hit home. You were . . ."

"Almost twenty years ago now. Took it right in the upper thigh."

"You mean the ass."

"I prefer to say upper thigh. Or lower back. Gang-banger got me from behind. It still itches sometimes in dry weather."

"Really? And I thought you were just unsticking your underwear all the time."

"I do that too. Jack . . ." Herb got serious on me. "We found another body about an hour ago."

My heart sank. "Another girl?"

"No. A boy. Stabbed twenty-three times with a hunting knife, left in a Dumpster behind Marshall Fields on Wabash. Blasky's doing the autopsy now."

"How do we know it's our perp?"

"There was another gingerbread man cookie. We ran the kid's prints, ID'd him as Leroy Parker. Two shoplifting convictions, wanted in connection with half a dozen more counts. His description and MO match the kid who pulled the seizure distractions. Perp also left another note."

Herb handed me a photocopy. The Gingerbread Man's familiar scrawl filled the page.

Hi JACK IM
Thinking oF YOU

"If I was only faster yesterday . . ."

"Our job is to catch him, Jack, not blame ourselves or take responsibility for what he does."

The nurse came, and went into a lecture about how I shouldn't be out of bed. To assuage her wrath I allowed myself to be helped back in.

"No more getting out of bed, Ms. Daniels, or I'll have you tied down."

"Kinky. I may like that."

The nurse picked up my tray and smiled her nurse's smile. "At least your appetite is healthy."

I eyed Benedict. "Just like Mom used to steam."

The nurse left, and I made Herb get me my clothes.

"You're not leaving."

"I'm leaving. I hate being coddled. I'm a grown woman, and I can fend for myself. Now help me put on my pants."

After ten minutes of sweating, grunting pain, I managed to get changed into the clothes Herb had brought me the night before. I was even able to tie my own shoes without ripping my stitches.

"There's a media circus waiting outside the front entrance for you to come out," Herb said. "Should we find a back way?"

"Hell, no. Our man isn't making any mistakes, but maybe if I piss him off enough, he will."

"So—you're going to anger the psycho?"

"Not at all." I called the surveillance team and told them I was getting out of there. "I'm simply going to give an honest, bare-bones interview."

After fighting with two doctors and four nurses, I was finally discharged against hospital recommendation and had to sign a paper absolving them of responsibility if I died after stepping off their property. Then I ran a brush through my hair, wiped the crud from my eyes, grabbed my aluminum hospital cane, and went to meet the press.

Benedict hadn't been exaggerating about the media circus. At least two dozen reporters were hanging around outside the hospital entrance, all waiting around for the off chance that I'd appear. I'd had big cases before, and had been on TV. At first I was impressed. But then I saw myself on the tube, which added twenty pounds, made me look short, and somehow distorted my fine speaking voice into something squeaky.

"I have some things to say, and then afterward I can answer a few questions," I told the crowd, giving them a chance to switch on their cameras and focus. "First of all, I was shot by the criminal that the press is calling the Gingerbread Man. He'd broken into my apartment last night. As you can see, my injury isn't serious. He couldn't aim the gun properly, because he was hysterical, crying for his mama."

Herb gave me a slight nudge in the ribs, but I was just warming up.

"Besides the obvious emotional problems, the killer is also very stupid. The only reason we haven't caught him yet is because he's been lucky, and because he's a coward who runs away when confronted. I fully expect that with the combined efforts of the Chicago Police Department and the FBI, we should have him in custody soon. Now I'll take questions."

The questioning went well. When it was over I'd also called the killer a bed-wetter, said he was impotent, and predicted that when we found him, he'd probably be picking his nose. I explained I felt no anger toward his attack on me; rather I felt sorry for him, like a sick dog. When asked if I was afraid of him going after me, I laughed and said he would be too scared to make another attempt.

At that point my cellular phone began to ring, and I had a pretty good idea who it was. I excused myself from further questions and walked away from the crowd before answering.

"Daniels."

"Why didn't you clear this with me before broadcasting live on five channels?"

Captain Bains.

"I was live? Did I sound squeaky?"

"You sounded like you're provoking him. Dime-store psychology is not the way to run a headline case."

"You left me in charge, Captain. This is how I want to run it."

"And when this guy kills a dozen people because he's mad you called him a mama's boy, how do you figure we'll still be employed after the lawsuits come rolling in?"

"I'm provoking him to come after me. The only one I put in danger is myself."

"And what if you don't catch him? You just promised the city you'll have him in custody soon."

"I'll catch him."

"If you don't, it's your ass."

He hung up. That was two conversations with Bains in two days. Maybe now was a good time to ask for a raise.

"Jack . . ." Herb caught up to me. The reporters had snagged him for a few questions after I'd jetted out. "You sure poked your stick at the hornets' nest back there."

"Hopefully the hornet will come out. Can you do a crippled girl a favor?"

"Sure. You bought dinner."

"See my tail?" I nodded in the direction of the two plain-clothes cops, following our path twenty feet behind us. "If they were any closer they'd be wearing my clothes. Ask them to loosen up."

"You got it."

Benedict waddled up to them, giving a mini lecture on the art of being inconspicuous. I gave them a big smile and a thumbs-up to smooth it over. Don't want to anger the guys guarding your life.

Herb drove me home, first stopping at the Salvation Army on my request, where I wanted to replace my antiseptic aluminum hospital cane with something more distinguished. I found a polished piece of hickory that fit the description.

"Very distinguished," Benedict commented.

"We ladies of good breeding demand nothing less than the best. Lend me fifty cents so I can buy it."

He forked over some pocket change and then insisted on seeing me into my apartment.

"If you're looking for a good-night kiss, I'll whack you with my cane."

"Just want to make sure you can work your burglar alarm okay."

"Since when did a bullet wound make a person feeble-minded?"

I couldn't work the burglar alarm, so Herb had to show me.

"You press the green button first, then the code."

"Thanks. Want a drink?"

"Can't. It's Sunday."

I waited for more.

"Lasagna night," Benedict explained. "Got to get home."

"See you tomorrow, Herb. Thanks again."

"Get some rest, Jack."

He left me to my empty, quiet apartment. The lab team had taken half of my possessions, including the phone, which saved me from having to take it off the hook. The free press has no qualms about around-the-clock harassment.

My leg was throbbing as if it had its own heart. I limped into the bedroom to get undressed and froze stock-still.

Dread crawled over my body.

My blood was still on the mattress. The bullet holes were still in the wall. The closet door was closed, and I had an unrealistic fear that the Gingerbread Man was still hiding in there. It was silly and stupid, but a fear nonetheless.

I forced myself to open the closet, and left it open. Then I gathered up every bit of clothing that was in the closet and arranged for dry cleaning. I had no desire to wear anything that might have touched him.

Afterward I took four Tylenol, grabbed my blanket, and went to go sleep in my rocking chair.

Well, attempted to.

The apartment was too quiet. So quiet that I could hear myself breathe. So quiet that when a car honked outside, I almost wet my pants.

I turned on all the lights and flipped on the TV to keep me company. *The Max Trainter Show* was on—local talk soup at its basest level. Whereas other shows relied on melodrama to keep the viewer interested, Trainter went for shock value and violent confrontation. Six bouncers were on the set at all times, necessary to keep the guests from beating one another silly. Which they did, several times a show.

I tried to relax, losing myself in the wonderful drama of human nature. A white-trash couple confronted their daughter's lesbian lover. The lover fought back with a folding chair, which seemed as if it had been placed on stage for that very purpose. I counted four felonies and a dozen misdemeanors on screen before tiring of the show and switching it off.

When sleep finally came, it came with nightmares.

CHAPTER 22

THE PAIN WOKE ME UP. My leg had stiffened overnight, and I felt like a piece of twisted licorice from my big toe to my bottom. I admit to some less than heroic yelping as I got out of the chair and hobbled to the bathroom in search of drugs. I'd gotten a prescription for codeine at the hospital, but hadn't bothered to fill it, big tough girl that I am. Luckily I still had some of Don's medication from when he'd had his wisdom teeth pulled. Vicodin. I took two.

Showering was an awkward, painful affair that involved a garbage bag, duct tape, and more patience than I thought I had. When I was finally clean and dressed, an hour of my life was irretrievably gone.

Using the cellular, I informed my shadow that I was awake and well. The Vicodin in my system almost prompted me into song. I felt good. Very good. The drug even seemed to cure my sniffles.

Later, I blamed the drugs for my decision to skip work

that morning and reschedule my appointment with Lunch Mates.

The bruises on my face from the bar fight were yellowing, but I opted for the natural look rather than concealer. Clad in loose-fitting chinos, my L.L.Bean sweater, and a pair of drugstore sunglasses, I left my building sans cane and hailed a cab, informing my tail I was following a lead to a dating service. Let them snicker. I felt too high to care.

The taxi driver, a young Jamaican with a hemp beret, initiated a conversation about the Bulls, a topic that I'm normally lukewarm about but today happened to be bursting with opinion. I tipped him five bucks when he spit me out on Michigan and Balbo a dozen minutes later.

The building that housed Lunch Mates had recently been made over. I remembered it years back to be a hotel for men, complete with dirty brown bricks and tiny yellow windows. Now it was all chrome and polish, replete with green plants and a fountain in the lobby. Chicago, like all big cities, was a cannibal. Something must die for something else to grow.

I limped up to the information desk and was directed to the third floor. The elevator was mirrored, and I checked myself from every angle. Not bad for a forty-something cop who'd just been shot.

But that might have been the meds talking.

Two thick glass doors allowed me entrance to Lunch Mates, where a handsome man with perfect hair flashed me a smile from his reception desk. I smiled back, though not as electrically.

"Good morning."

"Good morning. I'm Jack Daniels. I have an appointment."

"Nice to meet you, Jack. I'm Frank. Coffee?"

I declined, thinking about coffee breath. He bade me take a seat, and motioned to the leather couch on my left. I sunk into it, extending out my bad leg in a way that I hoped looked demure. A windsurfing magazine caught my eye on the coffee table. Since I windsurf on practically a daily basis, I picked up the mag and perused an article about getting more hang time when it's choppy.

"Jack? I'm Matthew. I'll be your Lunch Mates agent."

He was even cuter than Frank. Blond, baby blue eyes, a model's square jaw. I wondered if the Gingerbread Man had actually killed me, and I'd died and gone to hunk heaven.

I stood and took his hand. It was soft and dry, making me even more aware of how unkempt my hands were. I'd never broken the habit of biting my nails. It seemed so much easier than clipping them.

"Pleased to meet you."

"I love that sweater. It brings out your eyes."

"A recent purchase. The sweater, not the eyes."

Chuckles on both our parts. He led me through the carpeted hallways of Lunch Mates. It resembled any other office, with generic artwork on the walls and the obligatory Habitrail of cubicles where employees pecked away on computers between coffee breaks. It could have even been my workplace, except it was brighter and everyone looked happy.

We made small talk about the weather and current news events, and then I was led into a corner office complete with view, fireplace, and a decor that made it look like a cozy den. We sat across from each other in two deep suede chairs, our knees almost touching. He reached over on the table next to us and picked up a leather binder.

"What we're going to do, Jack, is have you answer a few questions about yourself and make a data sheet like this one."

Matthew held up a glossy piece of paper with a picture of a woman in the upper right-hand corner. It almost looked like a resume.

"This data sheet will be given to men who would be a likely match for you. I'll also give you data sheets of men . . . it is a man you'd like to meet, correct?"

"Yes. I've decided to give heterosexuality one more shot."

He gave me a million-dollar smile, and I flashed my five-buck grin right back. The Vicodin guide to better living through chemistry.

"So . . . if you and a man choose each other, we pick a place and set the date. If you'd prefer, you can fill out the data sheet yourself, but I like asking the questions because then I have a better idea of personality and compatibility."

"Ask away."

I leaned back and crossed my arms, held the pose until I realized I looked too defensive, then set my hands in my lap and crossed my legs. That was awkward as well, but I stayed that way rather than shift again so soon.

"You mentioned you were a police officer. For how long?"

"Twenty-three years. I'm a lieutenant. Violent Crimes."

"Tell me about your job. Do you enjoy it?"

I took a moment too long to answer. Did I enjoy it? How could I enjoy Violent Crimes? I dealt with the worst element of society, I witnessed atrocities that regular people couldn't even comprehend, I was overworked, underpaid, and socially retarded. But I still kept plugging away. Did I actually enjoy it?

"I like getting the job done." I crossed my arms in the defensive position again.

"Have you ever been married?"

"Yes. I was divorced fifteen years ago."

"Children?"

"Not that I know of."

Pleasant laugh. "Education?"

"Northwestern. Bachelor of Arts."

"What was your major?"

What the hell was my major? "Political science."

"Do you have any hobbies?"

Was insomnia a hobby? "I play pool. I like to read, when I have the time."

He paused frequently to write things down. I reviewed in my mind what I'd said so far and was less than impressed. I was coming off like the most boring person to ever walk the earth. Unless I wanted to get hooked up with someone who was comatose, I needed to spice up my answers.

"I got into a fight the other day. Bar fight. See the bruises?"

I pointed to my face and grinned. My painkiller high had overtaken my better judgment.

"And the other day I got shot. A maniac broke into my apartment."

"My goodness. Where were you shot?"

"My leg. It goes with the job. Maybe you saw me on the news yesterday."

And from there it went downhill. I talked about my acts of heroism. I talked about being a great kisser. The interview ended after I let him feel my muscle.

Then he led me to another room where he took my picture and my money; a chunk large enough to knock me out of my good mood. Before I had a chance to reconsider, I was handed a sheaf of men's data sheets, patted on the shoulder, and walked to the door.

I was silent during the cab ride home. Gradually the painkiller wore off and my leg began to throb again. Even worse than the pain was the growing sense of humiliation. I felt like I'd won the Kentucky Derby for horses' asses. I'm sure that when I left, Matthew had a firm opinion on why I needed a dating service in the first place. To add injury to insult, I was out almost eight hundred bucks, and all I had to show for it was a list of men who Matthew thought would be compatible with the idiot I'd become.

I put the Vicodin in the medicine cabinet and took four aspirin. My cell phone rang, and I flipped it to my face, half hoping it was my surveillance team calling to say the Gingerbread Man was standing behind me with a gun. I would have let him shoot me.

"Jack? Herb. I know you're resting, but you'll want to hear this. We've got a positive ID on the second girl. Her roommate called in. Are you up to move on it?"

"I'm up. I'll see you in ten."

I called my team and told them the news. Much as the job was wearing me down, it did help me to forget my life, which was what I needed at that moment.

Clearheaded, I managed to start my car on the third try. During the drive I tried to shake the image of being the last kid picked for a backyard football game.

I couldn't.

CHAPTER 23

HE KNOWS WHAT JACK IS DOING. All those lies. All those insults. She's trying to flush him out. Force him to make a mistake. It's a clever move on Jack's part, and even helps her save face after the pain she suffered the other night.

But it still burns. The city isn't likely to tremble in fear if they have an image of the Gingerbread Man being cowardly. He has to correct that image, and make Jack pay for the lies. It's all about power. That's all it has always been about.

He knew he was different at a very young age, after he tied up the family cat with yarn and poked at it with a stick until its insides oozed out. Father beat him with a studded belt when he found out, demanding to know how he could do such a horrible thing.

But it isn't horrible to him. It's exciting. Thrilling. The fact that he knows it's wrong makes it even more so.

Throughout adolescence he continues to pull the legs off

frogs, and throw lit matches at his sister, and call people up and say he's going to kill them. Because it's fun.

Sometimes he tries to determine why he is the way he is. Throughout his life he's never felt anything. Certainly no love for anyone other than himself. No guilt, no empathy, no passion, no pity, no happiness. It's a sad thing not to know how to laugh, when everyone around you is laughing. Humans could have been a completely different species, for all that he understands their interactions, their society, their culture.

As he grows, he learns how to fake emotions so he doesn't stand out. He's a spectator in a strange world, a chameleon that can blend into the scenery but is never truly part of it.

Until he learns to feel something, by killing the cat.

It's enthralling to kill the cat. It makes his heart pound and his palms sweat. The feeble escape attempts of the cat are genuinely amusing, and Charles laughs for the very first time. And when the cat finally dies, when it's lying there inside out with its blood turning the ground to mud, he feels something more than amusement. He feels sexual arousal.

Why does the death of a simple kitty cat bring out all of this in him? Charles has only one answer—power. Power over life and death. Power over suffering. Suddenly, he can feel. The blind can see and the deaf can hear and he knows what his purpose is.

All of these people, with their silly relationships and their bullshit lives, are only here for his amusement. He isn't less than they are. He is more. More intelligent. More evolved. More powerful. He embraces the feeling like a miracle drug.

As he gets older, he learns to hide his obsession from others. Neighborhood pets disappear, but it rarely leads back to him. He has a little place, out in the woods, where he takes the animals. Where no one will hear the screeching. Where he can bury them when he's finished.

Fantasy often accompanies his mutilations. He imagines himself the ruler of the world, with all creatures trembling before his might. Like Satan on a throne of bones, torturing the meek, laughing at their pain. Dragging it on, sometimes for days, keeping the animal alive.

Or sometimes the animals represent people. His classmates. His teachers.

Father.

It's invigorating to pretend that the dog he's tied up and castrating is his father.

From what he's read about serial killers like himself, there are several features they all share. Kind of like a big fraternity, everyone conforming to a basic set of rules.

Most apply to him as well.

Fantasy plays a big part in recreational murder; in fact the stalking and the planning and the dwelling on it are almost as much fun as actually ending someone's life.

Most budding serial murderers show evidence of the triad when they're children; bed-wetting, starting fires, and hurting animals. He lays claim to all three, wetting the bed until his late teens.

There are also stressors and escalation.

A stressor is an event that unleashes or sets off a murder spree. This particular spree in the Gingerbread Man's career of slaughter can be linked to a very specific occurrence. And as for escalation . . . like any drug, the more you get, the more you need later to feel the same high.

The majority of serial killers were also abused as children, physically or sexually . . .

He didn't like to think about that.

At age fifteen he gets a job at an animal shelter.

His fantasy world quadruples overnight.

There are plenty of things to do at the shelter to amuse himself. This is where he learns to give injections—too many injections, poisonous injections, eyeball injections; at one point he keeps a log of different things he injects into animals, with descriptions of what happens.

The stressor comes when he gets caught mistreating one of the animals and is immediately fired. His rage is all-encompassing. He continues to visit at night, letting himself in with his keys, but it isn't enough. He needs more.

So he decides to kill a human.

He picks a girl at school. A freshman. Fat and pimply. He watches her for a week to make sure she doesn't have any friends.

Then one day at lunch he sits down next to her and asks if she wants to see the puppies where he works.

She does.

Don't tell anyone, he warns her, or he could lose his job. She promises she'll keep it quiet, thrilled that someone is actually paying attention to her.

They walk there after school. He tells her they'll enter the back way, takes her into the alley, and sticks her with an animal sedative.

When the shelter closes for the night, he lets himself in.

After trying unsuccessfully to rouse her, he uses her sexually, and then pulls her into the crematory.

That wakes her up. For a little while, at least.

Three young women disappear from his town that year.

No one ever questions him.

And now, many deaths later, he's ready for the big time. Headline news. National attention. All the murders that came before were practice, a warm-up for the main event.

After he kills the last whore, the one who started it all, he'll write a long letter to the media. Explaining what they all had in common. Explaining the reason he leaves the cookies. Making a mockery out of Jack and the CPD.

Promising more deaths someday soon.

It will go down in history as the greatest unsolved case of all time. And with good cause. All of the planning and preparation, the stalking, the plotting, the violence, and the surprise ending will make this the crime of the century. Worth all the time he's spent hunched down in his truck, following these whores around. Worth all the pain that lousy bitch has caused him, her and all the others like her.

When he was a child, nothing ever made him cry. Not even the time Father made him kneel on tacks and beg for penance.

"You have the devil in you, boy," Father would say.

Father was right.

CHAPTER 24

NOW THAT I WAS VICODIN-FREE, stairs posed a real problem. The pain was bearable, but the muscle I'd injured was apparently essential for climbing, and it wouldn't do what I commanded. To get to my office I had to ascend them sideways, like a crab, using both my cane and the handrail.

"We do have an elevator, Lieut," mentioned more than one of the uniforms who passed me going up or down.

"It's not the destination so much as how you get there." I'd grin through my sweat, but after the twentieth stair I began to doubt my own wisdom.

Benedict was waiting for me when I reached my office. "I see you took the stairs. Or are you fresh from the sauna?"

"The leg keeps stiffening up. I need to stretch it."

"That's a nice sweater."

"Just got it. Thanks."

"Are you wearing perfume?"

"Maybe a touch. Why?"

"No reason. So how'd that lead pan out at Lunch Mates?"

Smart-ass. "Shouldn't you be eating something about this time of day?"

"That does sound tempting. We'll stop on the way. I'll drive, if you don't mind. And unless you'd like me to carry you on my shoulders, I think we should take advantage of modern technology and use the elevator."

"If it's convenient for you, who am I to argue?"

We took the elevator, and Herb's car, and after a quick stop at the local Burger King drive-thru we headed for Theresa Metcalf's apartment.

"So, did you join up or not?" Herb asked, finishing off his last bite of burger.

"I don't want to talk about it."

"Must have been expensive."

"It was. Now let's pretend for a moment that we're both cops and we have other things to discuss."

"Sure. You gonna eat those fries?"

I gave Herb my fries.

Benedict turned off Addison and on to Christiana. The houses here were city houses; two-story, built in the late forties, with concrete porch steps and just enough front lawn to be able to mow with scissors. Unlike the suburbs, where every fourth house was the same model, these were each unique in their design, brickwork, and layout. Herb had a house like one of these. I might have had one, had I made some better decisions in my past.

Herb found the address and parked by the nearest fireplug. Theresa's roommate, Elisa Saroto, answered the door after the fourth knock. She was in her mid-twenties, thin, wearing jeans and a white blouse. Her dark brown hair hung down to her shoulders, framing a face that would have been pretty if not for the expression of grief.

After introductions she led us into the kitchen, where she sat down in front of a cup of coffee. Next to the mug was a photo album. She'd been reliving memories.

"We went to Fort Lauderdale last year." She opened the album and began to flip through it. After finding the right photo she pulled it from its slot and handed it to Herb. A close-up of two women, obviously Theresa and Elisa, both smiling and sporting deep tans. I thought of the picture in my pocket that we'd taken of Theresa at the morgue. We'd found our second Jane Doe.

"These two surfer guys tried to pick us up," she continued. "Bob and Rob. It was so funny, Theresa and Elisa and Bob and Rob."

We lost her to sobbing. Herb located a box of tissue on the counter and offered her one.

"Ms. Saroto." I eased it in while she was catching her breath. "What kind of person was Theresa?"

Elisa wiped her nose and snuffled.

"She . . . she was my best friend. We met in college. We've been roommates for five years."

"Did she have enemies?" Benedict asked. "Ex-boyfriends who couldn't let go, problems at work, with the family . . . "

"Everyone loved her. I know that sounds stupid, but it's true. She was a great person."

"Did anyone ever call and make threats? Obscene phone calls?"

She shook her head.

"Had she been acting strange lately? Afraid?"

"She's been fine . . . Shit. Why did someone do this?"

A new round of sobs. Benedict and I stood there, uncomfortable with her show of grief, wishing we could take it away. You never get used to people's suffering. If you do, it's time to get out of the job.

"How about boyfriends?" I broke in. "Was she dating anyone?"

"No one steady since Johnny. He's her ex-boyfriend . . . fiancé. They were going to get married. I was her maid of honor. She pulled out a month before the wedding."

"Why was that?"

"He was cheating on her. When she found out, she dropped him cold. He kept calling, begging her to reconsider. Jerk."

"And when was this?"

"Six, eight months ago? Her wedding was set for May, so a month before that."

Herb asked, "What was the boyfriend's name?"

"Tashing. Johnny Tashing. But he didn't kill her. He's a loser, but he still loves her. There's no way he could kill her. Not like that. Not horrible like that."

We went on for twenty more minutes, asking more questions, handing her more tissues. Theresa Metcalf had been a waitress at a club named Montezuma's. The last time Elisa had seen her was three days ago, when Theresa was leaving for work. Elisa had spent the last few days at her boyfriend's apartment, and hadn't known Theresa was missing until seeing her photo on television. She didn't recognize the picture of the first Jane Doe. She didn't know who killed her friend. She didn't know why anyone would.

After the inquisition, we walked down the hall to Theresa's room. It was neat. The bed was made. The closets were organized. Nothing appeared out of place or unusual.

Benedict and I busied ourselves looking through drawers and shelves for anything that could give us a clue as to Theresa's life and schedule. We found a box of letters, an appointment calendar, and some canceled checks. Nothing else warranted further attention.

Then we checked all the doors and windows, looking for signs of forced entry. We found nothing.

"Did Theresa have a purse?" I asked Elisa.

"Sure."

We searched the bathroom and the rest of the house and came up empty-handed. Theresa must have taken her purse with her. That meant she probably wasn't dragged forcibly from her house. So our working assumption was she'd either been grabbed by surprise somewhere else, or she went willingly with someone she knew.

Benedict gave Elisa a receipt for the items we took, and we asked her if she would stop by the morgue sometime tomorrow to identify the body. Normally we'd ask next of kin, but according to her roommate, Theresa was an only child and her parents were dead. Elisa agreed to come in around ten.

"So where to?" Benedict queried as we climbed back into the car.

"Two choices." I grimaced, trying to get my leg into a position that didn't hurt so much. "Work or the ex-boyfriend."

"I'd like to read through the letters we took before we tackle the ex. I saw his name on a few of them."

"Then it's off to work we go."

"You can adjust the seat, Jack. It's all electric."

Comfort won out over ego and I began pressing buttons. By the time I'd found the perfect combination of tilt and lift, we'd reached Theresa's place of employment a few blocks away.

"They don't look open." Herb pulled in front of the club. We couldn't see any lights on through the tinted windows.

"Alley entrance. I'm sure someone's inside, setting up for the day."

Herb parked on the street, refusing to leave his nice car with electric seats in the alley. We walked around and banged on the back door until one of the kitchen workers answered. Our badges got us inside, and after an intense session of question and answer with the manager of the club, we learned that Theresa did indeed work there, but she hadn't shown up for her last four shifts.

We got an employee list, along with the current work schedule, and asked if any other employee had been missing shifts lately. None had. Neither had any employee been dating or harassing Theresa. Had any customers? Well, the wait staff got hit on all of the time, but none fit the stalker category. We'd have to talk with the other servers to be sure. No reaction to the picture of the first victim.

Benedict and I walked back to the car. Routine dictated that every employee had to be questioned and checked out. We'd run them all through the computer for priors, and then we'd begin the lengthy and time-consuming process of interrogation, checking alibis, running down new leads. Hopefully something would break loose, but I wasn't crossing my fingers. The more we turned up, the more it seemed that Charles picked women at random. Maybe all a girl had to do to get on his list was be young and cute.

We (Herb) stopped for doughnuts on the way back to the station, picking up a dozen and the obligatory coffee. Since Herb's tongue had been mangled, he'd actually been eating more than usual.

"I once knew an overweight woman who was anorexic," he told me. "She refused to give in to her disease, so she ate nonstop. I refuse to let a little mouth pain deter my eating habits."

"Who said overcompensation isn't healthy."

"Pass me another cruller."

I was unable to talk Herb into taking the stairs when we got back to the station, even when using big words like arteriosclerosis and myocardial infarction. It was a good thing I saved my energy, because waiting for me in my office were the men in gray, ready to save the world and document it in triplicate.

"Lieutenant Daniels," Agent Coursey said. Or maybe it was Dailey. "We've got good news."

I hoped it involved them being reassigned.

"Vicky worked up a new profile of the suspect, and we're 77.4 percent sure that he's French Canadian, and most likely owns a horse."

"Our killer is a Mountie." Herb said it deadpan.

"A what? Hmm, that's good. We hadn't thought of that."

They looked at each other, and Benedict and I took the moment to do the same.

"How about the candy," I asked. "Did you get anything?"

"There have been over six hundred recorded cases of food tampering in the last fifteen years. More than two hundred of those were with candy. By limiting the search to individuals who used razor blades, fishhooks, and needles, we narrowed it down to forty-three cases. In only two reported cases had a perp used all three. Both in Lansing, Michigan. On consecutive Halloweens, in 1994 and '95."

I felt, for the first time in this case, the stirrings of excitement. This could be a solid lead.

"Arrests? Suspects?"

"None."

The hope leached away.

"Both times, a bowl of candy had been left at an unoccupied house. No prints, no witnesses, no confessions, just several dozen kids taken to the emergency room, and one terminal occurrence."

"Have you gone through the Lansing files, found anyone arrested there in the past who might be our man?"

"We've cross-referenced arrest records with anyone fitting our profile, but no one came up who was French Canadian. Several suspects owned horses, and we're checking them out."

Patience, Jack.

"How about apart from your profile? Anyone arrested in Lansing for kidnapping women? Raping stab wounds? Leaving notes for the police? Any unsolved murders that involved abduction, torture, and mutilation? This guy has killed before. You've pretty much confirmed he's been in Michigan. Did you follow up on any of this?"

"We're checking," the one on the right said, hooding his eyes in a manner that could only be described as sheepish. "However, if you could spare the manpower, we'd like to check out some local livery stables and investigate this horse angle."

I blinked. Twice. I was a deep breath away from spouting off, when a uniform knocked on my open office door. It was Barry Fuller, a large patrolman who used to be on the Chicago Bears. He was assigned to the Gingerbread Man task force, though in what capacity I'd have to admit ignorance.

"Officer Fuller." I bid him entrance, happy to be interrupted.

Fuller came in, giving the FBI a sideways glance.

"We . . . I took a call this morning." I now remembered that Fuller had been assigned to work the phones, sorting out fake confessions and tips. "It was Fitzpatrick, the owner of the second 7-Eleven. He wanted to add to his statement."

"Add what?"

"He remembers hearing an ice cream truck before he saw the body."

"Like one of those Good Humor trucks with the music?"

"Yeah. It was playing one of those pipe organ songs, he thinks it was 'The Candyman.'"

I rolled this around in my head. We knew the perp drove

a truck. An ice cream truck would be practically anonymous; there had to be hundreds in Chicago. I turned to Herb.

"We need a list of all ice cream trucks registered in Illinois and Michigan. And we need to find out if any special kind of license or permit is needed, and check that list for priors; stick with assault, rape, burglary . . . don't bother with traffic violations. Then we need the list cross-referenced with Dr. Booster's patient list. And we need to talk with that kid Donovan, who found the first body."

"I did that," Fuller said. "I called him. He remembers hearing an ice cream truck as well. I've also gotten started on the DMV reports. The problem is, they only register make, model, and year. An ice cream truck is a Jeep, and there are thousands of Jeeps in Illinois. More in Michigan, I can guess. We can't break it down by drivers, because anyone with a standard class D can drive a Jeep. If the guy has a business license, it could be possible to find him through that, but that goes by village, not state. It could take weeks to check every suburb."

"What about companies that sell ice cream that have drivers?" Benedict was thinking out loud.

"There are six in Illinois," Fuller answered, surprising us. "I'm having them all fax employee lists as well as driver routes."

"Nice job, Officer," I told him. "We'll put someone else on phones, and you're in charge of gathering all of this information. I want a progress report every morning, and I'll need Donovan's and Fitzpatrick's depositions ASAP."

Since I liked initiative in my men, I also threw him a bone.

"There's an extra case file on my desk, go through it, see if anything shakes loose."

He grinned, I suppose from the opportunity presented to

him, and then left. In two minutes' time, an ex-football player who walked a beat proved to be of more help than two federal agents with years of experience. It didn't surprise me.

"Maybe he's selling ice cream on horseback," Benedict offered to the Feebies.

"Parlez-vous Fudgsicle?" I added.

"His driving an ice cream truck does not preclude ownership of a horse," the one on the left said, "but we'll need time to assimilate this new data and consult with Vicky."

"Maybe you should do that."

"We are well aware of the fact that you don't like us, Lieutenant. But we're all trying to do the same thing here. We're trying to catch a killer. We do it by analyzing data and comparing it to thousands of other documented cases, in order to get a picture of the unsub. You go on the news and talk about bed-wetting and cowardice. To each his method."

Then they turned as one and left.

"Ouch," Herb said, "that was awful close to an actual insult."

"I may need a hug, Herb."

"I'm here for you. At least until Lunch Mates sets you up with someone. Did I mention how darling you looked in that sweater?"

"Aren't there any doughnuts left you should be attending to?"

Benedict's eyes lit up and he attacked the box. I washed down two aspirin with the last of my coffee, and then was forced to refill it with the sludge from the hallway vending machine. When I returned, Herb had valiantly triumphed over an éclair and had begun poring over the letters we'd taken from Theresa Metcalf's room. I sat down, stretched my leg, and attacked the appointment book.

It was a typical Day-Timer, every date in the month with

a page of its own. There was an address book at the beginning, which was mostly blank except for a few unlabeled phone numbers that would have to be checked out.

Going page by page, I came across many notes and appointments involving her canceled wedding. She'd met with several caterers, bakeries, florists, photographers, etc. Again, all would need to be interviewed.

Every seven days she wrote down her work schedule, which hardly varied one week to the next. Birthdays for both Elisa and Johnny Tashing, her ex, were labeled in advance. There had been two dentist appointments and a doctor's visit, but it hadn't been to the late Dr. Booster's office. She'd also written in her dates with Johnny, which ended abruptly on April 29, when she wrote *PIG!* next to his name and underlined it.

Also in April were two meetings with someone named Harry. Just that name and a time—six o'clock in both cases. Once was on the twentieth, and once on the twenty-eighth. Nothing else about Harry, or Johnny, from then until present.

I called up Elisa and asked if she knew anyone named Harry, from back in April. She said she didn't.

"Any mention of anyone named Harry in the letters?" I asked Benedict.

"Nope. But her ex-boyfriend had a real flair for the romantic. 'Your breasts are like two ice cream scoops, and I want to lick them up.'"

"Isn't that Shakespeare?"

"Yeah. *King Lear.*"

"Does he seem like a wacko?"

"No more so than any other hormone-crazed guy who wants to get laid. He says 'I love you' a lot, and it seems sincere. Most of these letters are from when they just started dating. They'd been going out for a few years."

I set the appointment book aside and dove into the canceled checks. There was a big stack of them, dating back to 1994. Luckily they were in chronological order.

There was nothing unusual for the last few months. Rent, gas, phone, electric, groceries, clothes, all the normal things people pay for. Then, when I got to April, something abnormal.

She'd written two checks for two hundred dollars each to a man named Harry McGlade.

I frowned and showed them to Benedict.

"Sounds familiar. Cop?"

I nodded. "Used to be. Private now."

"You know him?"

I nodded again and extended my frown. I hadn't seen McGlade in fifteen years.

Fifteen very pleasant years.

"So Theresa must have hired him for something. I wonder what for."

"The mind boggles. I can't see anyone hiring Harry for anything."

"Something to do with the boyfriend?"

I shrugged. Only one way to find out, unfortunately.

"I'll go pay him a visit," I conceded. "You want to tackle the boyfriend?"

"I may do just that. You sure you don't want to tag-team them?"

"I'd rather meet with McGlade one on one."

"I sense some history here, Jack, that you aren't telling me about."

"Let's just say he's not my favorite person."

Which may have been the understatement of my life.

CHAPTER 25

THE ASPIRIN WASN'T HELPING MY LEG much and I felt every bump and crack in the road during the ride to McGlade's. A call to the phone company had confirmed his address to be the same as it was fifteen years back, when I'd last busted him.

He lived in Hyde Park, near the Museum of Science and Industry and the University of Chicago. Hyde Park wasn't really a park at all, but a multitude of apartment buildings sectioned off from shops and stores, sort of like a housing development.

I parked in front of a hydrant next to his building. A group of teenagers hanging out on the corner made me as a cop and walked off as I struggled to get out of my car. I suppose I was just cursed to look like an authority figure.

After finding the appropriate buzzer, I pressed once and waited, half-hoping he wasn't home.

"Harry's House of Love. You buying or selling?"

"I'm gagging. Lieutenant Jack Daniels, Violent Crimes. Buzz me in, McGlade."

"What's the magic word?"

"Now."

"Nope. Try again."

"Open the door, McGlade."

The door buzzed, but only for a second. By the time my hand reached the knob, it had stopped.

"McGlade . . ."

"When did you become a lieutenant, Jackie?"

Harry was the only person who called me Jackie.

"The nineties. Now you can either buzz me in or I can shoot the lock off and then arrest you for destruction of property."

He buzzed, but only for a millisecond like before. I was ready for it this time, and pulled the door open.

The lobby was dim, the carpet worn, the heat barely on. I saw a roach scurry along the wall and blend into the peeling paint.

Harry was on the fifth floor, and since I hadn't brought my cane, I took the elevator. When I located his apartment, the door was already open. He was standing in the middle of his den, pulling on a pair of pink paisley boxer shorts.

"Normally I don't dress until later in the day, but I don't want you getting any ideas."

He was as I'd remembered. A little older. A little chubbier. But he still had the same three-day beard, the same unkempt shock of brown hair, the same twinkling brown eyes that always seemed to be laughing at you.

"Christ, Jackie, you look old. Aren't they paying you enough to afford Botox?"

Exactly as I remembered.

I took a step inside and looked around. It was a pigsty. Laundry and garbage and junk covered every inch of the floor. Empty cans and wrappers and moldy socks and sour food were strewn around in such abandon that it seemed like someone had blown up a landfill.

"Jesus, McGlade. Do you ever clean up?"

"Nah. I pay a girl to come in once a week. But every time she comes over we just hump the whole time and she never has a chance to clean anything. Want to go into the kitchen, have a seat?"

"I'm afraid I'd stick to something and never be able to leave."

"No need to be rude," Harry said. Then he belched. I closed the door behind me and noticed the aquarium against the wall. That must have been where the smell was coming from. Moldering fish corpses and chunks of multicolored rotting things bubbled around in the brown water, buoyed by the tank aerator. I watched a corn dog float by.

"Some kind of fish disease wiped out my whole gang within twenty-four hours," McGlade explained.

"There's a shocker."

"I like it more now. There's always something new growing, and I save a bundle on fish food."

I pulled my eyes away.

"I'm here to talk about Theresa Metcalf. She was a client of yours. Back in April."

"Got a picture? I can't place the name."

Theresa's roommate had given us some snapshots, but I'd forgotten them back at the station. Instead, I handed McGlade one of Theresa done up by the makeup artist, with the digitally added eyes. It was as close to lifelike as we could get it.

"Yuck. Ugly."

"She's dead."

"Then she'd smell bad too."

"Do you remember her?"

"Not offhand. No. But then I have a hard time remembering last week. How long has it been, Jackie?"

"Not long enough."

McGlade raised an eyebrow.

"You're not still mad at me, are you?"

I took the picture back, careful not to touch his hand.

"If you don't feel like cooperating . . . " I began.

"You'll drag me in. Can't it wait? I was watching the new *Snow White* DVD, the director's cut with the extra footage. The gang-bang scene is next."

I frowned, wondering how to play it. I needed the information, but taking McGlade in would mean having to drive with him.

"Do you keep files?" I asked.

"Sure. At the office."

I let out a breath. My head was beginning to hurt, probably because I'd inhaled something toxic, and I was quickly losing the little patience I'd brought along. I took another cautious step forward, and something crunched underfoot.

"Hey, watch out for the pizza, Jack. I'm not done with it."

"Get dressed," I ordered. "We're going to your office."

"Kiss my piles. It's my day off. I'm not going anywhere."

"Then you're under arrest."

"For what?"

"For being an asshole."

"You can't do that. I've got an Asshole License."

"Okay. How about for assaulting an officer?"

"I haven't laid a hand on you."

"Seeing you in your underwear qualifies as assault."

McGlade shook his head.

"When are you going to get over it, Jackie? It was a long time ago. I paid for it, didn't I?"

"You have the right to remain silent, and I sincerely hope you do."

"This is ridiculous."

"Good. Resist arrest. Maybe you'll find someone down at County General that likes your boxer shorts more than I do."

Harry sighed. "Fine. You win, O Mighty Lieutenant. We'll go. Just help me find some socks."

"Find them yourself."

He bent over and picked some pants up off the floor. After sniffing the crotch, he deemed them okay and put them on. Years ago, I learned that the best way to deal with Harry was excruciating patience, punctuated by occasional outbursts of hostility. It still held true.

"What's the big deal anyway?" he asked, smelling a sock.

"She was murdered."

Harry gagged and dropped the sock back on the floor.

"I didn't do it."

"I'm sure you didn't. It was the Gingerbread Man."

"No shit? No wonder you've got your undies in a knot. If you told me that earlier, I would have been much more helpful."

"I bet."

Harry picked the sock back up and put it on.

"Can we stop for coffee on the way?"

"No."

"Maybe a bagel too."

"No."

"I know a great place nearby. If you don't like it, I'll pick up the tab."

"I hate it already," I said.

McGlade found a stained shirt and a suit jacket that didn't match his pants. He buttoned up the shirt incorrectly and had to redo it. I needed more aspirin.

"So what's with the limp?" Harry asked as we walked to my car. "Boyfriend wearing you out?"

"I got shot."

"Who would shoot a sweetheart like you? You sure you can drive okay? We could take my car. It's a lot nicer than yours."

"Shut up and get in. The more you talk, the more I feel like arresting you again."

"So nasty, Jackie. When was the last time you got laid? Pretty thing like you should be able to find a guy."

Following Harry's lousy directions, our meandering took us to a corner bakery, where I got coffee and McGlade got a large orange pop and blueberry bagel.

"Hell, where did I leave my wallet?"

I paid. From there, it was to his office, a merciful five blocks away.

"I'm on the sixth floor. Sorry, Jackie—no elevator. Want a piggyback ride?"

I ignored him, tackling the stairs with as much dignity as I could. It wasn't much. By the third flight I was a sweating, shaking mess.

"You don't mind if I go on ahead, do you, Jackie? No offense, but I don't like watching the Special Olympics either."

I nodded, gasping for breath.

"Just three more flights, last office on the left. I'll come check your progress in ten minutes or so."

He trotted off, and I bit back the pain and doubled my efforts. I reached the top sopping wet with perspiration. A circle of blood had seeped up through my pants leg. I had to put my head between my knees so I didn't pass out.

McGlade had left the office door open for me. He was sitting at his desk, leafing through a magazine called *Plucky Beaver*. It had nothing to do with wildlife.

"Glad you could drop by, Jackie. You want some club soda for those pants? I think I've got some bandages too."

"Don't trouble yourself."

"No trouble, just take a minute."

"Thanks," I managed. Though God knew why I was thanking him. I took a seat opposite his desk and struggled out of my sweater. His office was tidy compared to his apartment. Almost respectable. The blinds matched the carpet, four lamps shared the floor with several healthy ficus trees, and his desk and file cabinet were stained oak. The only Harryesque touch was the painting on the wall, a cubist portrait of a nude woman with large blue triangles for nipples.

I got my breathing under control, and Harry returned with a roll of gauze and a bottle of liquid.

"Out of club soda. I've got Diet Sprite. Does that take stains out?"

"I don't think so."

Harry shrugged and took a pull off the bottle. I took the gauze and was directed to the bathroom. Ten minutes later I was freshly bandaged and the bloodstain had been scrubbed out.

"Did you find her file yet?"

"Huh? I hadn't been looking. Check out this Rack of the Month." Harry showed me the centerfold. "Think those are real?"

"McGlade . . . "

"Think of her back problems . . . "

"Harry. The files."

"Yeah. Okay."

He tore himself away from the magazine and went to a file cabinet in the corner of the room.

"What month was it?"

"April."

From the top drawer of the file cabinet he removed an open box of Cinnamon Toast Crunch cereal. He upended it over his desk, and a sheaf of papers spilled out. I picked one up and he snatched it from my hand.

"Don't mess with my organization. This is a complicated filing system."

"It looks like you just stuffed all of your April reports in an empty cereal box."

"To the layman, yes, that's what it looks like. But to my computerlike brain it is infinitely more complex. Aha!"

He held up a slip of paper.

"That's a coupon for baby oil," I told him.

He put it in his jacket pocket and kept searching.

"Let's see. Metcalf. Theresa Metcalf. Here we go."

He scanned through the report, which had been hand-written on notebook paper. I took a glance at it myself and couldn't make out the chicken scratches.

"Okay. She hired me to follow her boyfriend. I can't make out his name. It looks like Tommy. Or Johnny. I think it was Tommy."

"It was Johnny."

"That's what I said. Johnny. She gave me two hundred up front. Wanted to know if he was cheating on her. Gave me another two bills when I finished the job."

"What did you find out?"

"Hey, my client has a right to privacy."

"She's dead."

"Oh, yeah. To hell with her privacy then. Her boyfriend was dipping the wick in another pot. I shot two rolls of film on them. I think I still have some copies. Want me to look?"

"No, thanks."

"They're pretty good. I took an amateur photography class last year. You should see what I can do with a zoom lens."

"Maybe some other time."

"Yeah. Call me. I'll have some slides made up. Is that all you needed?"

"How did she come to you?"

"Walk-in, I think. Saw my ad in the phone book. Pays to advertise."

"What was your impression of the boyfriend?"

"He had the endurance, but came up short in the size department, if you know what I mean. That's why I needed the zoom."

"What kind of person was Johnny?" I rephrased, a temple of infinite patience.

"Besides a cheater? He seemed okay. Worked for some mutual fund company. Good dresser. Ritzy apartment. Up-and-comer yuppie type. Met with the bimbo on his lunch breaks. She worked in his office."

"What did he drive?" I was hoping for a Jeep.

Harry checked his sheet.

"White Lexus. About four years old."

"Do you recognize her?" I showed him the photo of our first Jane Doe.

"I don't think so. Kind of looks like an aunt I had. But she had a mustache. You gonna give me the skinny on these two?"

"They were both kidnapped, tortured, and had their stab wounds raped."

"Yuck. It's a sick world. I had a case once, jealous wife took a needle and thread . . ."

"Did you get any impression at all from Johnny Tashing that he could be a killer?"

"Naw. He was a typical preppie type, probably piss himself if he saw blood. No connection between the vics?"

"Can't find one. They're both young, pretty. Maybe that's the only criteria the killer needs."

"Look harder. Raping stab wounds seems like a punishment thing. Almost like revenge. Maybe he's going after every girl that ever dumped him. Anyway, this woman's husband was passed out on the couch, drunk. So she took a needle and thread and sewed . . ."

I tuned him out. In his limitless stupidity, Harry had said something smart. What if these women had offended the killer personally in some way and he was out for revenge? Could he have been a customer that Theresa snubbed, or an old ex-boyfriend?

" . . . so when the guy tried to take a leak . . ."

I got up to leave.

"Don't you want to hear what happened?"

I walked out the door, my head swimming with ideas. We'd been dwelling on the who, what, where, when, and how. But maybe the why needed further attention.

"Don't be a stranger, Jackie," he called out after me. "Maybe we can do lunch sometime."

I was convinced now that the killer knew these girls. That he was out for revenge. People like Bundy and Gacy, they killed for pleasure. For sex. Our perp was using sex as a form of punishment. These vics had something in common.

But what?

Before I knew it, I'd reached the bottom of the stairs. I hadn't even broken a sweat.

Mind over matter.

CHAPTER 26

IN HIS LIFETIME, HE'S KILLED TWENTY-THREE people. He did two stretches in prison, totaling eight years. Neither was for murder. If he hadn't been behind bars, he believes his body count would be double.

He has a knack for it. The fact that he's never been caught is proof. There are several tricks he uses, so suspicion never falls on him. Never leave evidence. Never establish a pattern. Keep a respectable cover and have an alibi ready. And always plan ahead.

Hookers are easy. No one misses hookers. Murder is an occupational hazard.

Or kids. It's simple to grab kids. Tell them their mommy was hurt, they'll always come with you. Or dress up like a cop. Or in a big dinosaur costume. Or as Batman.

But the most fun is grabbing a normal girl. To do that you need to take your time. Find out about her. Stalk her. Abduct her. Bring her someplace private, where no one will hear.

It's tougher than picking up a whore or a little kid. It's also more rewarding.

The best screamers are the twenty-something bimbos who think they're too good for you. Like these bitches he's working on now. Like his ex-wife.

Soon he'll be finished. Then he'll move on. Fade into the background. Do his killing on a more private level. Maybe in a few years he can resurface, terrify an entire city one more time, but this performance is a strictly limited engagement.

The question is, what to do with Jack? After the comments she made on the news, she's proven herself no better than the other whores. What Jack needs is a nice long session in his basement.

She's a little old for him, but it's an intoxicating thought.

Will the lieutenant be a screamer? Will she beg?

Of course she will. Eventually, they all beg.

Since killing the cat as a child, Charles has felt superior to all humans. But here's one he feels a kinship with. Here's one who, by chasing him, is trying to be his equal.

In a way, it makes Jack endearing. Almost lovable.

Love is an emotion still alien to Charles. From years of murdering, he knows excitement, and fun, and pleasure, and disappointment and sadness when a victim dies too quickly. But love has been beyond his grasp. His marriage was for cover, for money, for convenience. But he hates the stuck-up slut more than anything. He hates her voice, he hates her personality, and he hates her goddamn face.

But Jack's face . . .

Thinking of it makes him smile. He wants to see it again. Wants to somehow get in touch with her. He knows Jack is being watched by the police, but there has to be a way.

There's always a way.

In the meantime, he has a schedule to keep. Girl #3. He wants to have her by tonight. He knows her route, knows he has two possible places to make the grab.

The syringe is in his pocket. He tries focusing on her face. Instead he sees Jack's.

CHAPTER 27

It was nice to get away from Harry. Sometimes the past should remain in the past.

I got to the station at a quarter past three, using the elevator so I didn't open up my wound again. Benedict was already in my office when I walked in, back from interviewing the boyfriend. The tired expression on his face probably mirrored my own.

"How'd you make out?" I asked.

"He cried from start to finish. If that wasn't enough, he also had an alibi. Out of town for a week until this morning. Business trip. It checks."

"He have any ideas?"

"Everyone loved Theresa, him included. He wanted to get back with her. Admitted his affair was stupid. He couldn't think of any reason anyone would want to kill her. No reaction to the computer sketch, or the picture of the first Jane Doe. I got a list of some mutual friends, most of them the same ones Elisa gave us. We've got a lot of ground to cover. How about you?"

"Harry was hired by Theresa to confirm Johnny's cheating. He took pictures. But he said something interesting— maybe the perp is punishing these women for something they did to him. It would help if we had an ID on the first Jane Doe. Somehow, they both managed to piss our man off. That's why he's leaving them out in public, rather than hiding the bodies. He's leaving them on display, as a message to others."

Herb thought it over. "Okay. We delve more deeply into Theresa Metcalf's life. Make a list of all the places she went to—bars, shops, movies, et cetera. Then flash around pictures of the first Jane Doe, see if we get any hits."

"The two women may not have known each other well, but maybe they've met. Like belonging to the same health club. They both did something, probably the same thing, to our man to set him off. Maybe something minor, like rejecting his advances, or laughing at him. Or maybe they both dated him in the past, and dumped him."

"Lots of maybes."

"Then let's narrow them down."

We spent the next hour with the task force, delegating authority, giving assignments, following leads. Officer Fuller had done an admirable job gathering information on ice cream trucks, and the lists of possibles were divvied up to be checked out. News came that the semen found in the stab wounds had been typed as A positive. A DNA print was forthcoming, and would take several weeks.

"You look like hell, Jack." Benedict eyed me when we'd finished our powwow. "Maybe you should go home and rest."

"Nonsense. I'm at the top of my ability."

"Jack," Herb said, startling me.

"Huh? What?"

"You just fell asleep sitting up. Go home."

"Maybe you've got something there, Herb."

"You need a ride?"

I shook away some cobwebs. "No, thanks. The pain will wake me up."

That it did. Hauling myself out of my chair was akin to getting cold water splashed in my face. By the time I'd made it downstairs to my car, sleep was the last thing on my mind.

On the way to my apartment I stopped at a neighborhood grocer, securing a frozen pizza guaranteed to rise in the oven, two cans of spray-on carpet cleaner, and some aspirin. Another hot night of adventure in the life of the swinging cop.

The pizza did rise, to about the thickness of an apple pie. I devoured half of it, along with two whiskey sours, trying to remember the last time I'd actually had a home-cooked meal. Once in a blue moon I'd fry up some burgers, or make spaghetti, but I couldn't recall when I'd last had a dinner where different food groups were represented by different dishes.

Don liked to cook, but he was a health nut and it always involved sprouts and tofu. Soy somehow lacked the homey feel of a five-course turkey dinner, or even pancakes and sausage.

I put the rest of the pizza in the fridge, then hit the bedroom to clean up my blood.

I needed both cans of cleaner and another drink to get the stains out. It helped that the carpet was brown. When I finished, I had to throw away the rags I'd used, and I made liberal use of some Lysol to kill the gamy smell.

With no more tasks to complete, I sat down at my dinette set, and looked through the Lunch Mates data sheets that Matthew had given me.

The first was a redhead. Forty-two. An accountant. Five feet ten, 170 pounds, green eyes. He was looking for a woman with a sense of humor who liked to take chances. His name was Latham.

The second had brown hair. Forty-six. A managing director for a steel production company. Five eight, 165, glasses, and a very cute face. He was looking for a woman with a lot of money. I filed his data sheet in the garbage.

The third was forty, but he looked too much like my ex-husband, so I filed him as well. This was like catalog shopping.

I scanned through the others, coming up with several possibles, rejecting others mostly based on their jobs and their appearance. Beggars shouldn't be choosers, but I was paying so much, I didn't consider it begging anymore.

After compiling my list of six, I whipped out the cellular and gave my Lunch Mates agent a call.

"Thanks for calling, Jack. I've been trying to reach you, but the line's always busy."

"Hollywood agents, trying to get me to sell the story of my life."

Matthew laughed his musical laugh. "You've had a chance to look through the data sheets?"

"Yes. I had some time off this afternoon after my skydiving lesson got canceled."

"What did you think of Latham Conger?"

He was the redhead who liked to take chances.

"I had him picked out, yes."

"I faxed him your data sheet, and he'd love to meet you. Shall we make a lunch date?"

"Sure. Tomorrow?"

"Let me check his schedule . . . yes, he is free tomorrow, at one. Do you like Chinese food?"

"That's fine."

"How about Jimmy Wong's then? On Wabash? One o'clock tomorrow."

"Great."

"I'll call Latham, tell him the good news. If for some reason you can't make it, call me here as soon as possible. Have fun tomorrow!"

He hung up. That was the easiest date I'd ever planned. I hadn't even needed to show a little leg.

I read Latham's data sheet again, and then once more. The whiskey was working its magic, and once again I felt the drowsies sneak up on me. While that would normally be a cause for celebration, it was scarcely six o'clock. Falling asleep now meant I'd be up again around midnight.

The drowsies won out. I shed my clothes and crawled into bed, letting exhaustion take over.

I woke up a little past eleven.

Five hours was as long a rest as I'd had in recent memory, but there was no way I'd sleep any longer than that. I peeled myself out of bed, changed my bandage, and spent the rest of the night watching program-length commercials.

I spent some money. Late-night advertisers knew that exhaustion zapped willpower. Five hours later I'd bought a buckwheat husk pillow, guaranteed to provide me with a good night's sleep; an Ab Cruncher, guaranteed to transform my abs into a six-pack in only five minutes a day; and a set of nonstick cookware, guaranteed to turn even the most inept chef into a world-class gourmet. Because I ordered early, I got a free cookbook and a bonus spatula worth $19.95.

I managed, through sheer force of will, not to call any psychic hotlines.

By the time the sun peeked over the horizon, my Visa was maxed and I felt like an idiot. It wouldn't be the first time. Over the years I've amassed enough mail order junk to open up my own business. Those tricky niche marketers. There should be a law against television broadcasts after two in the morning.

I wrapped my leg in plastic and took a shower, deciding my morning workout would have to wait a while until I healed. Or until my Ab Cruncher came in four to six weeks. I dressed in old jeans and a polo shirt because my good clothes were all still at the cleaners, and then headed for work.

During the drive I thought about the case, and the two dead women, and the Gingerbread Man. And then I did something I hadn't ever done on a case. I made myself a promise.

"No one else dies," I said aloud in the car. "I'm going to catch you, and you won't get anyone else."

Even if I go down in the process.

CHAPTER 28

HE'S FURIOUS.

He paces back and forth in his basement, holding the rag to his bleeding face, stopping to give the body a kick.

Bitch. Lousy bitch.

The grab is perfect. He pulls up next to her, asking her directions, even offering her a free ice cream for her assistance. When she takes the cone he grabs her arm and sticks her with the needle. No witnesses. No struggle. No screaming. A textbook abduction.

Then he quickly ties her up in his basement and waits for her to wake up.

But she wakes up too fast. He's making himself a sandwich and suddenly she's running up the stairs, naked and frantic.

He grabs her, trying to pin her down, but she scratches him across the eyes. He loses his temper and backhands her, sending her tumbling down the stairs.

And she breaks her lousy neck.

Such a waste! All the time and planning, ruined! She dies not even knowing who he is, or why she's being punished.

Charles kicks her again, then goes to take care of his face. His eye burns, an ugly red mark bisecting the cornea. It requires treatment, but a doctor is out of the question. The scratch marks on his face look like scratch marks. There would be questions, and he would be remembered.

He makes do with iodine and gauze pads. Later he'll get some kind of eye ointment at the store. He has some things to do first.

With his anger soaring and his face hurting like hell, Charles has no desire to violate the body. Sex is the furthest thing from his mind. But he has a reputation to uphold, and for the next part of his plan it's necessary.

At first he can't get aroused. But Jack helps him with that. Thinking of Jack's face when she discovers this body. Thinking how Jack will scream when he has her in the basement, doing this to her.

Thinking of being inside Jack.

He finishes, grunting in satisfaction. Then he begins.

They're probably on to his disposal method and undoubtedly watching all convenience stores. But he has something different in mind. Something audacious.

First he removes the hand that scratched him. He knows there's DNA evidence under her fingernails, but he's already left DNA samples with his semen and he doesn't care. He does care, however, about alerting the authorities to the fact that she scratched him. He'll have this bandage on his face for a while, and doesn't need to have that bit of information added to his description.

After the hand, he begins to dissect the rest of the body. He works on a plastic tarp, with a cleaver and some wire cutters.

When he finishes, he loads everything of size into a fifty-gallon thermos cooler. There's plenty of glop left over, which he disposes of outside.

In the vacant lot behind his house there is a manhole. He's been dropping things down there for years, feeding the rats. He uses a butcher's hook with a T-shaped handle to pry up the cover, and dumps all the little parts still on the tarp into the sewer.

He listens to the soft plops in the darkness, followed by squeals of delight from the rodent populace.

"Snack time." He giggles.

He takes a quick but thorough shower, using a tooth-brush to get the blood out of his fingernails, carefully avoiding his bandage. Then he spends twenty minutes getting the cooler up the stairs and into his truck. Another ten minutes are used up removing all of the pictures and descriptions of ice cream along the side panels and replacing them with signs that say "Mel's Plumbing," complete with a bogus phone number.

He also has a three-foot-long metal plunger, which he picked up at an auto graveyard, that attaches to the roof. An ice cream truck is conspicuous after dark, but a plumber can come and go at all hours.

Coming up on two in the morning, he finishes polishing his press statement. He has a lot to say, but if it's too long, it wouldn't all be used on the news. He wants it short, succinct, and on the front page. After printing the final copy, he puts it in an envelope along with the parts he's saved from Theresa Metcalf.

It's a cold night, and with his heavy jacket and hat he feels anonymous. First he dumps the cooler under some garbage bags in an alley he's had picked out for some time.

Then he makes a stop at an all-night coffee shop and buys himself a cup. After nursing it long enough to become invisible to the other customers, he hits the bathroom and uses some duct tape to secure his envelope behind the toilet bowl, putting his gloves on to avoid leaving fingerprints.

Gloves still on, he leaves the diner and walks to the nearest pay phone, calling the tip line for the *Chicago Tribune*.

"This is the Gingerbread Man," he tells the rookie who picks up the phone, "and I'm going to make you famous."

He hangs around for the next forty minutes, until some guy strides into the diner in an apparent rush, walking out two minutes later with the envelope.

The cops will be coming soon. Maybe even Jack. He stays and watches the fireworks, from the window of a corner bar across the street.

There's plenty of excitement; four patrol cars, five news vans, dozens of oglers.

No Jack.

He fidgets, sipping his beer until closing time, wondering why Jack hasn't shown up. Her fat partner hasn't shown either. Maybe a few body parts and a letter don't warrant waking them from their beauty rest. At four in the morning, the bar kicks everyone out, and he decides to check for himself.

He parks three blocks away from Jack's apartment, not sure how close the surveillance on her is. He walks quickly, hands in his pockets, head down, looking as if he has a destination.

On Jack's street he spots the team; they're parked almost a block away, and the windows are tinted to prevent looking in. But their cover is blown. Because it's cold, they have the heat on, and the engine is running. Charles sees the exhaust from a hundred yards away, and turns in his tracks and heads back the way he came.

If Jack's tail is still there, then Jack is still there. So the easiest way to follow Jack is to follow her tail.

They'll be looking for someone stalking Jack.

But they won't be looking for someone stalking them.

The Gingerbread Man gets back into his plumbing truck and finds a parking space a block away from the surveillance team.

Then he turns off the engine, shoves his hands in his pockets, and waits.

CHAPTER 29

A S USUAL, HERB BEAT ME TO WORK.

"I didn't know you owned a pair of jeans," he said.

"I'm undercover."

"I don't think they make Bon Jour anymore."

"Are you saying I'm out of style?"

"Is that an Izod shirt? I haven't seen one in fifteen years."

Like Herb could talk. The tie he wore today had a pineapple hand-painted on it.

"You're fired," I told him.

Herb ignored me, turning his attention to a box of grocery Danish. The phone rang.

"Daniels."

"My office. Benedict too."

Bains hung up. His small talk needed work.

"We are to proceed directly to the office of our captain," I informed Benedict.

He nodded, stuffing the rest of the breakfast roll into his

mouth, basset hound jowls inflating like balloons. Canine to chipmunk in 2.2 seconds.

We walked down the hall, Herb madly chewing and me trying to keep pace, having judiciously left my cane in my office. No point in looking frail before the almighty Captain Bains. Herb did a big cartoon swallow and we went in.

Bains took off his reading glasses and nodded at us.

"Early this morning our man left a package for the *Chicago Tribune*. It contained some body parts, in a plastic bag, that have since been confirmed as Theresa Metcalf's. There was also a letter."

Bains glanced at the paper on the table, encased in a big plastic bag. Herb picked it up and we read.

> *Chicago,*
> *This is the Gingerbread Man. The lies must stop. My plan was to leave this city after the fourth, but now I may stay to take revenge for the things said about me. I let that Judas live, and she betrayed me. Now you will all pay the price.*
> *Let me make it clear. I am no joke. I will kill your daughters, Chicago. Your sisters shall suffer. I will continue to kill until I am shown respect.*
> *Fire Daniels. Let the truth come out.*

"Has this been run yet?" I asked.

"It will be, afternoon edition. We were able to hold it back until we confirmed the parts belonged to the second girl."

"Did we get anything?" Benedict asked.

"No prints. He left it in a bathroom at a coffee shop. A team is still taking the place apart, dusting for prints, talking to customers and staff. It was a busy place, even that early in the morning. No one remembers anything. We have a tape of the phone call to the *Trib;* they automatically record their tip line. Voice print is being done, but it won't help unless we catch him."

"Why weren't we called last night?"

I realized, as it came out of my mouth, that I already knew the answer.

"The mayor has given jurisdiction on this case over to the Feds. Officially, you are on a leave of absence pending charges of official misconduct. The paper will run a statement from the police superintendent alongside the letter."

"That's bullshit, Captain!" Herb had a mad-on, venting for both of us. "The Feebies couldn't catch a cold in a snowstorm."

"Jack is officially on a leave of absence. You, Herb, will still keep our end of things up around here. And whatever Jack decides to do, on her own time as a private citizen, is her business."

I smiled. I never liked the spotlight much anyway.

"Now bring me up to speed," Bains said.

Herb and I took turns, relating what we had so far, and what we were going after.

"So the women are connected," Bains said when we finished.

"We think so. Maybe not to each other, but definitely to our perp. He's not grabbing women of a certain type, he's grabbing women he knows and wants to punish. If we can find the link, perhaps we find him."

"In his note, he refers to the fourth. The Feds think it's the fourth of next month."

"Could be," I said. "Or it could be the fourth victim."

The phone rang. The chief picked it up, listened, and held out the phone for me.

"Daniels."

"This is Briggs, front desk. Don't want to bust your

chops in front of the boss, but we've got a guy on hold says something happened to your mom."

Panic exploded within me. "Put him through."

"Jack? Guess who."

I gave a quick nod to Bains and mouthed "It's him." He picked up his cell phone and gave word to trace.

"What's happened to my mother?"

"Just blowing smoke, Jack, so they'd put me through to you. But I did leave you something, in the alley behind your building. A picnic lunch. Enjoy it. See you soon."

The line went dead.

"He's off," I said.

"Pay phone on Michigan," Bains said. The days of long traces were in the past. The modern phone trace was practically instantaneous.

I relayed the conversation word for word, Benedict writing it all down. A minute later the chief's cell phone rang.

"They missed him," he told us. "Blended into the rush hour crowd."

"Let's go check the alley," Benedict said.

Bains came with us. We didn't bother to stop for coats.

The district building was on a street corner, and on the third side was the parking lot. The alley wasn't an official alley; just an enclave where the Dumpsters were kept. We approached it cautiously, eyes scanning everything. Since we both outranked Herb, he did the honors of rooting through the garbage.

"Looks like a cooler," he said, moving some bags. "Big one."

Bains gave the go-ahead to open it. Herb lifted the corner, holding the edge with a handkerchief.

"Christ."

It was bad. Real bad. This had surpassed murder and become butchery.

"Let's rope it off, get a team in here." Bains shook his head. The third body being found right behind his police station wouldn't help his career.

I left the scene, placing a phone call to Mom, just to make sure she was safe. Then I sat on the steps in front of the district building, still without a jacket, letting the cold be my penance.

I'd let another person die.

The team came, and the reporters, and a crowd of gawkers.

I thought about my job, and my mom, and my insomnia, and my date that afternoon, and Don.

I thought about Benedict, and Phineas Troutt, and Harry McGlade, and my past, and my ex-husband, and the dog I had when I was a kid that we had to put to sleep because he broke his leg chasing a rabbit.

I thought about the stars in the sky. I hadn't seen the stars in years. The smog in Chicago was thick enough to blot them out. For all I knew, they weren't there anymore.

I wondered what the point was. No one was happy. Every day brings some new annoyance, some new problem, some new pain. And if you managed to avoid cancer, and AIDS, and drugs, and car accidents, and malevolent acts of God, there was still the chance that some wacko would grab you, or your kid, and torture them to death for no reason.

I tried to remember the last time I laughed so hard it hurt. I tried to recall a day where I went to bed happy.

I couldn't.

Special Agents Dailey and Coursey, in matching black trench coats, materialized from the crowd and walked briskly up to me. They moved in step, left foot, right foot, as if they were doing a Wrigley's Doublemint commercial. I didn't hide my disappointment when they stopped in front of my stoop.

"We hope there's no hard feelings," Dailey said.

I gave him a blank look.

"That you're off the case. We know what it's like, and we'll do our best to keep you in the loop."

How about that? An olive branch.

"In return, we'd like to use some of your men."

The left hand giveth, and the right hand taketh away.

"What for?"

"We believe we've found the horse. We'd like to put it under twenty-four-hour surveillance."

Both waited for my reply. I took a moment, then gave it to them.

"You're out of your minds."

"Excuse me?"

"I've got another girl murdered here, and you want me to pull my people off the case so they can stake out a horse? You're out of your goddamn minds."

"Lieutenant, I'm sure you're aware—"

"I'm aware that you're wasting my time. I don't give a rat's ass what Vicky says, or what your boss says, or what the cross-dressing ghost of J. Edgar Hoover says. Stay out of my way, or I'll arrest you and toss you in general population wearing gang colors."

They looked at each other, then back at me.

"Perhaps it's best that you've been removed from the case," the one on the left said.

I stood, twenty years of pent-up anger swelling in my chest.

"Get the fuck away from me."

It must have been a startling transformation, because they both flinched. Then they got away from me. I sat back down, content to follow the self-pity route a bit longer. Eventually Benedict found me, handing over my coat.

"What did Abbott and Costello have to say?"

"They want to borrow some uniforms to stake out a horse."

"Which house?"

"Not house. Horse. Like with four legs and John Wayne on top."

"They think a horse did it?"

"Their profile. Remember their French Canadian Connection?"

He seemed to think about this.

"Did you tell them to fuck off?"

I nodded, putting on my coat. Then we walked back into the fray.

Herb and I, the crowd, the media, and the world, watched as the contents were removed from the cooler.

It was a scene from a horror film, but the sadness in me outweighed the shock.

Then I stood along the sidelines while Herb took control of the crime scene.

CHAPTER 30

BENEDICT WAS THE ONE WHO TALKED me into keeping my date.

"All we can do now is wait for the reports to come in. Go have lunch."

"There are a million things to do."

"And a million people to do them. This is your job, Jack, not your life. Go eat. Everything will be here when you get back."

"My clothes are still at the cleaners."

"You look fine. Go. That's an order. Bains made me the senior on this investigation, remember?"

Traffic was good. I made it to the restaurant ten minutes early, and parked in front of a hydrant. The place did a moderate lunch, and the lobby was bustling when I entered. Jimmy Wong's was a Chicago landmark of sorts, famous in its day. The decor was pure 1950s, a throwback to the Rat

Pack era. It even had the requisite wall of fame. I eyed a signed picture of Klinger from *M*A*S*H* and checked my hair in the glass. After some brief finger fluffing, I went to the host desk.

A Chinese man wearing a red bow tie informed me that my date had not yet arrived, and directed me to the bar, where I could wait. I ordered a Diet Coke, becoming increasingly uncomfortable as the minutes passed. The last thing I needed was time to sit and dwell.

I watched him come in, seeing his reflection in the mirror behind the bar. He wore a tailored suit, dark blue pinstripe, with a light blue shirt. His smile was pleasant and seemed genuine when his gaze fell on me. He had a good walk, confident, with a slight bounce, toes pointed straight ahead and not out to the sides like a duck. I never found duck walkers attractive.

I stood to meet him, hoping my smile didn't look dopey.

"How do you do, Jack." He offered his hand, his grip firm but gentle.

"Very nice to meet you, Latham. Great suit."

"Do you think so? Thanks."

We let the host seat us at a dimly lit corner booth. Almost immediately a busboy set down a pot of tea. Neither of us touched the pot, or our menus. I tried to look relaxed, but wasn't sure if I was succeeding.

"So, where do you work?" I asked. It seemed like a good way to get the conversational ball rolling.

"I work for Mariel Oldendorff and Associates. Head accountant. It's about as exciting as it sounds. You're a police captain?"

"Lieutenant, actually."

"What kind of police work do you do?"

"Uh, violent crimes."

"Oh. Interesting, I bet. Are you undercover now?"

"Excuse me?"

"You know. Those old clothes. I haven't seen an Izod in years."

Ouch. "Oh, it's laundry day. Everything I own is at the dry cleaners, with the exception of this ensemble. Believe it or not, these jeans are Bon Jour."

"Really?"

I showed him the stitching on the pocket, regretting it immediately. Three minutes into the date and I'm showing the guy my ass.

"This is great." He was grinning.

"That I'm twenty years behind in fashion?"

"That you're confident enough to come as you are. The last woman I went out with wore way too much hair spray and perfume. When she lit a cigarette I ducked for cover because I thought she was going to ignite."

I laughed.

"I knew a guy like that. I swore he used to bathe in Aqua Velva. When we slow danced I got high off the fumes."

He had a pleasant, easy smile, and deep-set wrinkles when he crinkled his eyes. Definitely cute; even better than his picture.

"So why did you become a cop?"

"Because I like . . ." I searched for the word. ". . . fairness. My mom was a cop. She always did the right thing. That's what I want to do."

"You find fulfillment in fairness?"

My life had never been so succinctly defined before. "I like justice, and I like doing my part to make sure things turn out the right way. How about you?"

"I'm not that deep. I'm fulfilled by simple pleasures. Music. Food. Good conversation. Right here, right now, I'm happy."

He leaned in closer. Was he actually flirting? I felt the familiar schoolgirl tingle in the pit of my belly, and I realized I was interested in him. I leaned closer too.

"I wish I was like that. More carefree."

"Anyone can be. People aren't carved out of marble. We're all works in progress. The trick is to define ourselves, rather than let outside influences define us."

That's when I noticed my ex-boyfriend Don walking over to us. Dragging him along was a woman so pumped up with muscles, it looked like someone had stuck a tube up her rear and inflated her. Roxy, his personal trainer and new roommate.

"Speaking of outside influences," I said to Latham, "there's about to be a scene."

The couple stood next to our table, Roxy big and blonde and angry, Don embarrassed and maybe a bit scared.

"You're right, Donnie, she is old." She snorted through her large nostrils, giving me a blast of warm air.

Four million people and two thousand restaurants in Chicago . . .

"Take it somewhere else, Roxy. We're busy."

"Roxy . . ." Don tugged on her well-defined arm. "Just leave it alone."

But Roxy wasn't having any. Perhaps the steroids had gotten to her brain. She puffed up her chest and struck an impressive pose.

"You got a lot of nerve, tossing his stuff in the hall like that. Maybe you'd like to show me some of that nerve outside."

Latham frowned. "I don't think—"

"It's okay, Latham." I patted his arm. "I can handle this one."

I stood up, giving Roxy cop eyes. I had to look up to do so. She had a few inches on me.

"Showing off for your boyfriend isn't worth getting arrested, Roxy. Take off."

Don tried to pull her away, but she was practically his size.

"You scared, bitch? Scared I'll beat your ass in front of your pimp here?"

I smiled and pointed at her chin. "You missed a spot shaving."

She swung at me, but I was ready. In a single, efficient move I slipped the punch and came up behind her. Using her momentum I got her wrist in a hammerlock and shoved her on top of the table, pinning her down with my weight.

"Assaulting a cop is a felony, Roxy. Three to five, hard. If this big show of testosterone is simply because you need an apology, I'll offer it. I'm sorry. Now take off, or I'll stop being this nice. Got it?"

I gave her wrist a little extra twist to make my point. Roxy grunted and gave me an enthusiastic nod. When I let her up, she was beet red, and Don was studying his shoes. Neither said another word, and they moped off without further incident.

I sat back down and wondered how badly I'd ruined my chances with Latham. Could I be any less demure?

"I'm sorry," I muttered. "I'm really not a violent person."

"Don't be sorry." Latham looked flushed. "This is actually the most exciting date I've ever had in my life. What are you doing tonight?"

"Pardon me?"

"I get off at six. Can I make you dinner?"

"Uh, that would be great."

"Eight o'clock?"

"Fine."

He grinned. The waiter came by and we ordered our entrees.

Maybe all that money I spent on Lunch Mates was a good investment after all.

CHAPTER 31

HE KEEPS FALLING ASLEEP, WAITING FOR something to happen.

The discovery of the body in the cooler is exciting, but he has to stay too far back for fear of being seen. By the time the excitement dies down, Jack is back inside her office.

And now, the effects of a sleepless night are taking their toll. His eyelids keep closing. His head keeps lolling forward. Even the anger, the fuel that spurs him on, has been replaced by fatigue.

He uses the cigarette lighter to keep himself awake.

Charles knows he's grasping at straws. The surveillance on Jack is tight. Even the weak point, the shift change, proceeds smoothly. No matter where Jack goes, there's a team following her. But there has to be some kind of way.

He almost nods off, and again has to apply the lighter. He concentrates his efforts on his chest, where the burns will be out of the public view. Pain works so much better than caffeine.

Lunchtime comes, and his stomach rumbles. He hadn't expected to go on a stakeout, or he would have packed something. There's ice cream in the truck's freezer, but he hates ice cream. Maybe he can step out and grab a bite at—

The sedan he's following takes off. Jack is on the move. He starts the truck and follows, having to keep closer than he had last night because traffic is heavier. Once, he loses them at a red light, but they continue down the same street and he's able to catch up.

The destination is Jimmy Wong's on Wabash. Did Jack and her fat partner come here for a bite? He parks at a bus stop and watches.

An hour passes. He opens the door a crack and pisses on the street. He eats a Popsicle. He burns his chest again. He thinks about having Jack to himself, keeping her alive for days. Jack is the closest anyone has ever come to understanding him. Having her undivided attention would be delicious.

He knows Jack will just die for it.

Jack leaves the restaurant—not with Herb Benedict, but with another man. They shake hands, and she gives him a peck on the cheek. Friend? Lover? Brother?

There's only one way to be sure.

The man begins to walk away. Charles starts the truck and tails him for a block.

"Hey, buddy." He rolls down the window, pulling up close. The syringe is in his pocket. "I'm lost. Can you tell me how to get to Belmont?"

CHAPTER 32

I WAS FEELING PRETTY GOOD ABOUT myself. In one fell swoop I'd shaken off the vestiges of Don and had met a man who was attractive, interested, and much better suited for me. Even being grilled by Herb upon my arrival at the station hadn't hurt my mood.

"You're welcome."

"What for?"

"I seem to recall sending you off to Lunch Mates in the first place. The thank-you doesn't have to be formal. You can express your gratitude in a gift."

"Something to eat, perchance?"

"By happy coincidence, I've got a Mario's pizza menu in my pocket."

Benedict handed over the menu with instructions on what he liked on his pie. I wasn't shocked to find out he liked everything.

Formalities aside, we dove into the paperwork pool, gathering and collating information, trying to gain a better perspective on our perp.

We had yet to get any reports back on the third victim. The ME did a cursory inspection on site and drew several conclusions. She was a white female, late twenties to mid-thirties, blond hair, blue eyes, between five four and five six based on the length of the femur. She'd been hacked apart, Maxwell Hughes guessed, by some kind of heavy-bladed knife or sword. All of the dismemberment appeared to be postmortem. Her right hand was missing, as was a good deal of tissue.

Cause of death was unknown. There was a large abrasion on her head consistent with a blow by a heavy object. There was also a stab wound in the left upper thigh, and we all could guess what it contained.

Other than that, there were few similarities to the other victims. She had ligature marks on her wrists and ankles, but the body bore no evidence of torture. The others hadn't been hacked up like this. The method of disposal was different. The killer had completely changed his MO. The million-dollar question was, Why?

My concentration was shattered by a knock at the door. It was a bony little man wearing a brown bow tie and matching sweater vest. He had fair blond hair balanced delicately on an ovalish skull. Tiny eyes were distorted behind thick glasses, and a thin mustache rested on his lip like a string of uneaten spaghetti.

"Detective Daniels?"

"Lieutenant. That's Detective Herb Benedict."

He came in without being asked. "I'm Dr. Francis Mulrooney."

"Congratulations," I said.

He stood there, expecting more. "The handwriting expert?" He flashed a grin. I held my applause and picked up the phone.

"Hello, Bill? Jack. Can you have someone run up the notes from the Jane Does? Thanks."

I motioned for Francis to have a seat, and Herb scooted his bulk to the side to let him near the desk.

"So far on the case we've—"

Mulrooney held out his palm. "Don't tell me. I don't want to know anything until I've seen the samples. It could influence my judgment."

I gave Herb a look. He returned it. The FBI was bad enough. Why not just go medieval and hire a phrenologist?

"It's always exciting to work with the police." Mulrooney grinned. His teeth were uneven. "Is this a forgery case? Never mind, don't tell me. I'd rather see if I can figure it out. Forgery fascinates me. You see, handwriting is like fingerprints, and no two samples are exactly the same. But it's also a window into the part of the brain that understands and comprehends language. Your signature changes, for example, when you're under stress or if you succumb to mental problems. So, is this a forgery case?"

A uniform walked in, carrying the notes. The first two were in cellophane envelopes, each stained murky brown with dried blood. The third was sandwiched in an old encyclopedia.

"We store it in a book in the freezer," I told Mulrooney. "The cold takes away all the moisture without ruining the physical evidence. If we let the blood dry naturally, the paper will begin to rot."

All the color drained from Mulrooney's face, making his thin blond mustache appear translucent.

"Excuse me a second." He stood and bolted for the door. The uniform shrugged and followed him out.

"Think he'll be back?" Herb asked.

"Unfortunately."

The pizza came, and Benedict attacked it with a ferocity often seen on PBS specials involving carnivores.

"Doesn't your tongue hurt?"

"Not so much anymore. I think eating all the time has sped up the healing process. Maybe it will work with your leg."

Benedict offered me a slice so stacked with toppings, it had begun to topple. I declined, consuming several aspirin instead.

Our resident handwriting expert reappeared, his cockiness replaced by a serious expression.

"I apologize." He drew his hand across his mouth. "When I got the call I wasn't told what I'd be analyzing. Is this the Gingerbread Man case?"

"Yes."

He sat back down, averting his gaze from the pizza Herb was devouring.

"I've read about it. Terrible. If I may?"

I offered him the notes, as well as a photocopy of the one left for the *Tribune*; the original was still at the lab. Mulrooney slipped on a pair of white cotton gloves. From his vest pocket he removed a leather case.

"Can I take them from the cellophane?"

I nodded, making note of it on the evidence seals. First he simply read the notes, frowning. Then he unzipped his case and removed a jeweler's loupe and some long tweezers.

I watched him work, going over the notes line by line, scribbling in a pad constantly, handling them with the utmost care and professionalism.

After about fifteen minutes, during which Herb had finished his pizza and joined in the observation, Dr. Mulrooney let out a deep breath and sat back in his chair.

"You've got one sick puppy here." He met my gaze, intense. "First I'll tell you what I know for sure. The same person wrote all four notes. Block printing is not as easy to analyze as script, and in court it's harder to prove, but there's enough here to be absolutely sure of it."

"Go on."

"He's right-handed. He clubs, which means that the ends of his pen strokes are thicker than the beginnings. That's a characteristic usually found in sadistic personalities. You can see it on the down strokes of his *t, l, f, i,* and on the bottoms of the *y* and *b.*"

He showed us examples. I found myself becoming interested.

"The *t*'s have descending bars, which are also clubbed. This can be a sign of mental imbalance. Many violent schizophrenics have descending *t* bars. In the second note he also mentions *us,* which might indicate disassociative identity disorder. But I don't believe in multiple personalities. It's a psychiatric fairy tale. I think the *us* was deliberate, either a ploy or a nod to an accomplice."

So far, all on the money.

"His pressure and angularity are very extreme. Again, indicators of violent behavior and aggression. The *d* is the social self-image letter. His *d*'s are slanted to the right and clubbed. This usually means an inflated ego, along with a desire to control situations."

"Keep going, Doctor."

"He refers to himself in capital letters. I'd call that the mark of a grandiose narcissist. He refers to the police department in lowercase letters, minimizing your importance. That's all I can get from a handwriting analysis, but I'm also a psychiatrist. From what he's written, and from the little I know about the case, I can make some assumptions."

"Please do."

"You're dealing with a sexual sadist. He's a control freak, and mastery over life and death is the ultimate high. He's got severe delusions of grandeur. I would guess that he may also be a sociopath, without remorse for his actions. He will be able to fake emotions, but won't be able to truly feel them. Can you tell me anything about the case?"

I ran it all down for him, from the discovery of the first Jane Doe until he showed up.

"The idea that he's punishing these women is a good one," he said when I'd finished. "The amount of pain he inflicted on them would also indicate that he knew them personally, rather than just grabbed them at random."

"Why did he change his MO for the last one?" Herb pondered aloud.

"Do you know the cause of death yet?" Mulrooney asked.

I shook my head, and then I had it.

"He didn't change intentionally," I realized. "Something went wrong. Maybe he gave her too much Seconal and she went into a coma. Or she tried to escape and he had to kill her. But her body didn't show evidence of torture. I bet he wanted to torture her, but didn't get a chance, so instead took his punishment out on her dead body."

Mulrooney eyed me. "You'd make a good shrink."

"Thanks. Any other insights?"

"He's killed before. Probably many times. This isn't an amateur. He's just decided to go public with it. There's too much planning, preparation, and thought put into these crimes to make them his first. The only evidence he leaves is what he wants you to find. This is a game to him. But there must have been something that set him off on this spree. Some reason he's decided to go public. Maybe he got divorced, or lost his job."

"The triggering event."

"Right. And there's something else too. I'm sort of surprised you haven't caught it yet, Lieutenant."

"Caught what?"

"He's sent you letters, broke into your apartment, called you on the phone, and now demands that you get fired." Mulrooney gave me a pained look. "This man has a crush on you."

"A crush? He wants to kill me."

"Sociopaths can't express emotions normally. In the letter to the *Tribune*, he even refers to you in capital letters, maximizing your importance. He's a stalker. Now he's fixated on you. Perversely fixated. I think all of this is his way of courting you."

Golly. Other guys just send flowers.

"I have a surveillance team keeping an eye on me."

Mulrooney rubbed his mustache. "Do you know how hyenas find a carcass? They follow the flight patterns of vultures. The vultures lead them to the food."

"Christ," Herb said. He was thinking the same thing I was.

"The perp could be watching the watchers."

CHAPTER 33

"WE GOT A JEEP."

"Does the suspect fit the description?"

"There's some resemblance. No ID on him, but he's mentioned your name."

I nodded at Herb. The dragnet had been his idea. We ordered six teams to sweep a ten-block radius around my surveillance tail. Trucks and vans were stopped. Parked cars were searched. People on foot were questioned.

"We're on our way in, Lieut. Where do you want him?"

"Bring him to room C." I hung up the phone and reached out my hand to Dr. Mulrooney. "Good suggestion. We may have our man. Thanks for all your input."

He shook and gave me his card. "I'm glad to be of help. Feel free to call if I can be of further assistance."

Herb and I took the elevator, conserving my energy. This was all a bit anticlimactic, but that was how most cases ended; with a whimper, rather than a bang. As long as we got the guy, I was happy.

My hopes were dashed once I saw who was brought into the interrogation room.

"Hello, Lieutenant."

Phineas Troutt sat down in the lone wooden chair and smiled patiently at me.

Herb gave me a nudge. "This the guy that broke into your apartment?"

I frowned. "No. His name is Phineas Troutt, two *T*'s. Pull his record."

I closed the door behind me and shook my head at the legion of cops sitting behind the one-way glass. Then I turned my attention to my pool partner. "What's going on, Phin? Have you been following me?"

"I saw you on the news. You're purposely trying to get the Gingerbread Man to come after you."

"What does this have to do with you?"

Phin shrugged. "I had some free time, thought I'd see what your setup was. You've got three teams of two guys, each pulling eight-hour shifts. They hang back no farther than two hundred feet, and couldn't be more conspicuous if they tried."

The room smelled like smoke and sweat and desperation. Phin, however, seemed relaxed and even amused.

"You still haven't told me why you were following me."

"I figured the killer would make another try for you, but he'd see your surveillance just like I did. So I hung back to see if anyone was doing what I was doing and watching your surveillance team."

I still didn't know his angle, but I felt a tingle of excitement.

"Did you notice anything?"

He nodded.

"Two cars and four trucks, all with solitary male drivers. All acting suspicious. I wrote down the makes, models, and plates."

"Where did you write it down?"

"We're friends, right, Jack?"

I frowned. Why did he suddenly get coy?

"I'd like to think so, Phin."

"And friends do each other favors."

"So this is a favor?"

"Sure. I don't like seeing my friends get hurt. I'm sure you feel the same way."

Now it made perfect sense.

"You're in trouble, aren't you?"

"Possession. Cocaine. Trial is coming up next month. I'll do time." Phin scratched his bald head, an obvious ploy to make me aware of his cancer. "And the time they want me to do, I don't have left."

I didn't answer. The silence dragged. I knew the state's attorney, and the Gingerbread Man case was weighty enough that he'd trade his wife and mother for an arrest. But I disliked bargaining with criminals, even helpful ones who played pool with me.

"I'll be right back."

I left the interrogation room and met up with Herb in the hall. He handed over Phin's rap sheet.

There were several charges for assault, two for attempted murder, one for manslaughter, and two for murder in the second degree. No convictions—in every case charges were dismissed, dropped, or he was acquitted.

"You busted this guy once?"

"Yeah. He was jumped by some gang-bangers. Killed two of them, put three more in the hospital. Self-defense. Phin wasn't even armed."

The other victims of Phin's crimes had case numbers after their names; they all had criminal records as well.

The single nonviolent crime on his sheet was for the cocaine. This was recent, only five months old. The amount was substantial enough for the state's attorney to charge him with dealing rather than straight possession.

I went back into room C. Phin had his legs crossed and looked completely at ease.

"What do you do for a living, Phin?" I asked.

"I get by."

"By selling drugs?"

He made a face. "I don't sell drugs."

"You were arrested with thirty grams of cocaine in your possession."

"I wasn't selling it."

Herb snorted. "That was for personal use?"

Phin sized up Herb. "Morphine makes you sloppy. The coke helps with the pain and I can still stay alert."

"Where'd you get the coke?" Herb asked.

Phin ignored Herb and focused on me. "Are we helping each other, or are we going to keep pointing fingers?"

I stared into Phin's eyes. His personal life was none of my business, but I really disliked drugs, especially those who used them and sold them. On the other hand, he saved my ass back at Joe's Pool Hall, and he also may have just given us our biggest break.

And, even though I was a professional who never let personal feelings influence me, I kind of liked the guy.

"Deal. I'll get it squared with the state's attorney."

"Can I get that in writing?"

"You have my word."

He nodded, then handed over the notebook. The first entry was "White Jeep, Ice Cream Truck, F912 556."

"Herb, run these plates. This may be our guy."

Benedict disappeared with the notebook. Phin stood up and put his hands in his pockets.

"I can go?"

"Yeah. Thanks."

"Thank you. I heard you got shot. Leg okay?"

"I've got a spare."

He grinned.

"You're a pretty tough chick. Maybe I'll see you around. We never got to finish that last game."

"I'll check my social calendar."

"I'll save a table for you."

He turned and left.

I met up with Herb in his office. His expression told me everything I needed to know.

"Plates belong to a Chrysler Voyager. Reported stolen six months ago."

I let out a deep breath. There wasn't any way to trace stolen plates. At most, we could put out an APB and hope someone picked him up.

"Did you run any of the others?"

"In the process. In the meantime, we should keep going with the dragnet. The perp may still be watching our guys."

It was a long shot, but all we had for the time being.

"Agreed. I'm going to my office to tune in."

The scanner on my desk let me follow the action. Short, staccato bursts of cop talk in between long stretches of static. Several other suspects were questioned, but none were brought in. After two hours of feeling like a spectator on my own case, I switched off the radio.

Depression settled on me like a heavy blanket.

"You hungry?" Herb popped in with a bag of BBQ pork rinds.

"No, thanks." I had no appetite at all. Even the prospect

of a home-cooked meal held no appeal for me. I should probably call and cancel my date with Latham.

"We'll catch him, Jack."

"I don't want to spend the rest of my life obsessing about the one that got away."

My friend sat across from me.

"Then don't obsess."

"It's different with you, Herb."

"How so? I want to catch the guy too."

"But you have a life outside the force. This is all I have."

Herb set the bag down. You knew Benedict was serious about something when he pushed away food.

"You're the total of all the choices you've made in your life, Jack. This is what you have because this is what you chose."

I looked at him. "I've spent more than twenty years working hard at being a cop. I don't have a social life. I ruined my marriage. All I can do is this job. But if I'm not good enough for this, then what the hell is the point of my life?"

I bit my lower lip, my eyes welling up. I hated being weak, and I hated self-pity, but Herb's words really hit home.

I was here because this was the life I chose.

But what if I'd made the wrong choice?

My partner put his hand on my shoulder. "Jack, you're the best cop I know. If anyone can catch this guy, it's you."

I took a deep breath and held it, hoping in my heart of hearts that Herb was right.

CHAPTER 34

AFTER THE MAN LATHAM ANSWERS ALL of his questions, he ties him up with some extension cords and locks him in his own closet.

A dating service. How mundane. But how convenient for him.

Rather than try to circumvent Jack's surveillance team, all he has to do is wait here at Latham's house, and she will come to him.

He closes his eyes and imagines Jack in her bathroom. Putting on lipstick. Picking out a sexy dress. Perhaps she's even hoping to get laid tonight.

He decides that she will, whether she wants it or not.

The clock creeps up on eight o'clock.

The spider sits in his web and waits.

The fly will be here soon.

CHAPTER 35

BY SEVEN O'CLOCK I'D HAD MY fill of feeling sorry for myself. I stopped at the cleaners on the way home, but they hadn't even begun my order. After yelling for five minutes at a man who probably didn't deserve it, I got them to do a rush job on one of my pantsuits.

In my book, yelling was always more therapeutic than crying.

By the time I got home and showered, rebandaged my leg, and got dressed, I was late for my date. I called Latham on my cell to tell him.

The line was busy. After putting on perfume, grabbing the bottle of wine I bought Don an eternity ago, and strapping on my gun, I tried again. Busy.

Well, if his line was busy, then at least he was home. I informed my surveillance team of my destination and got on my way.

I was kind of excited. A home-cooked meal with an attractive man was the perfect way to get my mind off things.

After some torturous stop-and-go-stop-and-go, I made it to Latham's home half an hour late. He lived in a charming two-story brownstone, not too far from Benedict's house. I found a fire hydrant, parked the heap, and gave myself a final look-over in the rearview.

Not bad. Maybe I could do with a rinse in the near future, but not bad.

I grabbed the wine and hobbled up his porch. The doorbell rang with a Big Ben chime.

"Come in!"

I opened the door, assuming he was still on the phone. The house was dark, quiet. I sniffed the air, but couldn't make out any cooking aromas.

Next to me, on the foyer floor, a chair was overturned.

Warning bells went off in my head. What if the killer had been following me, and saw me with Latham?

What if the killer was here?

I let go of my wine and reached for my gun—stopping when I noticed the one already being aimed at me.

"Hi, Jack." The Gingerbread Man stood at the foot of the staircase, several feet to my left. "Take out the gun, slowly, and toss it over here."

Fear swam up my spine, like a cold and clammy fish. My feet had frozen to the floor.

"Where's Latham?" I managed.

"He doesn't matter. The gun. Now."

The killer smiled and moved two steps closer. He looked vaguely like our composite picture, but more wolfish and grubby. A bandage covered most of his left profile, and his one black eye bored into me.

"I won't ask again. The gun."

But I wasn't going to play by his rules. In one motion I

dropped to my knees and yanked out my .38. My injury screamed at me, but I managed to squeeze off two rounds.

My shots went wide, and the killer ducked into the next room. My leg felt like it had been snapped in half. I watched blood seep through the bandage, but saw no other holes in my body. Had he even fired?

I scooted across the floor and got behind a sofa, my gun trained on the kitchen. The cellular was in my pocket, and I took it out with my left hand.

"Hey, Jack!"

He was behind me. I turned, bringing around the .38, pulling the trigger . . .

Latham.

He had tape over his mouth, and the maniac was using him as a shield, the gun jammed under his jaw.

I managed to jerk my shot over their heads.

"Drop it. Now, or he dies."

Latham's face was pure panic, eyes unbelievably wide, moans coming from his throat.

I let the gun fall.

"Good girl. Now get up."

I pulled myself to my feet, using the sofa. My bad leg was shaking so hard, it could barely support me.

"The phone. Put it away."

I stuck it in my pocket. Had my surveillance team heard the shots? Doubtful. They were over a block away.

"What happened to your face, Charles? Cut yourself shaving?"

"Such bravado in a hopeless situation. You're a hero to the end, Jack. But how are you going to handle this, hero?"

He shoved Latham in front of him, aiming his weapon. I watched, helpless, as he shot Latham twice in the back.

Latham flopped forward, his head bouncing off the floor. Then he was still.

"Any more smart comments?"

I limped to Latham, but the killer rushed over and kicked me in my bad leg. I howled, dropping to the carpet.

"Do I have your attention now, Jack?"

He kicked again, this time at my head. Motes of light burst in my skull, a fireworks display of pain.

"Looks like the coward is kicking your ass. Maybe you're the one who's going to cry for her mama. Isn't that what you said on the news?"

I tried to focus, looking for where I'd dropped my gun. He followed my gaze and picked it up.

"You know why I said those things." My head was swimming, my leg on fire.

"Naturally. To get me to come after you. You should be happy. It worked."

My cell phone rang. Neither of us moved.

"It's the team checking in."

"Keep it simple. You're making dinner. Everything is fine. One wrong word . . ."

He put the barrel of his gun to my bloody pants and pressed. I bit the inside of my cheek to keep from crying.

"Make it good."

I spoke through my teeth. "You want them to hear me scream?"

He relieved the pressure and I sucked in a breath before answering the phone.

"Yeah?"

"You okay, Lieutenant? We heard what might have been gunshots."

"We're fine. Making dinner right now. Everything is peachy."

"Peachy" was the code word. They'd be here to rescue me within a minute, if I lived that long.

"Just checking."

He hung up. They did know the code word was "peachy," didn't they?

"Good job, Jack. Now we'll go for a little ride. Where's your surveillance?"

"A block away. Down Leavitt."

"Okay. We're going out the alley. My truck is back there. Get up."

I struggled to get to my feet, putting all my weight on my good leg. He wound his hand in my hair and jerked me upward. Then he pulled my head to his face. I felt his breath on my neck, sour milk and rotten meat.

"We're going to get to know each other, Jack. Like only a man and a woman can. We're even going to make a little movie."

He licked my ear. The revulsion I felt was so intense, I had to pull away, ripping out some of my hair in the process.

"Oh, it won't be so bad. I'm going to make you famous, Lieutenant. Our video will be on every news show in America. They'll have to edit out the nasty parts, though."

My cell phone rang. The signal. I dropped to the floor and covered my head just as the door burst inward.

Gunshots. Breaking glass. A moan. One of my guys went down in the doorway, and Charles ran away through the kitchen.

I pulled myself along the floor, over to Latham, checking for a pulse.

Faint, but there.

"Harris!"

He was kneeling next to the fallen body of his partner, a cop named Mark.

"I'll call for backup!" I told him. "He has a truck out back. Go!"

Harris took off after the killer. I found my phone and dialed 911, saying the most dreaded words in police lingo.

"This is Lieutenant Jack Daniels out of the two-six, officer down . . ."

After giving them my badge number and an address, I crawled over to Mark, who was pitched face-first on the carpet. Shoulder wound, a bad one. I kept pressure on it.

A minute later the place was surrounded with cops. Latham and Mark were carted off in ambulances. They tried to take me too, but I put up such a fight, they gave up.

Harris came back. He'd chased the killer on foot down an alley, but the perp had gotten away in a plumbing truck. He got a plate number, and it matched the one Phin gave us.

Benedict arrived shortly thereafter. "You okay, Jack?"

I was sitting at the kitchen table, an ice pack pressed to my leg. "He got away again, Herb. Even worse—he got my gun."

The thought of him killing someone with my weapon was almost as sickening as the thought of him torturing me to death.

"On the way over, I got word from the hospital. Your date has a collapsed lung and internal bleeding. He's in surgery. But it looks pretty good."

"How about Mark?"

"Stable." Herb put his hand on my shoulder. His eyes were kind. "This wasn't your fault. We couldn't have known he was waiting here for you."

"Yes we could have. This would all be over now if I'd just used some common sense and thought about it. He'd been following me, Herb, saw me with Latham, and followed him instead. If he dies . . ."

"You aren't the bad guy here, Jack. You didn't pull the trigger."

"As if that makes a difference."

"It does, and you know it. Why don't you come over?

Bernice is keeping the pot roast warm for me. There's more than enough."

I shook my head.

"Jack, there'll be plenty of time to beat yourself up later. Come to my house and eat."

"I'm going to the hospital, check on Latham."

Herb frowned, but knew there wasn't any point in arguing. I stuck around for a bit longer, sulking, and then limped out to my car and went to the hospital.

Latham was in Recovery. The doctor said he was still critical, but the outlook was good. I'd found an address book near his kitchen phone and called his parents. They came about an hour later, crying. We all sat vigil late into the night. None of us slept.

At five in the morning Latham's eyelids fluttered, and he awoke briefly. His gaze met mine.

"I don't want you here," he said.

I went back to my apartment.

There was a bottle of whiskey in the kitchen cabinet.

Since sleeping wasn't an option, I hit the bottle until I passed out.

CHAPTER 36

I WOKE UP TO PAIN.

Leg pain. Headache pain.

Emotional pain.

One more layer on the shit cake.

It was almost two in the afternoon. My stomach was doing a mambo, protesting all the liquor I'd consumed. I dropped two Alka-Seltzer in a glass of water and drank it before they finished dissolving.

I called the hospital. Latham was stable. His parents didn't let me talk to him. Couldn't blame them, I guess. I considered sending flowers, or at least a card apologizing, but they would only be reminders of me, the person who put him through hell.

My stomach settled down some, so I swallowed three aspirin to help with my other aches. I was due for a day off, but didn't feel that I deserved one. After a shower I scrubbed the bloodstains out of my pants. Then I shelved the guilt for later, and went to work.

Captain Bains wanted to see me. I gave him the blow-by-blow, filled out the requisition form for a new gun, and picked one up at the Armory.

It was homecoming week for the media. The Gingerbread Man's letter was all over the news last night, as was the discovery of the third woman. The incident at Latham's fueled the fire. Internal Affairs began conducting an investigation of the loss of my weapon. Bains told me to keep a very low profile, and the word to the world was I'd been suspended pending an inquiry.

Unofficially, I was still on the case. I just wasn't allowed to be connected with it. We live in a political world.

After working with a police artist to improve our composite photo of the perp, I grabbed a vending-machine ham on rye and went down to the shooting range to try out my new .38.

I spent an hour there, shooting round after round into paper silhouettes, imagining each one was the Gingerbread Man. When I was finished, my gun was hot to the touch and the stench of cordite had penetrated my clothes and hair like cigarette smoke.

When I got back to my office, Benedict was waiting.

"We matched prints off the third Jane Doe. Army record. Reserves. Her name was Nancy Marx. You up for it?"

"Let's go."

We took the elevator because I wasn't anxious to start bleeding again. Benedict drove. Nancy Marx had lived in a townhouse on Troy, off Irving Park Road. Herb already had a search warrant, should there be a need to break in.

There was no need.

"May I help you?"

A woman answered the door. Elderly, gray, wrinkled, someone's grandmother. My heart clenched.

"I'm Lieutenant Daniels. This is Detective Benedict. Does Nancy Marx live here?"

"Did you find her? I called this morning, but I was told I couldn't fill out a missing person report until she'd been missing two days."

"Are you related to Nancy?"

"I'm her grandmother. What's going on? Where's Nancy?"

In less than two sentences I destroyed this woman's life. If there was one part of my job I hated the most, this was it. Herb and I stood there, awkwardly, while she went from shock, to denial, to hysteria, and finally to depressed acceptance, moaning like a ghost haunting an old love.

We took turns trying to comfort her.

After the initial outpouring of emotion, they always wanted to know how and why.

We told her the how. We didn't know the why.

"She didn't suffer," was all we could offer.

The autopsy report had confirmed this. Nancy Marx died from a broken neck. How the ME figured that out from examining an array of body parts amazed me.

"But who did this to her?"

"We don't know yet, Miss . . ."

"Marx. Sylvia Marx. Nancy's parents, my son and daughter-in-law, died in a car accident seven years ago. She was all I had left."

We lost her to sobbing again. Benedict made some coffee in the kitchen, and I sat with the old woman on the couch, holding her hand.

"Mrs. Marx, did your granddaughter have any enemies?"

"None. Not one. She was a good girl."

"How about a boyfriend?"

"No one steady for a while now. Nancy was popular, she dated a lot, but there hasn't been anyone serious since Talon."

"Talon?"

"Talon Butterfield. Didn't really care for him much. He fooled around on her. They were engaged too. Lived together for a while, and then she moved in with me earlier this year, after she broke up with him. It was nice to have her home."

Her gray eyes began to blur again.

"Did Nancy know anyone named Theresa Metcalf?" I showed her a picture.

"No. Can't recall. Is she dead too?"

"Yes, ma'am."

"Pretty thing, like my Nancy."

I had her look at other pictures, of the first Jane Doe, and of the recent composite of our perp.

"I'm sorry, but no. I don't know any of them."

"Do you have an address for Talon Butterfield?"

"No. I don't think Nancy does either. When she left, he moved out of town. They haven't been in touch, as far as I know. Do you think Talon was part of this?"

"That's what we're trying to figure out, Mrs. Marx."

"I never liked the boy, but he wasn't a killer. He loved Nancy. He just couldn't keep his drumstick in his pants."

Benedict brought us coffee, and we asked a few more questions. After they yielded nothing, we got permission to search Nancy's room.

It was small, modest, and neat. Her drawers held no secrets. There were no letters, no appointment books, no bills, no canceled checks, nothing at all.

It occurred to Herb that maybe Nancy's things might be somewhere else. Not too many people did all of their paperwork in the bedroom. We decided to ask Sylvia. She was in the den, petting a white cat, staring at a framed picture of her dead grandchild. The cat jumped off her lap and fled when we approached.

"Mrs. Marx, did Nancy have a checkbook?"

"She kept it in the kitchen, in the utility drawer."

"Canceled checks as well?"

"Nancy had one of those cards. Like a credit card, but it drew from her checking account. The bank keeps the canceled checks."

"How about an address book? Or credit card statements? Or personal letters?"

"She has a box of papers that she never unpacked after moving in. It's in the closet there. Did you find anything from Talon?"

"No."

"I didn't think so. Nancy gathered up everything, pictures, gifts, cards, and threw it away when she left him. But I was thinking. If you want to find out about him, you could ask that private detective."

"Ma'am?"

"Nancy hired a private detective to spy on Talon when she thought he was being unfaithful."

My heart rate went up.

"Do you remember his name?"

"Let me think. Nancy actually went out with him a few times, after Talon. She brought him to the house once, and he pinched my bottom."

Sylvia Marx giggled, tears still in her eyes.

"Henry, was it? Henry McGee. No, McGlade. Henry McGlade?"

"You mean Harry McGlade?" Benedict asked.

"Yes, that was it. Harry McGlade."

Jackpot.

CHAPTER 37

H E HAS TO GET RID OF the truck.

That isn't part of his plan. His fingerprints are all over the damn thing. Even if he spends an entire day wiping it down, he'll never clean it completely.

And his fingerprints will lead them to him. He's never taken the pains to establish a new identity. He never thought that they'd get close enough for it to be necessary.

He goes over it all again in his head, goes over what they have.

They know his face now. But with some hair dye and a shave, that can be changed. There's nothing connecting him to the truck; he stole it in Detroit and put stolen Illinois plates on it. He has no business license. His driver's license is current, but shows an old address, and he never bothered to update it after getting married and moving.

But there are some links to his present address. The

phone company and the electric company. The IRS. Credit cards. The bank. If the cops get his name, they'll be able to find him without much trouble. And once they find him, they'll be able to convict. In his cockiness, he's giving them his DNA. Not the smartest move, in hindsight.

He has to move quickly, establish a new ID. Maybe even go to one of those doctors who can laser away your fingerprints. He'll disappear, resurface someplace else. Maybe even leave the country. There were plenty of women around the world to have fun with.

But first he has to finish the job here.

He takes a bus back to his house after ditching the truck in an all-night parking garage. Jack isn't on his mind for the moment. All of his focus is on the last victim. She'll be the easiest of all. No stalking necessary. No need for the truck. If he plays it right, he won't even need the Seconal.

He picks up the phone, no longer worried about telephone records or paper trails. It will all be over by tomorrow.

"Hello?"

"Diane? This is Charles."

"Charles?"

"I know you're surprised to hear from me. We didn't split on the best of terms. How are you?"

"Good. I'm doing good. I'm seeing someone."

"Good for you. I hope he's treating you well. Look, I'm calling because my therapist . . ."

"You're in therapy?"

"Yeah. For about six months now. She's helping me deal with my anger."

He tries to keep the smile out of his voice.

"Well, good for you, Charles. I'm happy for you."

"I need a favor, Diane. After you left me, I did a lot of soul-searching. My therapist says I'm a different man now, but I still carry a lot of guilt over how I hurt you. As long as

I have this guilt, I won't be much good for anyone, myself included."

He was reading out of a notebook filled with chicken scratches, sentences rewritten over and over until they sounded right.

"I need to see you, Diane, to apologize in person. If I know you've forgiven me, then I can get on with my life."

"I forgive you, Charles."

"Then let me say it in person. Please. You don't owe me anything, but we were in love once. It's the final step in my recovery. Please. Let me see you once more."

He holds his breath, waiting for her answer.

"Fine. When?"

"What are you doing tonight?" the Gingerbread Man asks.

He grins. He'll finally get to use that soldering iron.

CHAPTER 38

I WANT MY LAWYER," SAID Harry McGlade.

He sat in interrogation room C, in the same chair Phin had yesterday, Benedict and I standing over him. I had a car pick McGlade up and bring him here after we left Mrs. Marx. So far he was the only link between the two identified victims. I wasn't about to set foot in his apartment ever again, so questioning him here was the logical course of action. I suppose the intimidation aspect was also a factor.

But McGlade was not easily intimidated.

"I told you, you don't need a lawyer, McGlade. You're just answering some questions. You aren't being charged with anything."

"So what's with the media circus? What do you think that's doing for my reputation?"

Before Harry arrived, I left anonymous tips with several individuals involved in reporting the news that a suspect was being brought in. They kindly waited in front of the station and took three thousand pictures of Harry as he entered. I figured it would help make McGlade cooperative.

And if I could admit to being small, I also thought it was damn funny.

"Do you recognize this woman?" Benedict held up the photo of the first Jane Doe.

"How many times do I have to say it before it sinks into that Pillsbury Doughboy head? I don't recognize her. I knew Theresa because she hired me. I knew Nancy because Theresa introduced her to me. I dated Nancy a few times."

"How did Theresa and Nancy know each other?"

"I think they went to the same health club."

"Which one?"

"I don't know. Look, Nancy came in one day, said she wanted me to follow her boyfriend, said Theresa referred her to me. I didn't pursue it."

"Are you sure you don't want to check your cereal box?"

Harry made a sour face and picked some crud off his jacket. There were so many wrinkles in his suit that he gave the impression of just crawling out of a washing machine, save for the fact that he was covered with stains.

"I don't know how they were connected, Jackie. But I do know a few big-city lawyers who get their rocks off suing cops for defamation of character and false arrest."

"You're not under arrest, McGlade."

"Then I can leave." McGlade stood up.

I got in his face, glaring. "Don't you care about these women?"

"That's not the point. This treatment is unnecessary, and I'm getting pissed off. All you and Tonto the Wonder Chimp had to do was drop by my office. But instead you drag me here, and I get my name splashed all over the news in connection with your lousy case. Would you hire a private investigator who was a suspect in three serial murders?"

Of course I wouldn't. That was the idea.

"If you cooperate, Harry, I release a statement saying you helped us catch the guy. That without your valuable insight and expertise, we never could have cracked this case."

McGlade batted this around between his ears. After a few seconds, his face split into a big-toothed grin.

"Smooth, Jackie. It's about time you learned how to play hardball. You were so straightlaced back when we were partners."

Benedict jerked his thumb at Harry and gave me the eyebrow. "He was your partner? That's awful."

"Thanks for the sympathy, Chubbs, but it wasn't so bad. I got razzed a lot, getting paired with a broad. But in the end, it all worked out okay. Didn't it, Jackie?"

McGlade winked, then blew me a kiss.

I made a fist, and Herb had to pull me away before I broke the little wiener's nose.

"Don't let him rattle you, Jack."

But Harry did more than just rattle me. Much more.

When we were partners, I actually thought he was an okay guy, hygiene aside. He pulled his weight, watched my back, and we had one of the best arrest records in the district.

This was right after my promotion to detective third class, and I was out to prove to the brass that I could play with the big boys. I worked twice as hard as the men, for only half the respect. To compensate for this, whenever I had any downtime, I worked cold cases. Murder had no statute of limitations, and unsolveds were never officially closed.

A particular case commanded a good deal of my attention; the rape/ murder of a fifteen-year-old girl in Grant Park. Witnesses claimed to have seen her talking with a homeless man in a red baseball cap half an hour before her death. This angle had been extensively followed up, and led nowhere.

I chose to look closer at her ex-boyfriend. Straight-A student, no record, plenty of friends. His alibi for the night of the murder was shaky, but no one could believe he was a killer.

He did, however, collect baseball caps. He had samples from every team in the Major League, with two notable exceptions: Boston and Cincinnati. I thought it a little funny, that an avid collector would be missing the only two hats in MLB that were red.

It took a year, and cost me my marriage, but I pieced together a good case against the kid. Before I sought a warrant, I shared my findings with my partner, to get his opinion.

Harry repaid my trust by getting a warrant first, then arresting the suspect himself on my day off.

Not only did Harry get credit for the collar and a subsequent promotion, but when I complained to my lieutenant, McGlade trumpeted that he made the arrest to protect me.

"He was a dangerous murderer. Sending a woman after him would have been really stupid."

The department rallied around him, and the chauvinism in my department plumbed new depths. All of my hard work, all of my fighting to be treated as an equal in a male-dominated profession, gone because my partner was a sexist, backstabbing jerk.

It was years before I earned back the respect of my squad. But I couldn't ever forgive Harry.

I took a deep breath, unclenched my fist, and put on a big smile.

"Remind me again why you were kicked off the force, McGlade."

His smile lost some wattage. "I wasn't kicked off. I quit."

"You mean you quit after you were forced to take a leave of absence. Something to do with taking bribes, wasn't it?"

"I wasn't on the take. Someone set me up."

"And who'd want to do that to a sweet guy like you?"

He frowned. "Was it you, Jackie?"

"No, Harry. But I wasn't too sad to hear about it. Whatever happened to those bribery charges?"

"Dropped when I left."

"Isn't your PI license up for renewal soon?"

McGlade folded his arms and scowled.

"I take one bust from you fifteen years ago and you want to mess with my livelihood?"

"No, McGlade. I want you to help us catch a murderer. Now sit, and tell us about your investigation of Talon Butterfield." I forced a tight smile and added, "Please."

Harry weighed my sincerity, then sat down.

"Not much to tell. Nancy pretended to go out of town for the weekend, had me follow him to see what he did. He went barhopping, picked up some little honey, and took her straight back to their place. Did it right on Nancy's bed. I had to climb the fire escape to take pictures."

"And how many times did you see Nancy after that?"

"I don't know. Three or four. I think she used me to help get over Talon. I was happy to be of service."

"Did you have sexual relations with Nancy Marx?" Herb asked.

"I don't kiss and tell."

"Yes you do."

"Oh yeah, right. I shagged her a few times. In fact, we shared a room the night of the Trainter show."

"The Trainter show?"

"Yeah. That was the first time."

"What about the Trainter show?" I asked. What did any of this have to do with the local talk show?

"When you're on the show, they give you a free hotel room the night before. Nancy shared her room with me."

"Nancy was on *The Max Trainter Show*?"

"Sure. She and Theresa both. A show about cheating fiancés. You guys didn't know this? Some detectives you are."

"Think carefully, McGlade. Who else was on that show?"

"I don't remember, Jackie. It was five, six months ago. The show was about women who were dumping their men because they cheated on them. There were one or two other girls, I think. It was a wild show, even for Trainter. They had to bleep most of it. Max and I are old beer buddies. I'm the one who persuaded them to go on, dump their guys on TV."

"Look at the picture again, McGlade. Was this woman on the show?"

I showed him the first Jane Doe photo.

"Are you deaf? I don't know. You're showing me a computer enhanced photograph of a dead chick, who I might have seen on a show months ago. I'm not good with faces." He grinned at me. "So, have you finally forgiven me, Jackie? Maybe we could have a few drinks later."

"You're free to go, McGlade."

Harry stood up and brushed his pants. The wrinkles didn't come out.

"Just make sure I'm mentioned in your press statement, or I'll have to bring a lawsuit against this fine police establishment."

He shot me with his thumb and index finger, flipped the mirror the bird, and walked out of the door. A second later he walked back in.

"You got a couple bucks for a cab?"

I fished in my pocket and came up with some change.

"Here." I handed it to him. "Take the bus."

"Cold, Jackie. That's cold."

But he took the money and once again left. I'm sure the press was waiting for him outside, and I could only hope he'd make himself look like an idiot in front of them.

I probably didn't have to hope too hard.

"It can't be this simple," Benedict stated.

"Only one way to find out."

We went into a conference room down the hall and grabbed a phone. A minute later I was on the horn with the network where *The Max Trainter Show* was taped. After being bounced around a few times I was put in touch with the technical director, a guy named Ira Herskovitz. Once I'd informed him of the situation, he agreed to send over a dub of the show in question. I told him to send the unedited master. He refused, stating that the master tapes never left the building.

I was the cop, so I won. A squad car with sirens blaring went to pick it up, and when it arrived twenty minutes later I already had a 3/4" videotape recorder set up in my office.

"Cross your fingers," I said to Herb.

I pressed the play button.

Color bars and tone. A graphic with the show name, date, number, and director. Opening titles. Cue Max.

Trainter introduced the first guest, Ella. Ella was actually Theresa Metcalf.

Theresa dumped her fiancé, Johnny Tashing, in front of the studio audience. Tashing had been unaware of the reason he was on the show, and when Theresa confronted him about his affair and tossed her engagement ring in his face, the crowd cheered. Tashing looked destroyed.

Next was Norma. Norma was our first Jane Doe, no doubt about it. She also dumped her cheating fiancé. He called her several naughty slang terms, and stormed off the stage.

Third was Laura, aka Nancy Marx. Her fiancé, a guy we guessed was Talon Butterfield, was similarly dumped with much audience applause. Talon grinned a lot and shrugged his shoulders.

Then Nancy's new boyfriend was introduced. He came out, gave her roses and a peck on the cheek, and was abruptly attacked by Talon. Talon got in a good smack to the face, but the new man knocked him down with an uppercut before the bouncers separated them.

The guy with the quick fists was our favorite private detective, Harry McGlade.

The last guest came on. The fourth woman. The one we hadn't seen yet. Her name was Brandy, and she was breaking up with her husband because he didn't come home some nights during the week. She suspected an affair, and couldn't take it anymore.

When her husband came out, I paused the tape.

There, frozen on the screen in midstride, was the Gingerbread Man.

"That's our guy."

Herb got on the phone with the studio, demanding the real names and addresses of the guests on this show. I let the tape run, watching as Brandy confronted the guy, watching as she dumped him, watching as the other girls on the panel called him names and teased him badly, watching as he picked up his chair, threw it at her, went into a screaming, swearing animal rage and attacked everybody on the set. Four bouncers and three security guards were needed to restrain him, and when he was hauled off the stage, the audience was on its feet cheering.

"Charles and Diane Kork," Benedict said. "Address in Evanston. Don't know if it's current."

I stood up and turned to face the eighteen other people in the room who were huddled around the TV.

"I need anything we can find on Charles Kork. Criminal record, DMV, phone, credit cards, aliases, everything. I want to know his life story and I want it now."

The next twenty minutes were a stampede of activity,

phone calls, and computer checks. My team would call out info as it came.

"Got a record. Two stretches for assault and attempted."

"Divorce papers, finalized three months ago."

"I have a Diane Kork at an apartment on Goethe."

"DMV has a Charles Kork owning a 1992 Jeep."

"Evanston address checks out. Kork still seems to be living there."

Herb got on the phone again, dialing Diane Kork's number.

"Answering machine."

"Warrants," I told him. I played authority figure and divvied up assignments, including picking teams to send to Diane's place and to the killer's.

Sometimes this was how it worked. Tracking countless leads into dead ends, and suddenly it all came together. The end of the road.

Dr. Mulrooney had talked about something setting our man off. I guess getting dumped on national television qualified as a good triggering event.

"Kork is on Ashland and Fifty-third," Herb said. "You want to go there, or Diane's?"

"There. Let's move. I want eight men, full armor, now."

The adrenaline was pumping so hard, I didn't even feel the pain in my leg. Herb and I helped each other into our Kevlar vests, snugging Velcro and adjusting the shoulders. Then we strapped on lapel radios and earpieces and headed for the patrol cars.

I had four teams coming with me, plus me and Herb. Evanston PD was meeting us there with more men. Herb placed an obligatory call to the Feds, but called the local branch to stall for time—it would take a while to get the message to Agents Dailey and Coursey, and by then it would all be over.

In the black and white, siren screaming, Dispatch filled us in on Chuck's record.

"He's thirty-seven years old. Eight arrests in the past nineteen years. Convictions for aggravated sexual assault and attempted murder. Last stretch ended in 1998. Since then he's been clean."

"Not clean. Just careful."

The team heading to Diane Kork's arrived first. She wasn't home, and her place showed no signs of disturbance.

I hoped we weren't too late.

Three miles from the target we killed lights and sirens. The houses here were one-story one-family dwellings, middle-class income. I was hyper-tuned to my environment, noticing many things at once; the streets were pitted with potholes, the dusk air smelled like leaves, my chest felt confined in the tight vest, Herb had sweat on his forehead.

This was it.

Benedict parked behind a row of squad cars, all waiting for his signal.

"Ready?" he asked me.

"It's your show."

We got out of the car.

Suddenly, tearing down the street with much squealing of tires, a black Mustang convertible bypassed the police barricade and bounced over the curb and onto the sidewalk. It screeched to a stop on Charles Kork's front lawn, digging up four rolls of sod.

A man in a trench coat, holding what looked like a gallon jug of milk, leaped from the car and ran up to the porch.

I cleared leather with my .38 and limped in pursuit. Someone with a megaphone yelled, "Freeze! Police!" At ten yards away I dropped into a Weaver stance and kept a bead on the figure.

"Freeze! Hands in the air!"

The man put his hands up, still clutching the jug.

"Turn around! Slowly!"

I felt my backup fill in behind me. There was a tense pause. Then the man slowly craned his neck around and stared at me.

"Kinda funny how history repeats itself, huh?"

Harry McGlade.

CHAPTER 39

WAKE UP, MY LOVE."

He slaps his ex-wife across the face, watching the blood rush to her cheek. She whimpers, eyelids fluttering.

"It's Charles, honey. Wake up."

Diane Kork opens her eyes and stares at the man standing above her. She tries to move but can't.

"Charles, what are you—"

He cuts her off with another cuff to the mouth.

"You talk too much, Diane. Always talking. Always criticizing. I don't want to hear it anymore. All I want to hear are your screams."

He walks away. Diane lifts her head, looking at what restrains her. Twine. Her ankles and wrists are bound with twine. She's in her bra and panties, stretched out on a cement floor. Her hands and feet are tied to posts that have been driven through the concrete.

"I've got four tapes." Her ex-husband is standing off to

her right, next to a video camera mounted on a tripod. "That's four hours. Most women can't scream anymore after the third hour, but I've got high hopes for you. You've got such a big mouth."

Charles Kork walks to a table and picks up a hunting knife.

"Charles, please, untie me. This isn't funny."

"You don't think so? I think it's high comedy. This is the American Dream, Diane. Killing the woman you married. For four years, I listened to you bitch and nag. And I took it. Why? First of all, because you were a perfect cover. Cops look for loners, not married guys. A single guy gets attention. A married guy is invisible."

"Charles—"

"I'm not finished!" He hits her again. "Do you want to know what I was doing on those nights I never came home? You thought I was cheating on you, right? That's why you left me."

Charles leans over her, gets in her face.

"I was really out killing people, Diane. Stalking and killing people. Not cheating. Not really, anyway. I may have fucked them before I killed them, but I wouldn't say I was having any affairs."

Diane squeezes her eyes shut. "This isn't happening."

"Was I a bad husband, Diane? I spent time with you. I took you places. We even baked cookies together. Remember?"

He grabs a lacquered gingerbread man from the table, the last one, and thrusts it before her eyes.

"Look familiar? I was your perfect little suburban husband. I mowed the lawn. I paid the bills. I went out with your stupid friends and took you to movies and bought you flowers. I kept up my end of the bargain."

He bends down and smashes the cookie in her face.

"And then, out of the blue, you decide to leave me. Leave me! On television, in front of millions of people! Who do you think you are? Nobody leaves me!"

She's crying now. "Charles, please—"

"You don't get it, Diane. I've killed almost thirty people. Your younger sister, who ran off? She didn't run off. I buried her in a shallow grave in a forest preserve in the suburbs. Sneakers the cat? I broke his goddamn little neck. Haven't you been watching the news? I'm the Gingerbread Man."

Diane's eyes get wide as Charles kneels beside her. She begins to hyperventilate.

"We've got four hours of tape to fill." He brushes the tip of the knife over her quivering lips. "Four hours of quality time."

"Please, Charles. I'm your wife."

The Gingerbread Man cackles. "Till death do us part."

His knife enters her flesh.

CHAPTER 40

D AMMIT!" I UNCOCKED MY PISTOL. "Hold your fire!"

I stormed over to Harry, who was smiling ear to ear.

"I hope you didn't scare away the bad guy with all that screaming, Jackie."

"Drop the milk and put your hands on your head, McGlade. You're under arrest."

"It's not milk. It's filled with concrete."

"This isn't a game, Harry. Now put—"

Before I had a chance to finish the sentence, McGlade rushed the front door, swinging the milk jug at the knob like he was bowling. The door burst inward, momentum taking McGlade into the house.

I saw the entire bust fall apart before my eyes, and without even thinking I hobbled in after him.

"Around the back!" I yelled to whoever was listening. "Cover the perimeter!"

The house was dark and silent. All the curtains had been

drawn. There was a sickly-sweet smell in the air, disinfectant masking something else. Something rotten. I tried a light switch, but it didn't work.

"He's cut the power." McGlade was halfway down the hall, moving in a crouch. He'd dropped his plastic jug in favor of a .44 Magnum. It was the kind of gun I'd expected Harry to have—big and loud.

"McGlade, you asshole!" I whispered viciously at his back. "You're blowing this arrest!"

"Just say you deputized me."

"I'm not Wyatt Earp, McGlade. Now put down—"

"Hey, Charlie!" he yelled. "You've got company!"

Somebody screamed. A woman.

"Basement." Harry rushed through the house opening doors. Closet. Bathroom. Stairway.

We peered down. The stairs were dark and old, curving slightly so we couldn't see the bottom.

Behind us, cops flooded in.

"Cover me." McGlade headed down the stairs.

"We've confirmed a woman in the basement," I said into my lapel mike. "We're going down." I followed him, keeping one hand on the railing, trying to keep the weight off my bad leg.

"Don't shoot me in the back of the head, Jackie."

We made our way down several more steps, the soupy darkness engulfing us. I heard a jingle of keys and tensed, and then a little light went on in Harry's hand.

"Key light. Best buck-fifty I ever spent."

The basement floor came into view, and the smell wafted over us like a fog.

"Christ." Harry wrinkled his nose. "Something dead down here."

A noise at the top of the stairs made us turn. Two uniforms.

"Flashlight!" I whispered.

They shook their heads. They'd taken off their flashlights when they put on the Kevlar.

"There's the circuit breaker." Harry played the light over a wall near the bottom of the stairs. "Go turn on the electricity. I'll cover you."

I cleared my throat and passed McGlade on the stairs. There was a sound to our left.

"Help me."

A growl followed, and then a heart-wrenching scream.

I ran for the circuit breaker.

CHAPTER 41

THEY'VE FOUND HIM.

He has barely started on her, barely even drawn blood, and now it's all going to end.

He curses, controlling the urge to cut her head off, forcing himself into action.

The Gingerbread Man can handle this. It isn't expected, but he's planned ahead far enough to foresee this possibility. He puts the knife in his belt, checks his pocket for the lighter, and grabs his gun.

He hears the front door burst in and he hits the circuit breaker, plunging the house into darkness. Someone yells his name.

Diane screams. He walks to her in the dark, guided by the flame on his Zippo.

"Scream again and I shoot you."

The gun goes into her mouth to drive his point home. Then he uses the knife to cut her free.

"Kneel, bitch."

She kneels on the concrete floor, whimpering. He flicks his lighter again and finds the master fuse on the floor, running along the back wall.

Voices.

Charles listens.

One is Jack's.

Light the fuse and get out of here, he tells himself.

But Jack is so close.

Charles wants to see her one more time.

He goes to his wife and crouches behind her as Jack and someone else descend the stairs.

One last time, Charles thinks. One last dance.

Before everything goes *boom*.

CHAPTER 42

I RUSHED THE CIRCUIT BREAKER, OPENING the panel door and flipping on the main.

The basement exploded in light. Spotlights. Set up on stands and hanging from the ceiling like a TV studio.

And in the center of the lights . . . our killer.

"Hi, Jack." He was squinting against the glare, hiding behind a kneeling half-naked woman. She had blood running freely down her torso from several dozen cuts. A gun was being pressed under her chin.

My gun.

"Take it easy, Charles."

"I've got him, Jack." McGlade assumed a shooting stance. "I can blow his head off from here."

Charles brought his free hand around to the woman's front and flicked a Zippo lighter. He held it next to her hand. In her trembling fist was a length of rope. I followed the rope to where it divided into six segments, each leading to the base of a large barrel. They were spaced far apart along the walls of the basement.

It wasn't a rope at all. It was a fuse.

"Hold it, Harry! Everyone fall back! I don't want anyone within fifty yards!" In my earpiece, I heard the commotion of my men complying.

"Such a good cop, Jack. Such concern for her people."

"What's in the barrels, Charles?"

"Gasoline. Enough to take out the whole block."

"Stand down!" I yelled into my mike. "Clear out the houses on both sides and call the FDP! It's all wired to burn!"

The word spread quickly. Panic. Evacuation. Herb came over the air, begging me to pull out. I ignored him.

Only McGlade and I remained.

"You can't get away, Charles. There's nowhere to go."

"You're wrong there. You're the one who can't get away. Once I light this, the whole place goes up. You won't have time to piss your pants."

"I'm shooting him," Harry said.

"Both of you drop your guns. Now, or I light it."

I took a step closer. "It's over, Charles. Give up. Maybe you can do a Trainter show from your cell, let him interview you live."

Charles Kork grinned, pure malice, pure evil.

"Good-bye, Jack. I'm sorry we never got to know each other. I guess I'll just have to look up your mother after you're dead."

He lit the fuse, and then dragged Diane backward, retreating to the other side of the basement. Next to the furnace was a back door. Charles yanked his wife through it and disappeared into the night.

But Harry and I had our own problems.

"Uh-oh," McGlade said.

I dove for the fuse, which was burning at about three inches a second. I grabbed and just missed, watching the fuse separate into six different flames, each one heading for its own full barrel.

Enough gas to burn the whole neighborhood.

I yanked at the nearest fuse, searing my hand but pulling it free of its gasoline tank. It harmlessly burned itself out.

Scrambling on all fours, I hunted down a second flame and pulled that out as well.

"It won't go out! It won't go out!" Harry stomped up and down on a lit fuse with both feet. He looked a lot like Daffy Duck throwing a fit.

"Yank it!"

I turned my attention to a barrel several feet away, the lethal flame streaking toward it. I took two quick steps, pain searing through my leg, and I launched myself into the air, ramming into the barrel, pulling out the fuse and watching the last six inches burn away in my hands.

I looked at Harry, who was standing on the far end of the room, tossing two burning fuses aside. His eyes tracked the floor, following the last flame as it snaked its way to the final barrel.

It was less than two feet from its target, and too far away for either of us to get to in time.

I drew my gun and aimed.

"Jesus, Jackie, ricochet!" Harry crouched down and covered his face.

I fired three times at the flickering spark, my .38 slugs bouncing off concrete and turning the basement into a deadly pachinko game. Cement chips peppered my feet. Harry howled with fright. I exhaled slowly and fired once more, my fourth bullet neatly severing the advancing flame from the rest of the fuse.

Stillness. I took a deep breath.

McGlade peeked through his fingers. "Are we dead?"

Herb's voice in my ear. "Jack, are you okay? Suspect on foot, in the backyard. Has a woman with him."

"Move in!"

McGlade walked over to the last barrel, examining it. He pulled out the remaining fuse, about the length of a cigarette.

"Nice shooting, Wyatt."

I limped past him, pushing through the back door. The backyard was cool and dark, and I couldn't spot any movement. Red and blue lights swirled from a few houses away, washing over the lawn in waves.

"The bomb is defused, Herb, close the perimeter. Perp ran out the back door. He has a hostage. Do you have a visual? Over."

"Negative, Jack. We were falling back. We're coming in now."

A hand on my shoulder. I spun, bringing around my gun. McGlade.

"Don't tell me you lost him."

I walked away before I did something I'd regret, like shoot him. The important thing was finding Charles.

I couldn't allow him to kill his wife.

In my ear, Benedict and his men swept the block, while I took a walk across the backyard lawn. I gripped the .38 in both hands, holding it at an angle away from my body, ready to point and shoot at anything that grabbed my attention.

"Jackie! I found something!"

McGlade was holding up some kind of hook.

"Nice work, Harry. Now sit on it and spin."

"It was right on the ground, next to this manhole."

It took a few seconds to register, and then I hobbled over. McGlade used the hook to pry up the cover, dragging it off to the side. He flashed his key light down into the hole.

"Stinky. Think he's down there?"

"Jack!" My earpiece buzzed. "We have a man and a woman, four doors down. Team is moving in!"

"Roger that, Herb. McGlade and I . . . Harry!"

Harry disappeared down the hole.

"Dammit! Herb, we found a manhole in the yard, Harry just went down. I'll contact you again in a minute."

I got on my knees and peered down into the sewer.

"Harry! Get up here!"

"Sorry, Jack," he called up. "You did this to me. I have to catch the guy to clear my good name."

"Goddammit, McGlade, you don't have a good name! Harry! Harry?"

He yelped once, then didn't answer.

I reloaded, told Herb my intention, and then went down after him.

CHAPTER 43

THERE IS NO *BOOM*.

Charles stops, hunching down in the sewer line, filthy water up to his ankles. He holds his breath and listens.

No explosion. No screaming. Nothing.

What's going on?

He wraps his hand in Diane's hair and pulls her along. If the cops aren't burning, they'll be coming after him. He has to hurry.

It's dark as ink, foul, claustrophobic. The narrow pipe forces him to run in a crouch. His wife whimpers, dragging her feet, slowing him down. He jabs her with the knife to get her to move.

"I told you to run!"

After the fourth or fifth jab, she falls down. Continued poking doesn't make her get back up.

Damn her. Charles hates to end it here, in a sewer where he can't even see her face. This isn't how it's supposed to be.

He wants to take his time, make it last, feast on a banquet of her agony.

A clang, in the distance. Someone opening the manhole cover.

Jack.

Charles reaches down, slashes at his wife in the darkness. Such a disappointing ending. She deserves so much more.

Then he scurries away from her. He moves by feel, counting his steps. Sight is minimal, but he's walked the route several times. Before he became a media darling, Charles always kept his kills hidden. The sewer is the perfect hiding place for corpses—he can bring them here without witnesses, no one notices the smell, and the rats take care of any evidence. Throughout these pipes are the remains of a half-dozen people he's killed.

After twenty-four paces he stops, feeling for the grating. It's two feet before him. Taped to it is a flashlight.

He crouches in the concrete tube and flicks on the light, briefly. Finding the clasp, he opens the rusty gate and slips down four feet into the main line.

Now he can walk upright rather than bent over. The sewer main is wide as an alley. Filthy water runs down the center in a putrid, brown stream. Charles doesn't know how deep it is, and has no desire to find out. On either side of the flow is a ledge, a catwalk that can be treaded upon when the water level is low enough.

His smartest escape route is to follow along the right wall, down to the end of the block, and then turn left and go eight blocks over. He'll pop up in an alley, right across the street from the public garage where he keeps his second car, and far from the searching pigs overhead.

But he isn't ready yet. He still has to deal with Jack.

The lieutenant can't be allowed to live. She found him. She'll find him again. Charles doesn't want to be looking over his shoulder for the rest of his life, waiting for her to pounce.

It will end here.

The Gingerbread Man checks his bullets and switches off his light.

Noises are coming from the sub main he'd exited moments before.

He hunches down and giggles, ready for the fun to start.

CHAPTER 44

THE LADDER WAS MADE OF STEEL bars, rusty and slimy. Descending was a complicated ordeal where I had to hop down each step, since my bad leg refused to bend. When I finally reached the bottom, I stepped on something.

"Jesus, Jackie!"

I was on Harry's leg. He shoved me off and flicked on his key light, pointing it in my face. McGlade was on his ass, in the middle of a large slick of gunk.

No—not gunk.

Blood.

"My God, Harry—"

"I slipped. It's not my blood."

My stomach churned. The wife.

I tried to radio Herb to say we were on the right trail, but the radio only gave me static. I played with it for a few seconds, but being underground probably put us out of signal range.

Harry stood up and banged his head on the top of the tube we were in.

"Christ! That's gonna leave a lump."

The smell was nauseating, human waste and rotting animal matter. Several rats scurried past, disappearing into the darkness.

I took the key light from Harry. The little beam barely penetrated the darkness, only allowing for a few feet of sight.

"So which way, Lieutenant? This tube goes both ways."

I focused the light at our feet. The trickle of sludge was moving to our left.

"This way."

"Lead on, Jackie. You've got the body armor."

I killed the light and we shuffled forward. The muck became ankle-deep after a few yards, and the smell was so foul, I could taste it in my mouth.

I stopped twice to listen. The only sound I heard was my labored breathing, which was amplified in the fetid air and made me sound asthmatic. Walking in a crouch with a bad leg was slow going and painful. I felt down in the darkness and discovered that my pants were soaked with blood yet again. This damn wound would never heal.

But that was the least of my problems.

"I think we went the wrong way," Harry whispered.

"Shhh."

"I'm going back. Be a dear and let me borrow your vest."

"Kiss my ass."

"You want to get romantic now?"

I strained my ears. There was noise ahead, like a water cascade. We were coming to the end of the tunnel.

How far ahead of us could he be? Assuming he knew these sewers, Charles could be hundreds of yards away by now.

Or he could be just around the corner, waiting in ambush.

"Help . . ."

A woman's voice, weak and pleading, coming from ahead of us. Diane Kork was still alive.

I moved faster, urgency prodding me on, overriding the pain. The radio was still all static. I also tried my cell phone, but couldn't get a signal surrounded by all this concrete. We came to her twenty yards later, lying half-naked in the filth, covered with blood and muck.

"Diane. Can you hear me?" I knelt down next to her, my wounded leg stretched out behind me. Her pulse was strong, steady. I eyed her wounds; several ugly slashes across the chest, and a deep cut in her collarbone that missed her throat by a fraction. Her eyelids fluttered, and she focused on me.

"He heard you coming, and ran off."

"Diane, we're going to get you out of here."

She shook her head. "You have to get him."

"We will. First we're going to . . ."

"No!" The power in her voice startled me. "Don't let him get away. You have to go get him. Please."

I looked at Harry.

"Give her your jacket."

He shrugged off the blazer, draping it over Diane.

I tucked the sport coat under her arms and chin.

"He won't get away, Diane. I promise. We need to get you to the hospital. Can you stand?"

She shook her head.

"We'll have to carry her, Harry."

"You can't even walk. How are you supposed to carry someone?"

"I'll manage."

No one else dies. Even if we had to drag her to safety an inch at a time.

Harry complied, gently lifting Diane under her armpits.

She groaned painfully. I positioned myself on the other side and lifted her knees, my legs trembling under her weight.

It would be tough, but we'd get her out of here.

"Jack!"

The voice came from behind us, loud and unmistakable. Benedict.

"Herb! We're over here!"

Thirty seconds later my partner came waddling down the tube, followed by a uniformed officer. His labored breathing and the coat of sweat on his face told me he wasn't any more comfortable in the sewers than I was.

"Kork is ahead of us," I called out. "Get Diane out of here, alert the troops. We need to cover all manhole exits for ten square blocks."

"You're going after him?"

I nodded.

"With him?" Benedict jerked a thumb at Harry.

McGlade sneered back. "Good to see you too, Tubby."

"Harry's going back with you. Place him under arrest for obstruction of—"

"My ass," McGlade said. Then he took off down the pipe.

Nothing's ever easy.

"Gotta go, Herb."

"Be careful, Jack. Backup is coming."

We exchanged a tense look, and then I went after Harry. A few feet into the blackness, I stopped and listened. The falling water sound was louder, and I could hear the echo of footsteps.

"Dammit, Harry! Wait up!"

My voice sounded small, hollow, as it echoed down the tube.

"I'm a few yards ahead of you."

When I finally caught up to him, I was sweating as much as Herb had been.

"Welcome back, Jackie. You gonna read me my rights?"

"When this is over, Harry, I swear—"

I felt the bullet at the same time I heard it. It hit me in the stomach, knocking me backward. I sprawled in the filthy water, my head bouncing on cement.

The feeling was unreal, like I'd been gut-punched by a speeding car. I sucked in the foul sewer air, my breath having left me. The pain was so bad, it made me forget my leg.

The tube exploded in a muzzle flash, and thunder erupted in my ears. McGlade was returning fire. Enclosed in the concrete tube, the gun deafened us both.

A long minute passed. McGlade knelt next to me and felt along my body. He pressed on my diaphragm and I yelped. Then he reached under my vest and felt the skin. I couldn't sense if there was a wound or not.

Harry released the pressure and a moment later the little flashlight was pointing in my face.

"The vest stopped the bullet." Or that's what it sounded like. My ears were still ringing. "Can you move?"

I tried to speak. "Yeah."

He offered his hand and helped me up. The darkness fractured into pinpoints of light, stars dancing in my vision. I blinked twice and swallowed.

"Kevlar worked pretty good." McGlade handed me the light and crouched behind me. "You go first."

I looked down at my gun hand and saw that I still held the .38. Then I moved, one foot in front of the other.

The water sound increased. I sensed the tube ending, opening up into a much bigger area. The sewer main. I listened, peering into the dark.

"You waiting for Christmas?" Harry nudged me. "Move it."

I flicked on the flashlight, looking for a foothold so I could climb out.

Bang! Bang! Bang!

Three shots went into the wall next to me, chips of concrete biting into my face and neck. I jumped, landing on a ledge several feet below, falling partially into the sewage water. My gun skittered off out of sight.

A bright flashlight beam trained on the tube where I'd been seconds ago. It made its way down the wall and hit me in the face. I squinted at the figure behind the light.

The Gingerbread Man grinned, his gun pointing at my head.

"Hello and good-bye, Jack. Looks like the best man won."

Then a shot rang out from the tube above us.

Harry.

The flashlight fell away from my face, and Charles Kork howled in pain. I felt around for my gun, instead finding the keys. I flicked on the key light and Harry dropped to the ledge next to me.

Charles moaned. I put the light on him. He was bleeding from the shoulder, clutching the wound with his good hand. His gun was gone.

I let out the breath I'd been holding.

The Gingerbread Man offered a lopsided grin. He looked small, petty, like the sewer rats that scampered behind him.

"Well, looks like you got me, Jack."

"Stand up, put your hands on your head."

"I can't get up."

I took a step closer. My reserves were almost gone, and my entire body ached and smelled like sewage. But I could honestly say I never felt better.

"Turn over on your stomach. Hands behind your back."

"How'd you find me?"

"You'll find out at the trial. Now turn over."

Charles Kork shook his head. "I'm not going back to prison."

And then he rolled off the ledge and into the river of muck.

The current began to take him away at a surprisingly brisk pace. He floated chest-deep in the sewage, his good arm flopping ahead of him in an effort to paddle.

"I'll see you again, Jack!" he called out to me. "Soon!"

Before I had a chance to consider my next move, there was a terrific *boom!* and Kork's head exploded in a plume of red.

I looked at McGlade. He holstered his .44 and shrugged.

"He was trying to escape. Were you gonna jump in that shit and go after him?"

The headless corpse of the Gingerbread Man floated off into the blackness on a river of filth. It bobbed in the gentle current once, twice, and then began to sink.

Following him were a swimming legion of rats.

Harry came over to me, eyes serious.

"Hey, Jackie—you're not pissed, are you?"

I didn't say anything.

"I mean, he was a scumbag. Think of all the money I just saved the taxpayers. Do you know how expensive those high-profile trials are?"

I found Charles's gun. It was a .38. My .38. I took a plastic bag out of my jacket pocket and put the gun inside, lifting it by the barrel with two fingers.

"Jack, you're not really thinking of arresting me, are you?"

"He died in the shoot-out, Harry. That's what's going into my report."

"You had me worried. I thought you were still pissed about me stealing your bust."

"You saved my life, Harry."

"Yeah. I guess I did. So we're even now, right?"

I made a fist and clipped him across the jaw. It was hard enough to stagger him back.

I shook my hand, the knuckles aching wonderfully.

"Now we're even."

Harry wiped at his mouth and grinned.

"It took you fifteen years to finally do that. Feel better?"

I thought about it. "Yeah, I do."

"Then let's get the hell out of this sewer. It offends my delicate sensibilities."

First we spent a few minutes finding my dropped gun. When it was safe in its holster, we took the nearest ladder up to the surface.

A few moments after we emerged through the manhole, a swarm of cops came running toward us. Several cops went down into the sewer after the body. My radio was finally working again, and I contacted Herb.

"The woman is okay," he reported. "Did you get him?"

The words felt so good coming out of my mouth. "We got him."

"Are you okay?"

"I'm perfect," I said, taking a big gulp of cold city air. "Perfect."

"Can I talk to him?" Harry reached for my headset. I let him have it, walking away from the commotion, away from the flashing blue and red lights, into the urban night.

The sky was a huge, black blanket, spreading out in all directions. I looked up, trying to see the stars through the smog. I couldn't make them out.

But I knew they were there.

CHAPTER 45

I KNOCKED THE EIGHT BALL INTO the corner pocket and Phin grunted.

"That's two more bucks." I let a smile creep onto my face. "What is that, five games?"

"How am I supposed to eat this week?"

"Don't play if you can't pay."

He frowned and rooted around in his front pocket, extracting a bill.

"Can you break a fifty?"

To his chagrin, I could. Then I sent him off to buy me another beer.

It had been three days since the death of the Gingerbread Man, Charles Kork. The papers were still running headlines. Most of them centered on Harry McGlade. He'd become a media darling, though I don't think "darling" is the right word.

How Harry found out about Charles was simple enough.

He had a copy of the show at his apartment. After he left the station, he watched the tape and drew the obvious conclusion. Then he called up his buddy Max Trainter, and soon had Kork's name and address.

McGlade had attempted to beat us to the scene and take all the glory for himself. Which, essentially, is what he did.

"That guy was the top layer on the shit cake," McGlade told five networks, plus CNN.

Diane Kork had lost a lot of blood and needed a few dozen stitches, but she was expected to make a full recovery. Physically at least. Mentally she was a mess.

I'd gotten to see her twice since that day, trying to fill in the remaining pieces of the puzzle.

She'd filed for divorce from Charles in May, right after *The Max Trainter Show*. He'd been neglectful and verbally abusive, but never physically. This may have sounded odd, but Dr. Francis Mulrooney told me later that many married serial killers aren't aggressive within the family unit. They saved it up for their excursions.

Diane had never known about his two stretches in prison, never met his family, and certainly had no idea that every time he sneaked out at night, he was stalking and killing people.

Charles's mother, Lisa Kork, died of cancer shortly after Charles was born. Attempts were made to locate his father, Buddy Kork, but to no avail.

A delve into Buddy Kork's past revealed he'd been arrested twice for child abuse, and acquitted both times. Apparently, his position as a reverend at a local church was enough to justify the beatings he gave his children.

He was fired from the church ten years ago, but a phone call confirmed that Dr. Reginald Booster was a regular parishioner—the same Booster whom Charles had killed for the Seconal prescription. Booster had known Charles was

Buddy's son. Hence the note he left on the pad at the murder scene.

Just to tie up loose ends, Dr. Mulrooney matched the Gingerbread Man's letters to samples found in Charles's home, and to the release form Charles had filled out to appear on *The Max Trainter Show*.

The search of Kork's rented house unveiled a cache of six hundred pictures and twelve home videotapes. They showed, in detail, Charles torturing and killing animals, children, and women. A task force was assigned to begin matching the victims with missing persons. I was offered the job to head the task force, but after watching one of the videos, I knew I wouldn't be able to sit through the rest of them. I declined.

Charles Kork's body, sans head, was fished out of the sewer four blocks from where Harry had shot him. In the ME's report, Phil Blasky commented that it was the best lobotomy he'd ever seen.

Diane Kork was able to shed light on the significance of the gingerbread man cookies. She and Charles had baked them during their first Christmas together. They'd lacquered them and hung them on the tree every year after that. She hadn't seen them since they split up.

Herb was invited over to the mayor's house for dinner, since he'd been the chief investigator on the case after the captain had kicked me off. I hadn't been asked to attend, but Herb related that he'd eaten enough for both of us. Though I missed out on hobnobbing with the powerful, I was allowed to return to work, the Internal Affairs investigation was dropped since I recovered my lost gun, and I even got a call from a very important news journalist with her own prime-time show. But she only wanted to ask me questions about Harry, and I hung up on her.

I pumped more quarters into the table, and Phin came back with two bottles of beer.

"Loser racks," I reminded him.

He racked the balls. I sipped my beer and chalked my stick. Then I engaged in a truly magnificent break, pocketing two stripes. Phin swore.

By eleven o'clock I was up about thirty bucks. Phin called me several choice names when I was leaving and made me promise I'd meet him tomorrow for a rematch. I agreed, telling him I could use the money.

It began to snow as I walked back to my apartment. The first snow of the season. It looked pretty, glowing in the street lights, contrasted against huge skyscrapers. Covering up all the dirt. I felt myself smile, and then the smile disappeared at the thought of digging out my car in the morning.

There were messages on my machine when I got back to the apartment. The first was from Latham, my ill-fated Lunch Mates date. He was doing well, and begged me to bring him a pizza when I visited him tomorrow.

"The food here is wretched. It tastes like they steam everything."

He held no resentment toward me at all, only expressing some joking disappointment that our third date couldn't possibly be as exciting as the first two were.

Great guy. I was going to enjoy getting to know him.

The second call was a reporter from *Time* magazine, who wanted to know if I wouldn't mind talking to him about Harry.

The last was from my worried mother, who hadn't heard from me in over twenty minutes and wondered if I was still doing okay. I called her back.

"I'm fine, Mom. Are you happy to be back home?"

"Yes, thank goodness it's over. I'm so sore, I can barely move."

A tinge of panic. "Is your hip getting worse? You told me—"

"My hip is fine, Jacqueline. I'm not nursing-home material yet. I'm sore because of that rascal Mr. Griffin. He's like the Energizer Bunny. He keeps going and going—I swear, I didn't sleep for three days."

Perhaps I was a bit hasty in worrying that Mom couldn't take care of herself.

After the call, I made myself a sandwich and sat down in my rocking chair with a recent Ed McBain paperback.

The next thing I knew, without any effort whatsoever on my part, I was asleep.

CHAPTER 46

I WOKE UP THE NEXT MORNING, refreshed, invigorated, and feeling good enough to exercise.

I took it easy, favoring my bad leg, but still managed to make it through my morning routine. I had to skip sit-ups because of the huge bruise on my stomach, the ugly aftermath of getting shot. But I did a few extra push-ups to compensate.

The snow from the night before didn't stick, so unearthing my car wasn't necessary. However, it took eight tries before the engine finally caught, and I stalled twice driving to the station.

I didn't let it hurt my good mood.

When I arrived, I found out Benedict was at the morgue with the relatives of JoAnn Fourthy, the first victim. She'd been identified through *The Max Trainter Show,* and her parents had been located in New Jersey. The Gingerbread Man case was officially closed.

Now I had to take on the backlog I had accumulated. A

knifing. A hit-and-run. A gang murder. A fatal shooting at a high school.

A Violent Crimes lieutenant's job was never done.

An undetermined time later, my concentration was broken when two men stepped into my office. Without knocking. It was Special Agents Dailey and Coursey, complete with matching suits, haircuts, and demeanors. I wondered if they called each other every morning to decide on what to wear that day.

"We never got to congratulate you on catching the unsub, Lieutenant," Dailey said.

Or maybe it was Coursey.

The other one added, "I know we didn't always see eye to eye on things, but we're glad everything worked out for the best."

Standard FBI procedure. Don't burn your bridges.

"Was Kork listed in your computer under known poisoners?"

They looked at each other, and then back at me.

"He was on a suspect list for the candy tamperings in Michigan, but Vicky didn't have him in her database. We did a follow-up with the investigating officers of that case and read through their reports. Kork was brought in for questioning and released on two different occasions, but there was never sufficient evidence for an arrest."

"I see." I tried to look appropriately smug. "And how did things go with the horse?"

One of them cleared his throat. The other looked at an imaginary spot on his sleeve.

"Profiling isn't a hard science, Lieutenant. Sometimes we're a little off-center."

"Ah."

"So—have you had a chance to look at the Hansen case yet?"

"Pardon me?"

"The high school shooting? It's almost identical to a similar homicide in Plainfield, Wisconsin, last year."

"And?" I feared where this was headed.

"And your captain wanted us to work together on it. A state line has been crossed."

Oh, no. "Look, guys..."

They headed for the door.

"We'll be by at two o'clock to discuss the case further. We need to have Vicky help us with a suspect profile before we can proceed."

And then they were gone.

So much for my good mood.

I resumed scaling Mount Paperwork, filing things, throwing out things, typing things. I always saved the typing for last because I'm so bad at it.

"Hi, Jackie."

I looked up from the keyboard and saw that Harry McGlade had walked into my office. Apparently no one believed in knocking anymore. Harry was wearing the typical Harry outfit: stained brown pants, beige jacket, fat tie, and more wrinkles than a retirement home.

I'd have to get a lock for that damn door.

"What do you want, Harry?"

I continued typing, trying to show that I was busy.

"You still haven't thanked me."

"For what?" I asked, and then looked at my 97-723 report and saw I'd typed "for what" on it. I swore and reached for the correction fluid.

"For leading you to the killer. Without me, you never would have connected Kork to the Trainter show. You'll probably get a big fat promotion out of this. 'Captain Daniels.' It has a nice ring to it. You owe me."

"I do, huh?"

I couldn't find the Wite-Out, so I went back and crossed out the mistake in pen.

"Sure. That's why I stopped by, so you can thank me and buy me breakfast."

"Maybe you should buy me breakfast. You're the one getting the movie offers."

"Funny you should mention that, Jackie. A Hollywood agent called this morning, interested in turning my story into a film. Guess who's going to play me?"

"Danny DeVito."

"Funny. Ha ha. Actually, Brad Pitt is interested. But before they can start shoveling money at me, there's a tiny little question about story rights."

McGlade pulled some folded paper out of his pants pocket.

"If you'll just sign here..."

"No way, Harry."

"Come on, Jackie. There'll be some money in it for you. I mean, not much, but you'd be doing me a huge favor."

"I don't think so."

"Let's at least discuss it over breakfast."

"I've got a lot of paperwork to finish."

Harry put his hands on my desk and leaned toward me.

"Screw the paperwork. It'll be here when you get back. Come out for breakfast with an old friend. You work too hard anyway. Enjoy life, Jackie. Stop being married to the job."

I wasn't sure eating breakfast with Harry would qualify as enjoying life, but what he said was very similar to what Herb had said. Did I want, at the end of my life, for my epitaph to be, "She was a good cop"?

I guess that I did.

But even a good cop has to eat.

"Fine. A quick breakfast. But I have no desire to see myself on the silver screen, Harry."

"Some big names are interested in your part, Jackie. I've heard the name Roseanne being bandied around. It's a Hollywood rule. All tough-guy heroes need a humorous sidekick."

"Now I'm definitely not going to sign that paper."

"Sure you're not."

He grinned again, and I got up and grabbed my coat.

"I know this terrific new pancake place, just opened." Harry held the door for me, the first gentlemanly act I'd ever seen him perform. "If you don't like it, it's my treat."

"I hate it already."

We walked out the door.

If You Loved *Whiskey Sour*,
Be Sure to Catch *Bloody Mary*,
J. A. Konrath's Newest Jacqueline "Jack" Daniels Mystery,
Coming in July 2005 from Hyperion.

An Excerpt, the Prologue and Chapter 1, follows.

IT WOULD BE SO EASY TO kill you while you sleep."

He rolls onto his side and faces his wife, tangling his fingers in her hair. Her face is shrouded in a dried blue mask; an antiaging beauty product that has begun to peel. The moonlight peeking through the bedroom curtains makes her look already dead.

He wonders if other people look at their partners at night, peacefully dozing, and imagine killing them.

"I have a knife." He brushes his fingertips along her hairline. "I keep it under the bed."

Her lips part and she snores softly.

So ugly, especially for a model. All capped teeth and streaked hair.

He wedges his hand between the mattress and box spring and pulls out the knife. It has a large wooden handle, disproportionate to the thin, finely honed blade. A fillet knife.

He places it against his wife's neck, gently.

His vision blurs. The pain in his head ignites, a screw twisting into his temple. It tightens with every heartbeat.

Too many headaches in too many days. He should, will, tell the doctor. The six aspirin he took an hour ago haven't helped.

Only one thing helps when the pain gets this bad.

He caresses her chin with the edge of the knife, shaving off some of the mask. Sweat rolls down his forehead and stings his eyes.

"I can cut your throat, reach in and rip out your voice before you even have a chance to scream."

She twitches, her head tilting away. Her neck is smooth, flawless. He clenches his jaw hard enough to crush granite, teeth grinding teeth.

"Or maybe I should go through the eye. Just a quick poke, right into the brain."

He raises the blade up, trying to control the trembling in his hand. The blade wavers over her lid, creeping closer.

"All you have to do is open your eyes, so you can see it coming."

She snores.

"Come on, honey." He nudges her shoulder. "Open your eyes."

He bites down on his tongue, the inside of his mouth hot and salty. His brain is a tiny clawed demon trying to dig its way out.

"Open your goddamn eyes!"

She shifts toward him, mumbling. Her arm falls over his bare chest.

"Another headache, honey?"

"Yeah."

He places the knife behind her head, at the base of her skull. He imagines jabbing it in, the tip poking through the front of her throat.

Wouldn't she be surprised?

"Poor baby," she says into his armpit. She rubs his cheek, her fingers cool against his burning ear.

He gives her a little prod with the knife, just under her hairline. Her head jerks away.

"Ow! Honey, cut your nails."

"It's not my nails, dear. It's a knife."

She snores her response.

He nudges her again. "I said, *It's a knife*. You hear me?"

"Did you take some aspirin, baby?"

"Six."

"They'll work soon. You should see a doctor."

She hooks a leg over his stomach. He feels himself become aroused, unsure if it's her touch that's causing it, or the thought of peeling off her face.

Or perhaps both.

He smiles in the darkness, knuckles white on the knife handle, ready to finally give in to the nightly temptation. But as he readies the blade, he notes that the pain in his head has begun to subside. Gradually, the sharp throbbing melts away into a dull ache.

Bearable.

For now.

"I'll kill you tomorrow." He kisses her on the scalp.

The knife goes back under the mattress. He holds her tight and she makes a happy sighing sound.

When he finally falls asleep, it's to the image of cutting her open and bathing his face with her blood.

CHAPTER 1

"D<small>AMMIT.</small>"

My fan had died. It didn't surprise me. The fan had ten years on me, and I came into the world during the Eisenhower years. It belonged in a museum, not an office.

Today was the first day of July, and hot enough to cook burgers on the sidewalk, though you probably wouldn't want to eat them afterward. My blouse clung to me, my nylons felt like sweatpants, and I'd developed a fatal case of the frizzies.

The 26th Police District of Chicago, where I slowly roasted, was temporarily without air-conditioning due to a problem with the condensers, whatever the hell they were. We were promised it would be fixed by December.

I hit the base of the fan with my stapler. Though I was the highest ranking female cop in the Violent Crimes Unit, I tended to be useless mechanically. My handyperson skills maxed out at changing a lightbulb. And even then, I had to read the instructions. The fan seemed to sense this, slowly wagging its blades at me like dusty tongues.

My partner, Detective First Class Herb Benedict, walked into my office, sucking on a soda cup the size of a small garbage can. It didn't seem to be helping him cool off. Herb weighed about two hundred and sixty pounds, and had more pores on his face than I had on my whole body. Benedict's suit looked like it had been soaked in Lake Michigan and put on wet.

He waddled up and placed a moist palm on my desk, leaving a streak. I noticed droplets in his gray mustache; sweat or diet cola. His basset hound jowls glistened as if greased.

"Morning, Jack."

My birth name was Jacqueline, but when I married my ex-husband, Alan Daniels, no one could resist shortening it to Jack.

"Morning, Herb. Here to help me fix my fan?"

"Nope. I'm here to share my breakfast."

Herb set a brown paper sack on my desk.

"Donuts? Bagels? Cholesterol McMuffins?"

"Not even close."

Benedict removed a plastic bag containing, of all things, rice cakes.

"That's it?" I asked. "Where's the chocolate? Where's the canned cheese?"

"I'm watching my weight. In fact, I joined a health club."

"You're kidding."

"You know the one that advertises on TV all the time?"

"The one where you get to work out with all of those Olympic bodybuilders for only thirty bucks a month?"

"That's the one. Except I've got the Premier Membership, not the normal one."

"What's the difference?"

He named a monetary figure, and I whistled at the amount.

"But with it, I get full access to the racquetball and squash courts."

"You don't play racquetball or squash."

"Plus, my membership card is colored gold instead of blue."

I leaned back in my chair, interlacing my fingers behind my head. "Well, that's different. I'd pay extra for that. How is the place?"

"I haven't worked out there yet. Everyone that goes is in such good shape, I thought I should lose a few pounds before I start."

"I don't think they'd care, Herb. And if they do, just impress them by flashing your gold card."

"You're not being very supportive here, Jack."

"Sorry." I picked up a file to fan myself. "It's the heat."

"You need to get in shape. I've got guest passes. They've got Pilates at the club. I'm thinking of taking a class after work."

Herb smiled, biting into a rice cake. His smile faded as he chewed.

"Damn. These things taste like Styrofoam."

The phone rang.

"Jack? Phil Blasky. There's, um, a bit of a situation here at County."

County meant the Cook County Morgue. Phil was the Chief Medical Examiner.

"I know this is going to sound like a paperwork problem . . ." He paused, sucking in some air through his teeth. ". . . but I've checked and double-checked."

"What's wrong, Phil?"

"We have an extra body. Well, actually, some extra body parts."

Phil explained. I told him we'd stop by, and then shared the information with Herb.

"Could be some kind of prank. County are a strange bunch."

"Maybe. Phil doesn't think so."

"Did he say what the extra parts were?"

"Arms."

Benedict thought this over.

"Maybe someone is simply lending him a hand."

I stood up and pinched the center of my blouse, fanning in some air. "We'll take your car."

Herb recently bought a sporty new Camaro Z28, an expensive reminder of his refusal to age gracefully. Silly as he looked behind the wheel, the car had great air-conditioning, whereas my 1988 Nova did not.

We left my office and made our way downstairs and outside. It was like stepping into a toaster. Though it couldn't have been much hotter than the district building, the blistering sun amplified everything. A bank across the street flashed the current temp on its sidewalk sign. *One hundred and one.* And the sign was in the shade.

Herb pressed a gizmo on his key chain and his car beeped and started on its own. It was red, naturally, and so heavily waxed that the glare coming off it hurt my eyes. I climbed in the passenger side and angled both vents on my face while Herb babied the Camaro out of its parking space.

"Zero to sixty in five point two seconds."

"Have you taken it up to sixty yet?"

"I'm still breaking it in."

He put on a pair of Ray-Bans and pulled onto Addison. I closed my eyes and luxuriated in the cool air. We were at County all too soon.

Cook County Morgue was located on Harrison in Chicago's medical district, near Rush-Presbyterian Hospital.

It rose two stories, all dirty white stone and tinted windows. Herb pulled around back into a circular driveway, and parked next to the curb.

"I hate coming here." Herb frowned, his mustache drooping like a walrus. "I can never get the smell out of my clothes."

Years ago, when my mother walked a beat, cops would smear whiskey on their upper lip to combat the stench of the morgue.

Sanitation had improved since then; cooler temps, better ventilation, greater attention to hygiene. But the smell still stuck with you.

I made do with some cherry lip balm, a small dab under each nostril. I passed the tube to Herb.

"Cherry? Don't you have menthol?"

"It's a hundred degrees out. I wasn't worried about windburn."

He sniffed the balm, then handed it back without applying any.

"It smells too good. I'd eat it."

The heat hit me like a blow dryer when I got out of the car.

A cop walked over and eyed the Camaro—there were always cops around County. He was young and tan and didn't give me a second glance, preferring to talk to Herb.

"Five speed?"

"Six. Three hundred ten horses."

The uniform whistled, running his finger along some pinstriping.

"What's under the hood, five point seven?"

Herb nodded. "Want to see?"

I left the boys with their toy and walked into the entrance, to the right of the automatic double doors.

The lobby, if you could call it that, consisted of a counter, a door, and a glass partition. Behind the counter was a solitary black man in hospital scrubs.

"Phil Blasky?"

He shot his thumb at the door. "In the fridge."

I signed in, received a plastic badge, and entered the main room.

Death overpowered the cherry, so strong I could taste it in the back of my mouth. It had a sickly-sour smell, like rotting carnations.

To the right, a mortician in an ill-fitting suit hefted a body off a table and onto a rolling cot. When he finished, he pulled off his latex gloves and shot them, rubber-band-style, into a garbage can.

Next to him, resting on a stainless steel scale built into the floor, was a naked male corpse, grossly obese, with burns covering most of his torso. The LCD screen on the wall blinked *450 lbs.* He smelled like bacon.

I held my breath and pulled open the heavy aluminum door, which led into the cooler.

The stench worsened in here. Bleach and blood and urine and meat gone bad.

Cook County Morgue was the largest in the Midwest. Indigents, unclaimed bodies, accident victims, suicides, and cases of foul play all came through these doors. It held about three hundred bodies.

Just my luck, they were running at capacity.

To my left, corpses lay stacked on wire shelves warehouse-style, five high and thirty wide. Stretching across the main floor was a traffic jam of tables and carts, all occupied. Some of the dead were covered with black plastic bags. Some weren't.

Unlike movie depictions of morgues, these bodies didn't lie down in peaceful, supine positions. Many of them had kept the poses they died in; arms and legs jutting out, curled up on their sides, necks at funny angles. They also didn't look like a Hollywood conception of a corpse. A real dead person had very little color. Regardless of race, the skin always seemed to fade into a light blue, and the eyes were dull and cloudy, like dusty snow globes.

The temperature hovered at fifty degrees, fans blowing around the frigid, foul air. It chilled my sweat in a most unpleasant way.

To the right, in an adjacent room, an autopsy was being performed. I focused on the figure holding the bone saw, didn't recognize him, and continued to look around.

I found Phil Blasky near the back of the room, and walked up to him carefully; the floors were sticky with various fluids, and all of them clashed with my Gucci pumps.

"Phil."

"Jack."

Phil was leaning over a steel table, squinting at something. I stood next to him, trying not to gape at the nude body of a toddler, half wrapped in a black plastic bag, lying next to him. The child was so rigid and pale, he appeared to be made out of wax.

"I went through every stiff in the place a second time. No one is missing arms."

I glanced down at the table. The arms were severed at the shoulder, laid out with their fingertips touching, the elbows bending in a big M. They belonged to a female, Caucasian, with fake pink nails. A pair of black handcuffs connected them at the wrists. There was very little blood, but the jagged edges to the wounds suggested they didn't come off easily.

"I suspect an axe." Phil poked at the wound with a gloved finger. "See the mark along the humerus, here? It took two swings to sever the appendage."

"It doesn't look humorous to me." Benedict had snuck up behind us.

"Funny," Phil said. "Never heard that one before, working with dead bodies for twenty years. Next will you make some kind of *gimme a hand* joke?"

"I did that one already," Herb said. "How about: *It appears the suspect has been disarmed?*"

"She was always such a cut-up?"

"Would you like a shoulder to cry on?"

"Can I go out on a limb here?"

"At least she'll get severance pay?"

Phil cocked an eyebrow at Herb.

"Severance?" Herb said. "Sever?"

I tuned out their act and got a closer look at the arms. Snapping on a latex glove, I pushed back the cold, hard fingers and peered at the handcuffs. They were Smith and Wesson model number 100.

"Those are police issue." Benedict poked at them with a pencil. "I've got a set just like them."

So did every other cop in our district, and probably in Chicago. They were also sold at sporting goods stores, sex shops, and Army/Navy surplus outlets, plus a zillion places over the Internet. Impossible to trace. But maybe we'd get lucky and the owner had etched his name and address on the . . .

I inhaled sharply.

This couldn't be right.

On the cuffs, next to the keyhole, were two small initials painted in red nail polish. I tugged out my .38, holstered under my blazer, and looked at the butt. It had the same two red letters.

JD.

"Herb." I kept my voice steady. "Those handcuffs are mine."

Ready for Another Shot?

New from J.A. Konrath, the latest intoxicating cocktail featuring Jacqueline Daniels.

Available wherever books are sold.

www.JAKonrath.com